Reading Power 系列

Advanced

★ 108課綱、全民英檢中／中高級適用

精選閱讀

附翻譯與解析

王郁惠、鄭翔嫚 編著

Main Idea

Details

Vocabulary in Context

Structure

Reference

Inference

三民書局

國家圖書館出版品預行編目資料

Advanced Reading：精選閱讀／王郁惠,鄭翔嬬編著.——
—初版九刷.——臺北市：三民，2021
　　面；　公分.——(Reading Power系列)

4712780665893 （平裝）
1. 英語 2. 讀本

805.18　　　　　　　　　　　　　97002352

 Reading Power 系列

Advanced Reading：精選閱讀

編 著 者	王郁惠　鄭翔嬬
發 行 人	劉振強
出 版 者	三民書局股份有限公司
地　　址	臺北市復興北路 386 號 (復北門市)
	臺北市重慶南路一段 61 號 (重南門市)
電　　話	(02)25006600
網　　址	三民網路書店 https://www.sanmin.com.tw
出版日期	初版一刷 2008 年 4 月
	初版九刷 2021 年 10 月
書籍編號	S807340
	4712780665893

三民書局

序

知識，就是希望；閱讀，就是力量。

在這個資訊爆炸的時代，應該如何選擇真正有用的資訊來吸收？
在考場如戰場的競爭壓力之下，應該如何儲備實力，漂亮地面對挑戰？
身為地球村的一分子，應該如何增進英語實力，與世界接軌？

學習英文的目的，就是要讓自己在這個資訊爆炸的時代之中，突破語言的藩籬，站在吸收新知的制高點之上，以閱讀獲得力量，以知識創造希望！

針對在英文閱讀中可能面對的挑戰，我們費心規劃 Reading Power 系列叢書，希望在學習英語的路上助你一臂之力，讓你輕鬆閱讀、快樂學習。

誠摯希望在學習英語的路上，這套 Reading Power 系列叢書將伴隨你找到閱讀的力量，發揮知識的光芒！

給讀者的話

　　增進英語能力最好的方法之一，便是大量閱讀好文章，這包含了廣泛地閱讀各種主題和文體類型的文章 (extensive reading) 與深入地分析和欣賞精彩的短文 (intensive reading)。同時在這雙向練習的訓練中，若能學會成功地運用各種閱讀策略，則能夠幫助學習者更有效、更有自信地完成獨立閱讀的過程，確實地吸收消化這些好的作品，並進而增進對英語的語感、訓練邏輯思考與批判性閱讀的能力。

　　然而許多學習者誤以為閱讀就等於翻字典查單字再加上逐字逐句做翻譯，甚至也有些學習者認為增進閱讀技巧就是不斷地做題目，訓練不需閱讀就能作答的解題技巧，這些都是對閱讀錯誤的迷思。學習者要有正確地閱讀觀念，瞭解自己閱讀的目的，培養良好的閱讀習慣，並反覆練習各種閱讀策略，如此才能厚植自己的英語實力。

　　本書的編寫目的即是希望透過介紹一些必備的閱讀策略，讓學習者在閱讀文章時有足夠的方法與技巧，包括快速掌握文章主旨、掃瞄文中細節、利用上下文推敲字義、確認指涉詞、找出作者隱藏在文中的含意以及理出整篇文章的脈絡等六大基本技巧。因此本書在編排上首先有一篇總論，分析探討這些閱讀策略，讓學習者學會主動積極辨認文章結構，瞭解主旨與細節之間的邏輯發展與概論與實例之間的鋪成，並揣測生字的意思與發掘文章深層的意涵，使閱讀從枯燥沉悶的練習，變成有趣且富挑戰的一種積極參與。

　　接著本書第二部份蒐集各種文體的文章，內容有人物介紹、科技新知、生活型態、性別議題、人文藝術等各類主題共五十篇。每篇皆有五道題目，其中每篇各有兩題分別針對推測單字意思與辨認篇章架構能力的題目，期望學習者透過充份及反覆的練習，強化各種閱讀技巧，提昇閱讀速度與能力。

　　此外，本書最後除了附上每篇文章的全文翻譯，同時還有深入的詳解，一一說明每一道題目解題的邏輯分析過程以及考題的出題方向與要測驗的能力，更方便學習者自修使用。

　　本書的編寫力求完善，但難免有疏漏之處，希望讀者與各界賢達隨時賜教。

Table of Contents

理論篇

Unit 1　辨認文章主旨 [Main Idea] ·· 2

Unit 2　掃描段落細節 [Details] ··· 6

Unit 3　利用上下文猜字義 [Vocabulary in Context] ······················ 9

Unit 4　辨認指涉詞 [Reference] ·· 12

Unit 5　推論 [Inference] ··· 14

Unit 6　段落結構 [Structure] ··· 17

測驗篇

Unit 1　Intelligent Design: Creationism Repackaged? ················ 22

Unit 2　From Scared Kid to the Best Storyteller ····················· 24

Unit 3　CAN One Enjoy Ballet?? Just Maybe... ······················ 26

Unit 4　Key to Our Survival? ·· 28

Unit 5　Five Foot 一 Something ·· 30

Unit 6　WHAT'S IN A NAME? ··· 32

Unit 7　Procrastination: A Barrier to Completing Work ············· 34

Unit 8　Exit the Dragon? ·· 36

Unit 9　The Cultural Impact of TV's Friends ··························· 38

Unit 10　Ang Lee's Path to Success ··· 40

Unit 11　Uncoding the da Vinci Surgery System ······················ 42

Unit 12　Stay-at-Home-Dads: A Kindlier, Gentler Society? ········ 44

Unit 13 The Puzzle of Memory ·································· 46

Unit 14 Pluto Gets Plutoed ··································· 48

Unit 15 What Motivates You? ······························· 50

Unit 16 Game On ··· 52

Unit 17 An Attractive Man ································· 54

Unit 18 Thumbs Down for BlackBerry ···················· 56

Unit 19 Vision Defects and Corrective Lenses ············ 58

Unit 20 Who Are Your Real Friends? ···················· 60

Unit 21 The Eyewitness Problem ························· 62

Unit 22 Dangerous Obsession ··························· 64

Unit 23 Lance Armstrong: Le Tour de France Didn't Make Him a Winner ··········· 66

Unit 24 Sneezing in Summer and Gagging on Plums ········ 68

Unit 25 The Bittersweet Truth about Sugar ·············· 70

Unit 26 And They Live Happily Ever After... ············· 72

Unit 27 Olive Oil: The "New" California Wine ············· 74

Unit 28 How Successful Advertising Campaigns Work ······ 76

Unit 29 Bullies: From the Schoolyard to Cyberspace ······ 78

Unit 30 Will Global Warming Cause Worldwide Political Conflicts? ·········· 80

Unit 31 Forget the Sting: Wasps Recruited for Explosives Detection ·········· 82

Unit 32 Catch-22: From Fiction to Real Life ·············· 84

Unit 33 And You Thought Sugar Was Bad For You! ········ 86

Unit 34 Don't Put Those Comic Books Away ·········· 88

Unit 35 Modelling Industry Today: All About the New ·········· 90

Unit 36 Woe Is Jan. 24 ·········· 92

Unit 37 Emails Can Make Cowards of Us ·········· 94

Unit 38 American Idol or Object of Ridicule ·········· 96

Unit 39 Eco-chic ·········· 98

Unit 40 Idiot or Savant? ·········· 100

Unit 41 Designing for Women ·········· 102

Unit 42 Feeding Baby Right ·········· 104

Unit 43 Round-the-World Plastic Surgery ·········· 106

Unit 44 Were the Lights on in Ancient Egypt? ·········· 108

Unit 45 Crossing Cultural Borders ·········· 110

Unit 46 True Love: A Short Course ·········· 112

Unit 47 Mom's Wisdom ·········· 114

Unit 48 LOHAS = "Happy Life": A Worldwide Trend for the

Good of the Planet? ·········· 116

Unit 49 Winning Handicap: Matthias Berg ·········· 118

Unit 50 Puppies Behind Bars ·········· 120

Answer Key ·········· 123

Acknowledgements:

The articles in this publication are adapted from the works by: Jason Crockett, Douglas Hinnant, M.J.McAteer, Karl Nilsson, Theodore Pigott, Amy Rashap, Paula Savvides, Charles Tracy, Han Tseng, Ming Wong, and Vanessa York.

理論篇

要增進英文閱讀能力，除了要大量閱讀，從中培養字彙的實力與閱讀的速度，更重要的是要從閱讀的經驗中累積閱讀的技巧，這其中包括：

(1)辨認文章主旨 (main idea)

(2)了解文中細節 (details) 的鋪陳是如何傳達重要論述

(3)試著從上下文中去推敲生字 (vocabulary in context)

(4)確認指涉詞 (reference)

(5)根據作者的陳述推論出隱藏在文中的含意 (inference)

(6)找出整篇文章的脈絡與結構 (structure)。

本篇將針對這六項重要的閱讀技巧分別說明。

ADVANCED READING 1

Unit 1　辨認文章主旨 (Main Idea)

在英文的寫作模式中，通常主題句 (topic sentence) 會出現在每個段落的第一或第二句，而文章的最後一句則多會摘錄重點或總結全文。因此快速略讀 (skimming) 這些句子有助於讀者找出文章的主題 (topic)，接著讀者要斷定針對此一主題作者所要表達的看法與觀點 (point of view)，這也就是全文的中心思想 (controlling idea)。

✳舉例而言，以下是從本書一篇文章中所節錄出來的句子：

第一段第一句

Most people feel relieved when they learn that even the world renowned Russian writer Anton Chekhov once said, "I don't understand anything about the ballet."

第二段第一句

Is this prejudice really justified, however?

第三段第一句

Try to adopt a different perspective upon ballet.

第三段最後兩句

Sit back. Let the music and grace engulf you.

　　從這幾個句子之中不難推測出文章的主題為 ballet，而作者對芭蕾的看法是鼓勵大眾去欣賞它，因此這篇文章的主旨為——Though ballet is hard to understand, people can still enjoy its remarkable skill and beautiful movement.。

✳然而有些文章沒有明顯的主題句，這時讀者就必須利用文中的<u>事實 (facts)</u>、<u>細節 (details)</u>、<u>舉例 (examples)</u> 等等歸納出主旨。此外透過找尋<u>關鍵字 (key words)</u>，意即作者反覆使用的字詞 (repetition)，也有助於辨認文章主旨。

以 94 學年度指考的閱讀測驗為例，試回答以下這題有關主旨的問題：

※ What is the main message of the passage?

　(A) A good speaker has to be fully prepared regardless of the audience.

　(B) A good speaker should display his learning to the audience in an enthusiastic way.

　(C) The more a speaker wants to please the audience, the more likely he will succeed.

　(D) The key to a successful speech is to make it meaningful and relevant to the audience.

　　Dr. Thompson was pleased. Just three months after moving to the small Midwestern town, he had been invited to address an evening meeting of the Chamber of Commerce. Here was the perfect opportunity to show his knowledge of modern medicine and to get his practice off to a flourishing start. With this in mind, the doctor prepared carefully.

　　On the night of his speech, Dr. Thompson was delighted to see that the meeting hall was full. After being introduced, he strode confidently to the lectern and announced his topic: "Recent Advances in Medicine." He began with a detailed discussion of Creutzfeldt-Jakob disease, a rare brain disorder that had recently been covered in the *New England Journal of Medicine*. Next he outlined the progress that had been made in studying immune system disorders.

　　Just about this time, halfway through his speech, Dr. Thompson began to notice a certain restlessness in his audience. People were murmuring and shuffling their feet. Someone in the fourth row seemed to be glancing at a newspaper. Nevertheless, Dr. Thompson plowed on. He had saved the best for last. He quoted extensively from an article in *the Lancet* about genetic research, feeling sure his audience would be impressed by his familiarity with this prestigious British medical journal.

　　Then the speech was over. Dr. Thompson had expected to be surrounded by enthusiastic people, congratulating him and asking questions. Instead he found himself standing alone. Finally the president of the Chamber of Commerce came up to him. "Something tells me," said Dr. Thompson, "that my speech was not very successful. I can't understand it. I worked so hard to make it interesting." "Oh, it was a fine speech," replied the president. "But maybe it would have gone over better with a different audience. Creutzfeldt-Jakob disease is not exactly a factor in these people's everyday experience. You know, here we are in January. If you'd talked about ways to avoid getting the flu, you'd have had them on the edge of their seats!"

解析技巧

此篇閱讀測驗的內容在敘述 Dr. Thompson 演講的經過，快速地看過加底線的這些句子可知，當 Dr. Thompson 受邀去演講時非常高興（第一段），演講那天整個大廳也座無虛席（第二段），但漸漸地聽眾越來越煩躁不安（第三段），而結束時也沒有人喝采或提問（第四段），文章結尾處有人建議 Dr. Thompson 若能以這裡的居民平日所會遇到的疾病，像是冬天常見的感冒問題，必定能引起觀眾的興趣。作者從這些描述與細節之中要傳達的訊息是：了解觀眾的背景與需求才能有成功的演講，故選(D)。

這類考題的題幹通常以下列幾種方式呈現：

What is the main/primary/general idea of this passage?

What is the subject/topic/purpose of this passage?

What is the best title for this passage?

The passage focuses on/centers on/mainly deals with _____ .

There is a lot to see and do in Bangkok if you can tolerate the traffic, noise, heat (in the hot season), floods (in the rainy season), and somewhat polluted air. The city is incredibly urbanized, but beneath its modern appearance lies an unmistakable Thai-ness. To say that

Bangkok is not Thailand, as has been claimed by some, is like saying that New York is not America, Paris is not France, or London is not England. Bangkok caters to diverse interests: there are temples, museums and other historic sites for those interested in traditional Thai culture; an endless variety of good restaurants, clubs, international cultural and social events, as well as movies in several different languages and a modern art institute for those seeking contemporary Krung Thep, the Thai name for Bangkok. As William Warren, an American author now living in Thailand, has said, "The gift Bangkok offers me is the assurance I will never be bored."（92 學年度指考閱讀測驗）

※ What is the main idea of this passage?

(A) The city of Bangkok is urbanized but it is also rich in traditional Thai culture.

(B) Visitors to Bangkok might find the weather, the heat, and floods unbearable.

(C) Bangkok is an international city, just like Paris, London, and New York.

(D) There are a variety of restaurants and social events in Bangkok.

解析技巧

仔細閱讀本段落的前兩句 (There is a lot to see and do..../The city is incredibly urbanized, but....)。第一句描寫曼谷的壅塞交通、噪音、悶熱氣溫、水患和空氣污染。第二句則明確指出，雖然這座城市已十分城市化，但在現代化的表面之下卻十分地泰國。由這幾句便可推知文章主旨為(A)曼谷市雖然已經十分都市化，卻也是個極富傳統泰國文化的城市。

在辨認出文章主旨之後，接下來便是了解作者如何支持、解釋或證明自己的論點。此時作者會說明 who、what、when、where、why、how 等，藉由提供例子、事實、描述、解釋、理由或統計數據等探討主題。因此讀者要仔細閱讀這些支持句 (supporting sentences)，才能徹底理解文意，通常在這些支持句前會出現一些承轉語詞 (transitional/signal words)，來引出新的理由或論證。

一般而言，在敘述文中常出現和時間相關的承轉語詞，如：first、second、next、later、then、soon afterward、suddenly、last、finally、at the same time、meanwhile、from then on、by the time、recently 等；在說明文中常出現和增添訊息相關的承轉語詞，如：first、second、moreover、besides、furthermore、in addition、also、next、last、last but not least、finally、the most important reason 等；在舉例之前常會出現的承轉語詞有 for example、for instance、such as、especially、specifically 等。此外許多連接副詞（如：therefore、thus、however、on the contrary、in other words、in fact、as a result、to sum up、in conclusion 等）也有指示文章發展方向的功用。因此在閱讀時若能多留意這些承轉語詞，也可幫助讀者在回答問題時，快速地找到該特定訊息出現的段落。

此外，在回答此類型的問題時，若能先知道所要找尋的特定訊息為何，像是人名、地點或時間等，接著便能預測出這樣的訊息會以何種方式呈現，如果考題考的是日期，便可快速掃瞄全文，鎖定文中有出現時間的地方，再進而找出所需的答案。

✳ 節錄以下 94 學年度指考閱讀測驗這個題目為例：

According to the passage, how tall will the Dubai Tower be?

　(A) At least 43 stories higher than Toronto's CN Tower.

　(B) 180 feet higher than Toronto's CN Tower.

　(C) At least 22 stories higher than the Taipei 101.

　(D) 160 feet higher than the Taipei 101.

In recent years, a craze for height has hit hard in industrializing Asian countries like Taiwan, Hong Kong and China, which boast seven of the world's 10 tallest buildings. The current tallest, at 101 floors, is the Taipei 101 in Taiwan, though Toronto's CN Tower is 180 feet higher, largely because of its huge antenna. Yet, in the Persian Gulf city of Dubai, the world's tallest building-to-be is already well under construction. Its pilings are already in place, plunging 160 feet into the earth. When it's finished, visitors will swoon over this city from 123 stories high, if not more. Currently, however, its exact height is still kept a secret to potential competitors in the world's race for the title of the tallest skyscraper.

> 問題考的是杜拜塔有多高,這道問題和數字有關,應此可快速掃瞄所節錄的文章中出現數字的部份,注意不要被和杜拜塔無關的數據弄混,最後可從文章倒數第二句 "When it's finished, visitors...." 得知杜拜塔落成後會有 123 層樓高,比台北 101 高 22 層樓,故選(C)。

Rice balls with folded plastic wrappers separating the rice from the seaweed; a dozen kinds of cold tea in a dozen different bottles—enter any convenience store in Japan, and you're immediately struck by the great variety and quality of the packaging!

Japanese companies have been accused of over-packaging; but within the Japanese cultural context, that's not really true. The Japanese tend to use more packaging because of a cultural emphasis on freshness and a lack of storage space at home. Moreover, they believe nice packaging adds value because it's a strong signal of quality. What's more, compared with Westerners, the Japanese are more connected with packaging as a symbol of appreciation, love and care. Packaging has, therefore, attained an important place in Japan's economy. The packaging market is worth over ¥ 7.4 trillion. New packaging is introduced to Japanese store shelves at a rate of 20 percent per year, the highest rate in the world. In such an environment, a product has to have more than just a nice graphic design to differentiate it from its shelf-mates. The product has to speak to the consumer's needs with both personality and practical value. In this changing industry, nothing is really certain except one thing. You can be sure that the goods out there on display on the shelves of the convenience store will soon be looking rather different.（95 學年度指考閱讀測驗）

※ Which of the following is NOT a reason for the Japanese to use more packaging?

　(A) Packaging helps to keep food fresh.

　(B) Packaging helps the Japanese to show appreciation.

　(C) The Japanese consider packaging a symbol of quality.

　(D) Packaging is a way to compete with Westerners in economy.

解析技巧

從第二段的第一句 "Japanese companies have been accused of over-packaging…."（也就是此段的主題句）可知，這一段要說明「為何日本人如此講究商品的包裝」，因此可多注意這段接下來和因果關係相關的字詞與承轉語詞，如：because of, moreover, what's more, therefore 等(A)(B)(C)分別出現在第二、第四及第三句中。而「包裝」的用意並非是與西方人在經濟上競爭的方式，因此(D)不是日本人重視包裝的原因。

Unit 3 利用上下文猜字義
(Vocabulary in Context)

　　在閱讀文章時若遇到不會的單字，讀者應學會利用上下文，也就是這個生字前、後的句子來揣測該字的意思。以下說明幾種常見的上下文線索：

1. 有時當作者在介紹一種新的事物或概念時，會直接給予定義 (definition)，這時讀者利用這線索就可猜出文中生字的意思。

✳ 以 93 年指考閱讀測驗為例：

Take "geocaching," for example. Hikers looking for something a little different on their treks created a global hunting game, hiding "caches"—packs filled with goodies like CDs, photographs, and journals—in obscure places throughout the world. They then post the coordinates at www.geocaching.com, where other hikers can use them, along with a global positioning system (GPS), to join the worldwide goose chase.

> 從這段敘述可知 geocaching，指的就是一種利用網路與科技 (a global positioning system) 的大地尋寶遊戲 (a global hunting game)。

2. 除了定義之外，為了使讀者更瞭解文意，作者也會透過舉例的方式來做說明，以上面 geocaching 這段敘述為例，作者對於何謂 cach 便有舉例說明：goodies like CDs, photographs and journals。

3. 有時文章中也會出現一些同義字 (synonym) 或反義字 (antonym)，此時讀者就必須仔細閱讀在文章中文意是承接上文或是出現轉折，同時透過觀察承轉語詞也能幫助讀者猜出生字的意思。

✳ 以 94 年學測閱讀測驗為例：

Jet lag, caused by traveling between time zones, is becoming a common problem for frequent travelers: for 49 percent it is only a nuisance and for 45 percent it is a real problem.

> 從文意的轉折，可知 nuisance 和 a real problem 為一相反詞，因此可知對於百分之四十九的人而言，時差只是個小麻煩，不是個大問題。

✳ 再以 95 年指考閱讀測驗考題為例：

They (Native Americans) respected the animals' endurance and hunting ability, and warriors prayed to hunt like them. <u>They draped themselves in wolf skins and paws</u>, hoping they could acquire the wolf's hunting skills of stealth, courage, and stamina. <u>Plaines Indians wore wolf-skin disguises</u> on raiding parties. Elite Comanche warriors were called wolves.

在 draped 一字之後，出現了另一個同義字 wore，因此讀者應訓練自己不要太過於依賴字典，善於利用上下文即可推測出單字的意思。

Queen Victoria was a stern and serious woman. One reason she was so serious was that she had suffered a great loss. When she was twenty years old, she married a German prince named Albert. Victoria and Albert were deeply in love, and their marriage was extremely happy. In 1861, after they had been married for twenty-one years, Albert died, leaving Queen Victoria heartbroken. For the rest of her life, the lonely Victoria **mourned** his loss. It was customary in those days for a widow to dress in black for a short time after the death of her husband. But Queen Victoria dressed in black for *forty years*. And for forty years, as another sign of her grief, she wrote her letters on white paper edged in black.

（節錄自 91 學年度指考閱讀測驗）

※ The word **mourned** here means _____ .

　(A) felt sad or sorrowful in a social situation

　(B) expressed publicly one's sadness because someone has died

　(C) checked regularly in order to find out what was happening

　(D) included in a group of numbers, ages, measurements with particular fixed limits

解析技巧

由此字的前文中提到 Queen Victoria 和 Prince Albert 兩人深愛對方 (deeply in love)、婚姻美滿 (extremely happy)，但當 Albert 死後，Queen Victoria 感到心碎 (heartbroken)，之後提到當時的寡婦在先生死後，會身著黑衣一段時間，但 Queen Victoria 卻穿黑衣長達 40 年之久，來表達她的悲傷 (grief)，故選(B)。

    Most shark attacks seem to have nothing to do with sharks' taste for human flesh. Their attacks are usually **prompted** by human invadinig their territory or interrupting mating. Also, underwater, swimmers resemble seals and sea lions, and their jewellery glinting in the sun can look like fish scales. Sharks may thus attack humans they mistake for marine mammals.

（節錄自 "Man-Eating Myths"《Enjoy Reading 悅讀 50》）

※ The word **prompted** in this paragraph can best be replaced by _____.

  (A) accepted   (B) denied   (C) caused   (D) prevented

解析技巧

由此字的前文及同一句可以知道鯊魚的攻擊是有其原因的 。 而該字後 "by human invading their territory or interrupting mating" 解釋了「引起、導致」的原因，因此可以推測 prompt 此字意為最接近(C)選項。

Unit 4 辨認指涉詞 (Reference)

在文章中，作者常會用指涉詞來代替前面提到的人事物。閱讀測驗的考題中，常出現要求辨認指涉詞的題目。指涉詞多半以代名詞 (one, ones, it, its, them, their, he, she, us, this, that)、助動詞 (do, does, did) 或副詞 so 的型式出現。在回答問題時，必須仔細閱讀指涉詞出現的句子，利用上下文推斷出所指涉的字詞，可從選項中代換，找出不影響原句意思的答案。需特別注意指涉詞不一定代表最接近的名詞，仍需由句意、單複數來決定。

✳ 以下是本書一篇文章摘錄下來的句子為例：

There were also no signs of the existence of any sort of device that could have been used for the battery to create light, until the discovery of rock carvings that resemble an ancient light bulb, now known as the Dendera light. So it is possible that the Egyptians may have had a working light source. Its design was copied many years later, and it worked. However, no other proof that **they** ever existed was found.

※ What does the pronoun **"they"** refer to?

⒜ Carving.　　　⒝ Light sources.　　⒞ Egyptians.　　⒟ Designs.

在回答問題時，可將四個選項代回 "no other proof that _____ ever existed was found." 的句子中，只有 "light sources" 符合原句表達的「古代埃及人的發電裝備並沒有留下實體證據」的句意，並不是代替最接近的名詞 "designs"，此句並非表示設計的證據沒有被找到。

在閱讀文章時，需養成習慣，注意關係代名詞所代表的先行詞，及同位語的使用，增進自己辨認真正主詞和指涉詞的能力。

Plastics used to account for as little as 10% of medical waste in the late 1970s, before disposables began rapidly replacing reusables. They now make up as much as 30%. The EPA estimates that the average levels of dioxin in all Americans are so high that we can expect to see a variety of health effects, including cancer. Given the harm caused by the burning of medical waste, physicians and nurses have the responsibility to take a lead in reducing the use of plastics in the hospitals. After all, they can't be treating cancer on the inside of hospitals and contributing to **it** on the outside.（節錄自 92 學測閱讀測驗）

※ What does **it** in the last line refer to?

(A) Dioxin.　　　　(B) Cancer.　　　　(C) Medical waste.　　　(D) Use of plastics.

解析技巧

此段主要說明醫院內過多的塑膠廢棄物。這裡的指涉詞 **it** 應該是代替前面提到的名詞(B) **cancer**，指醫生不能做這種事：在醫院裡治療 cancer（癌症），卻在醫院燒棄塑膠廢棄物來造成 cancer。

Unit 5　推論 (Inference)

　　一般而言，文章的作者在寫作時會直接陳述事實或自己的意見。但有時候作者並不會直接陳述意見或看法，此時則必須利用文章中所提供的事實訊息，來做合理的邏輯判斷 (inference)。

此類考題常出現的型式如下：

What can we infer from this passage?

What can be inferred from the second (first/third...) paragraph of the passage?

What is the author's attitude toward ＿＿＿＿＿？

It can be inferred from the passage that ＿＿＿＿＿.

What do we learn from this passage?

＊以 96 年指考閱讀測驗 ("Conflict diamonds") 題目為例，以下是從文章節錄出來的兩段，試回答此問題：

※ What is the author's attitude towards blood diamonds?

　(A) Indifferent　　　　(B) Threatening　　　　(C) Sympathetic　　　　(D) Disapproving

　　Conflict diamonds, sometimes called blood diamonds, are diamonds that are sold to fund the unlawful and illegal operations of rebel, military and terrorists groups. Countries that have been most affected by conflict diamonds are Sierra Leone, Angola, Liberia and the Democratic Republic of Congo. They are places where citizens have been terrorized or even killed by groups in control of the local diamond trade.

　　It's difficult for most of us to imagine what life is like in countries where diamonds are the source of so much chaos and suffering. Furthermore, the connection between terror and diamonds is not something that's reported heavily in the press. The 2006 movie *Bolld Diamond*, starring Leonard Dicarprio, should help make the issue more mainstream, if only temporarily. So, take some time to learn more about the problems that conflict diamonds create, and then follow your heart the next time you shop for a diamond.

解析技巧

作者雖然沒有直接說出對 conflict diamonds 的態度，但從 unlawful, illegal, chaos, suffering 等字的使用，可推論出作者對此種鑽石的不贊同。第二段最後也建議讀者要多了解 conflict diamonds 所造成的問題，並要本者良心去選購鑽石，因此可推斷作者關心此議題，對 blood diamonds 的態度應該是(D) **disapproving**（不贊同的）。

Try it!

These days, even a walk in the woods can be transformed into an "extreme" sport. Take "geocaching," for example. Hikers looking for something a little different on their treks created a global hunting game, hiding "caches"—packs filled with goodies like CDs, photographs, and journals—in obscure places throughout the world. They then post the coordinates at www.geocaching.com, where other hikers can use them, along with a global positioning system (GPS), to join the worldwide goose chase. Geocaching works on an honor system: When a geocacher takes something, he leaves a cache of his own behind. Vacationers can get in on this trend at resorts like Utah's Red Mountain Spa, where they can learn to use GPS and coordinates to find caches filled with spa products.（93 年指考閱讀測驗）

※ It can be inferred from the passage that _____.

  (A) geocachers like to chase geese all over the world

  (B) one can learn to be a geocacher exclusively in Utah State

  (C) geocaching requires that items be exchanged among its participants

  (D) caches are spa products hidden in remote places throughout the world

根據段落，此篇並非說 geocachers 喜歡追逐的是 geese（鵝），所以(A)不正確；而在倒數第三行中說明度假的人可以在猶他州參與這項活動，並非如(B)選項中只能在這州學習；而由 "caches"—packs filled with goodies like CDs, photographs, and journals—in obscure places throughout the world. 這句可得知，caches 並非只是 spa products，故(D)選項不正確；而由 "Geocaching works on an honor system: When a geocacher takes something, he leaves a cache of his own behind." 可推論出在拿到 caches 後，參加者必須留下一項自己的東西給別人，因此正確選項為(C)。

本書中的閱讀測驗試題，每一篇均有一題和篇章結構有關的考題。篇章結構主要是測驗讀者對整篇文意的連貫或句子和句子間的邏輯關係是否清楚了解，在作答時應先瀏覽一遍所有選項，再回來看一遍文章，每一個空格的前後句都看過後，仔細閱讀上下文，找尋承轉詞（for example, but, as a result, therefore, however, finally, in other words, moreover 等）或指示代名詞（it, they, he, she 等）所透露出來的線索，再去選擇選項。

✳ 以摘錄 96 年指考篇章結構片段為例：

Japan is dealing with a problem that is just starting to sweep the world—an aging population combined with a shrinking work force. _____(1)_____ By so doing, it is hoped that Japan's government will save its increasingly burdened pension (i.e., payment received after retirement) system from going bankrupt. In 2000, the Japanese could get a full pension from the government at 60. _____(2)_____ What's more, permiums paid by workers every month are set to rise while payouts they get after retirement fall.

⒜ The new policy could be a strain for employers.

⒝ Therefore, aged Japanese are now being encouraged to work longer in life.

⒞ And, unlike the U.S., Japan has no law against discrimination based on age.

⒟ But by 2025, they won't get any until they are 65.

⒠ These people born between 1947 and 1949 make up 5.2 million members of the work force.

由上下文得知 (By so doing...)，第一格應為一個可以用來解決日本政府退休金的辦法，故選⒝。第二格由後面的承轉詞 (what's more)，可得知此空格應該也是和後文一樣表示對勞工較為不利的情況，故選⒟。另外，⒜的前文必須要出現有關新政策 (the new policy) 的簡介，⒞的上下文應該會提到有關職場年齡歧視的內容，並且以 and 開頭一定有承接上文的作用，而⒠在說明某一些人，前文應該要有描述某一特定人群的文字。

✳ 另外一種練習如下：

He met his future wife while in America, and decided to stay there after they were married. His loving wife worked to support their family, while he continued to hone his craft. His first three Asian-themed movies, *Pushing Hands*, *The Wedding Banquet*, and *Eat Drink Man Woman*, were well received and got him noticed by Hollywood. He went on to display his versatility as a director in a wide range of movie genres, such as the period piece *Sense and Sensibility*, the dark drama *The Ice Storm*, and *Ride with the Devil*, a western. His first real taste of success came with his martial arts classic *Crouching Tiger, Hidden Dragon*. _____ His next film, the CGI-filled *Hulk*, was a major disappointment and he thought about retiring. However, he decided to continue and took a chance with a small independent film. This "little" film was the controversial *Brokeback Mountain*. The movie was critically acclaimed and gained Ang Lee every film director's dream, the Academy Award for Best Director.

※ Which of the following sentences can best fit into the blank?

　(A) It became the highest grossing foreign-language film ever released in America.

　(B) Martial arts movies are an unfamiliar genre for him and the Western audience.

　(C) The surprising success of the film opened the door to Hollywood for him.

　(D) The critics highly favored the film, but the box office was not so impressive.

解析技巧

　　此格根據上下文應為補充說明前一句有關《臥虎藏龍》電影成功的句子。(A)選項補充說明電影的成功，故為正確選項。(B)並無承轉上文電影成功的作用。(C)選項和本段前四行的內容衝突，《臥虎藏龍》並非讓李安第一次被好萊塢注意的片子。(D)選項和前句提到的 success 不合。

　　英文文章句子間的因果關係，排列的順序（比方說依時間或空間排列），推理的過程（從現象到呈現問題到提出解決之道，從簡單到複雜，從抽象概論到具體明確）

是有邏輯性的，每一段都有主題句點出該段主旨，同學在做篇章結構的練習時，要多注意文字語氣和意義上的連貫。

Try it!

Architects design new buildings and oversee work when old buildings are renewed. Carrie Jeffers is an architect whose job is making old buildings look like new. _____(1)_____ In today's cities, many old buildings are in need of repair. Sometimes bathrooms, kitchens, and electric wiring need replacing. Underneath, though, these houses are sturdy. If they could be fixed, many more people of the city would have good homes. _____(2)_____

As a young girl Carrie saw many beautiful old buildings and went to many museums. When Carrie was in college, she worked as a letter carrier in the small town of Newark, Ohio. _____(3)_____ One day she said to herself that she could make better houses than the new kind she saw going up.

Carrie studied art history in college. _____(4)_____ When she finished her studies, she found a job with a small company that mainly rehabilitates old houses in the city. She enjoyed working for the company because she got to do many different kinds of jobs.

_____(5)_____ But Carrie says you don't have to be a great artist or even very good in math to be a good architect. The one talent needed is an ability to see in your mind what a building will look like when it's finished.（93 指考）

(A) She got to look at the fine old houses as well as the new houses being built.

(B) Architects make drawings and careful plans of everything they do.

(C) The word for what she does is *rehabilitation*.

(D) Then she went on to study architecture.

(E) That is precisely what Carrie does.

1. _____ 2. _____ 3. _____ 4. _____ 5. _____

由第一格的上下文可得知主要在描述 Carrie 的工作內容，故選(C)。第二格的前文說明某種工作內容，下一段則接 Carrie 的生平，所以選(E)，來連結兩段。由第三格的後一句 "she could make better houses than the new kind she saw goingup." 可得知第三格應為和 Carrie 所看的東西有關聯，故選(A)。第四格由前文可知和學習有關係，所以選(D)，第五格選(B)來連結說明當建築師不一定要是很棒的藝術家。

參考解答：

1. C 2. E 3. A 4. D 5. B

測驗篇

　　測驗篇文章主題及題材多元，涵蓋名人介紹、科技新知、生活常識、性別議題、人文藝術等種類。

　　本測驗篇共有五十篇 250–300 字的文章，每篇文章搭配有五個問題。其中每篇各有兩題分別針對推測單字意思與辨認篇章架構能力的題目。讀者可以應用理論篇所介紹的六大閱讀技巧，來加強提升閱讀能力及速度。

ADVANCED READING 1

Intelligent Design: Creationism Repackaged?

In the early days of human history, man thought that any natural phenomenon or anything else that could not be easily explained was an act of the gods. <A> Or according to the Christian Bible, one almighty God, the Supreme Being, created everything in the universe, including man.

For many centuries, almost everyone continued to believe that God created everything on earth. Many early scientists were successful in understanding more about our world and dared to propose that there was more to it than just God. <B> However, they were often labeled as witches, sorcerers or **heretics** by religious groups who wanted to protect the belief of the existence of God. The debate went on for centuries between the people who looked at things scientifically, and those creationists who insisted that God was responsible for everything. Science eventually won and the theory of evolution is almost universally accepted.

Not to be defeated, the creationists came up with something called "Intelligent Design." Somewhat complicated, this theory basically says that science may prove some things, but it must be the work of God when a reasonable explanation can not be found. <C> Some followers of Intelligent Design go even farther and include supernatural beings and intelligent aliens. The scientific community has generally ignored this idea. Intelligent Design has only recently become an issue when its supporters pushed to have it taught in schools. Its opponents say that it is wrong to mix the pure science with religion or the supernatural and that it would be like equating astronomy with astrology.

The debate still continues. With advances in science and technology, maybe some day all of our unanswered questions will be answered, thus proving that creationism and Intelligent Design are both wrong. <D> However, Intelligent Design believers may have the last laugh with a challenge for the scientific community, "Prove that God doesn't exist."

_____ **1.** This article aims to _____ .

(A) describe the procedure of a discussion

(B) introduce a brand-new, revolutionary idea

(C) analyze a controversial subject and issue

(D) propose an explanation of a phenomenon

_____ **2.** A "**heretic**" may _____ .

(A) believe in a different religion from Christianity

(B) support the existence of one almighty God

(C) argue everything exists for a specific reason

(D) disapprove of the theory of evolution

_____ **3.** Which one of the following is TRUE of "Intelligent Design"?

(A) Scientists have doubts but generally accept it.

(B) Its followers hope it can be included in the curriculum.

(C) It excludes science in explaining phenomena on earth.

(D) Its opponents claim astrology has a great influence on it.

_____ **4.** What is the author's attitude toward the issue in the last paragraph?

(A) Eventually technology will help solve the dispute.

(B) Creationism is not likely to have many supporters.

(C) Intelligent Design believers may still gain the upper hand.

(D) The scientific community must try to prove God does not exist.

_____ **5.** The following sentence can be added to the article.

"**Ancient civilizations worshipped many different gods. The gods brought good fortune when they were pleased and punished mankind for any wrong.**"

Where would it best fit in the article?

From Scared Kid to the Best Storyteller

You know a kid like this: the scared, unathletic type. The kind of kid who is lousy at sports. The kind of kid who wails for his mother when trees brush against his house at night. The kind of kid who watches a TV program on snakes and has nightmares about it for weeks afterwards. <A> He wove amazing tales about those night-time trees, inventing one imaginative yarn after another.

Who is this person? Movie director and producer Steven Spielberg.

The young Spielberg loved to terrify himself as well as others. <B> He would push his sisters into a closet, in which a plastic skull glowed. As he locked them inside, he would turn off the light; the skull would eerily light up. Of course, his sisters shrieked. Spielberg's *Indiana Jones* movies, as well as his film *War of the Worlds* are filled with scenes that keep audiences spellbound—and frightened.

Spielberg was influenced by many other experiences that did not necessarily **go bump in the night**. <C> When he was four, the young Spielberg would spend hours meteor-gazing with his father. His movie *Close Encounters of the Third Kind*, is a tribute to this meaningful experience with his dad. A practicing Jew, Spielberg was greatly affected by the courage of Oskar Schindler, a German who saved 1,100 Jews from dying in World War II concentration camps. Spielberg won the Academy Award for best director of his 1993 masterpiece *Schindler's List*.

You never can tell what kind of adult a kid will become. Spielberg is the perfect example. <D> This scared kid became an adult who makes movies that continue to enthrall people and change lives worldwide.

_____ **1.** This article is primarily about _____.

(A) what motivates Steven Spielberg to attain his goal

(B) how experiences shape Steven Spielberg's films

(C) the biography of the storyteller Steven Spielberg

(D) the severe criticism Steven Spielberg has to face

_____ **2.** Based on the article, which of Spielberg's films might deal with the issue about Nazis soldiers and the Holocaust?

(A) *Indiana Jones.*   (B) *War of the Worlds.*

(C) *Close Encounters of the Third Kind.*   (D) *Schindler's List.*

_____ **3.** Which of the following statements is TRUE?

(A) As a sportsperson, Spielberg was very popular in school.

(B) As the only child, Spielberg liked to play jokes on his friends.

(C) Spielberg received the Academy Award for Best Actor in 1993.

(D) Spielberg's films owe much inspiration to his childhood memories.

_____ **4.** When something "**goes bump in the night**," it makes you feel _____.

(A) astonished   (B) frightened   (C) interested   (D) overjoyed

_____ **5.** The following sentence can be added to the article.

"**Yet this pathetic little person used stories to alleviate his fears.**"

Where would it best fit in the article?

CAN One Enjoy Ballet?? Just Maybe...

Most people feel relieved when they learn that even the world-renowned Russian writer Anton Chekhov once said, "I don't understand anything about the ballet." <A> They envision skilled athlete-artists leaping in the air and doing extremely stylized moves. The costumes, more often than not, look antiquated. And what's with this dancing on the points of one's toes!

Is this prejudice really justified, however? If someone said, "Are you afraid of watching ballroom dancing?" the invariable response would be, "Of course not!" We all admire the vigor of the tango, or the grace of a waltz. Why, then, does ballet—just another form of dance—instill such **antipathy** in most of us? Part of this cultural attitude is based on ballet's history. <B> No doubt, it's an elitist art form. From the glittering courts of Renaissance Italy to the grand French palaces of the eighteenth century, ballet has been funded and enjoyed by royalty and the privileged classes. <C> Ballet became known as an art form that only a few could really understand and appreciate.

Try to adopt a different perspective upon ballet. With his or her body, the ballet dancer performs incredible acts of strength, poise, and emotion. A ballerina taking flight in a jeté[1] looks as if she defies gravity. Years of astonishingly hard work and discipline have resulted in dancers' bodies that can turn, lift, and leap effortlessly like excellent acrobats. <D> So what if the moves are stylized or the plots old fashioned? Everyone can marvel at the skill involved. Go to a performance. Sit back. Let the music and grace engulf you.

[1]jeté: A leap in ballet in which one leg is extended forward and the other backward.

_____ **1.** The word **"antipathy"** in the 2nd paragraph is closest in meaning to _____.

(A) envy   (B) energy   (C) praise   (D) dislike

_____ **2.** Prejudice against ballet comes from the following reasons **EXCEPT** for

_____ .

(A) the unnatural moves   (B) the unfamiliar story line

(C) the out-of-date costumes   (D) the historical background

_____ **3.** The author probably would agree that _____.

(A) ballet is an entertainment for the rich

(B) ballet is a show of strength and beauty

(C) ballet originates from Italy and France

(D) ballet demands its audience's full attention

_____ **4.** What is this article mainly about?

(A) Though ballet is hard to understand, people can still enjoy its remarkable skill and beautiful movement.

(B) People find it hard to identify with ballet dancers because their bodies seem to exceed physical limits.

(C) If you get some proper training in watching ballet, you will learn to enjoy this complicated art form.

(D) The prevailing opinion is in favor of ballroom dancing because it is fun to learn as well as to watch.

_____ **5.** The following sentence can be added to the article.

"In fact, many people hold a similar opinion of this dance form."

Where would it best fit in the article?

Key to Our Survival?

A toothpick is something that is usually taken for granted, a trivial thing that you can do without in your daily life, but at times it's **indispensable**. It costs next to nothing, but when you really need one, it can be priceless. <A> On top of all that, nobody is sure who invented it. It is also probably the oldest instrument used for dental hygiene and may have played an important role in the survival of humans as a species.

Historical records date the first use of toothpicks, or some form of wooden instrument, back to somewhere between 500B.C. and 700A.D. by Buddhist monks as part of their cleansing ritual. <B> This practice was then adopted by the nobility, and then spread to the general public as awareness of the importance of good dental hygiene grew. This concern for having clean and healthy teeth leads to dental innovations such as the toothbrush and dental floss.

Anthropologists studying the teeth of early humans found curved grooves near the base of the teeth, which they believed were caused by some sort of tool used to clean the teeth. <C> More recent studies found similar grooves in fossilized teeth dating back even earlier to 1.8 million years ago!

These findings have led many to believe that the toothpick ranks up there with things such as fire as a key to our survival. The reason is that if one of our prehistoric ancestors hadn't got really annoyed with a little piece of food stuck in his teeth and hadn't been smart enough to find something to use to pick it out, his teeth would have rotted and fallen out. <D> Without teeth he would not have been able to eat. If he hadn't been able to eat, he would have died. And if he had died, we wouldn't be here today.

_____ **1.** What is the article mainly about?

    (A) The sanitary condition of our prehistoric ancestors.

    (B) The origin and inventor of dental floss.

    (C) The importance of dental hygiene.

    (D) The practice and significance of a cleansing tool.

_____ **2.** Which evidence proves the existence of tooth-picking in ancient times?

    (A) The use of fire.

    (B) The curved grooves.

    (C) The intact fossilized teeth.

    (D) The finding of dental floss.

_____ **3.** The following facts about toothpicks are correct **EXCEPT** _____.

    (A) The use of toothpicks has never been documented.

    (B) Early humans may have used wooden toothpicks to clean teeth.

    (C) Toothpicks have once carried some symbolic religious meaning.

    (D) Toothpicks are related to the physical health of human beings.

_____ **4.** In the 1st paragraph, which of the following words is closest to the meaning of the word "**indispensable**"?

    (A) Avoidable.   (B) Disposable.   (C) Vital.   (D) Lethal.

_____ **5.** The following sentence can be added to the article.

    "**It seems that our early human ancestors may have used grass, which was easily found and ready to use, to floss between their teeth.**"

    Where would it best fit in this article?

Unit 05

Five Foot-Something

What's *five foot-something*? It's the average adult human height. Actually, there isn't an exact figure; however, statistics show that the average falls somewhere between five and six feet (153 cm～183 cm). If your height is a little above or below this range, you're considered normal, unless your height is more than 20 percent above or below this range. Many things, such as furniture and doors, are usually designed to suit the average-sized person. Being too tall or too short may be ridiculed or have problems finding suitable clothing, but it can also have advantages, especially in sports such as basketball, horse racing or auto racing.

But what determines a person's height? <5> Researchers claim that the genes passed on to you from your parents account for about 60～80 percent, while the environment you live in and your standard of living and level of nutrition as you mature, account for 20～40 percent. Historically, people in western countries have always been taller than Asians, but as the standard of living and level of nutrition improves, people in some Asian nations are quickly catching up with their western counterparts. For instance, according to the latest statistics, in the United States the average American male is 5'10" (178 cm), while the average American female is 5'4 1/2" (164 cm). In Taiwan, the average height of men and women are 5'7 1/2" (171 cm) and 5'2 3/4" (159 cm), respectively.

Studies also show that average human height is slowly increasing as more and more countries are becoming better developed. But the studies have also revealed a strange trend in the western world; the average height in Europe is increasing, while in America it's actually decreasing. Some people, especially Europeans, theorize that it's because of Americans' **obsession** with junk food, which is making them fatter rather than taller.

_____ **1.** The author introduces the main idea by _____ .

(A) clarifying a misconception

(B) explaining the meaning of a phrase

(C) providing the result of an opinion poll

(D) analyzing some statistics

_____ **2.** Which of the following can be inferred from the article?

(A) Average-sized people can live a carefree life.

(B) Europeans are worried about the problem of obesity.

(C) Better developed countries may have taller citizens.

(D) Compared with men, women generally lack proper nutrition.

_____ **3.** If you have "**obsession**" with something, that means you _____ it.

(A) love   (B) resent   (C) make use of   (D) are wary of

_____ **4.** According to the statistics provided here, which one is TRUE?

(A) 20% of people in the world are above or below the average height.

(B) The living standard plays a major role in determining people's height.

(C) On average, women in Taiwan are shorter than their American counterparts by 5 cm.

(D) Those who are not five-foot something usually excel in designing furniture and horse racing.

_____ **5.** Which one of the following can be best added to the blank in the 2nd paragraph?

(A) Height variations within a population are mostly genetic.

(B) Researchers have shown that height loss is linked to heart disease.

(C) Biologists point out that genetics and environment are two decisive factors.

(D) In human world, the average height is indicative of the social class.

WHAT'S IN A NAME?

What's in a name? That which we call a rose

By any other name would smell as sweet.

—*Romeo and Juliet*, Act II, Scene II

According to Shakespeare, our names do not define who we are. But they certainly identify us and follow us throughout our lives. <u><A></u> Thus, parents take special care when naming their children.

Boys are often given names that convey a sense of strength and tradition. Of the ten most popular boys' names in the United States in 2005, nine come from the Bible. <u><B></u> Also, it is somewhat common for firstborn sons to take the full name of their fathers, thus carrying on the strength and tradition of the family.

Only five of the top ten girls' names in 2005 are from the Bible because, unlike boys' names, girls' names are often chosen for beauty or sentimentality. One way girls' names become popular is through movies and the arts. <u><C></u> The fifth most popular name in 2005, Olivia, originally appeared in Shakespeare's comedy, *Twelfth Night*.

In the Black community, some parents draw strength from their African **heritage** when naming their children. Names might be chosen from words in African languages that mean king, queen, strong, beauty, or the like. <u><D></u> But other times, Black parents mix African words and syllables to create new, unique names.

So while a name might not define who we are, it is often the first thing people learn about us and the last thing people remember. It is no wonder that we look to our names for strength, beauty and pride.

_____ **1.** Which of the following can also be used as a title for the article?

(A) Why People Need Names

(B) How Parents Name Their Children

(C) How People Like Their First Names

(D) Why Boys and Girls are Named Differently

_____ **2.** Which of the following is an example of the naming practice to pass down one's family customs and spirits?

(A) Mrs. Joan White named her daughter Joan White.

(B) Mrs. Jane Stevenson names her son John Stevenson.

(C) Mr. James Smith named his firstborn son James Smith.

(D) Mr. Martin King named his firstborn daughter Olivia King.

_____ **3.** Based on the article, what is the author's viewpoint on the quotation from Shakespeare's *Romeo and Juliet*?

(A) The author believes that the quotation is out of date.

(B) The author agrees with the implication of the quotation.

(C) The author does not understand Shakespeare's intention.

(D) The author expresses different opinions of the quotation.

_____ **4.** The meaning of the word "**heritage**" is similar to _____.

(A) creation　　　(B) definition　　　(C) invention　　　(D) tradition

_____ **5.** The following sentence can be added to the article.

"**Madison, the third most popular name in 2005, was virtually unheard of until a character took the name in the movie, *Splash*, in 1984.**"

Where would it best fit in the article?

Procrastination: A Barrier to Completing Work

<A> **W**ith many jobs and school courses requiring meeting deadlines, sometimes people put off doing their work. There's even a word that describes the lack of motivation to getting things done: it's called "procrastination." And though some people may mock others who procrastinate, it can cause profound **distress** and despair.

<B> Psychological professionals believe that procrastination can be caused by either physical problems with the brain or by mental difficulties. The physical causes of procrastination may be that the part of the brain that deals with organizing work is damaged or not working properly. The mental or psychological problems that cause procrastination can include low self-esteem, a vague feeling that things aren't going to turn out right, or mental depression, from which people feel sad and hopeless, making it very difficult for them to get anything done.

<C> There are also two main types of procrastinators: those who worry a lot about the work they're not getting done, and those who are calm about their procrastination. The first type of people have many negative feelings about not completing their work, and the relaxed type of procrastinators will generally not worry about the work they're not getting done.

<D> Understanding why you procrastinate is the first step in stopping the behavior. Another helpful method is to prioritize your tasks and pay close attention to time management. Setting goals and promising to meet these goals are also ways of avoiding procrastination and increasing work and schoolwork productivity.

Regardless of someone's reason for procrastinating, he or she should try to consult with a counselor to learn about what may be causing their procrastination and how to overcome it.

_____ **1.** The word "**distress**" in the 1st paragraph is closest in meaning to _____.

    (A) anxiety   (B) contempt   (C) ecstasy   (D) serenity

_____ **2.** Based on the expert's explanation, which of the following is **NOT** a possible cause of procrastination?

    (A) Brain malfunction.   (B) Lack of self-confidence.

    (C) Poor working habits.   (D) Pessimistic attitude.

_____ **3.** Which of the following statements is TRUE?

    (A) Procrastinators are constantly worrying about the unfinished work.

    (B) Putting off doing things may cause people much stress and torment.

    (C) The first step in stopping procrastination is to manage one's time well.

    (D) Counselors are not able to help procrastinators with physical problems.

_____ **4.** Which of the following writing mode is **NOT** used in the article?

    (A) Cause and effect.   (B) Problem and solution.

    (C) Compare and contrast.   (D) Classification and division.

_____ **5.** The following sentence can be added to the blank in the article.

    "**Though chronic procrastination can be overwhelming, thankfully, there are some ways to modify one's procrastination behavior.**"

    Where would it best fit in the article?

Exit the Dragon?

For thousands of years, dragons have played an important and beneficial role in Chinese culture. In China, the dragon acts as a positive symbol, conveying peace and prosperity. <A> Nonetheless, some officials now fear that it is hurting the country's image in the West, where dragons are considered evil. This has led to a debate within China about how to preserve the country's cultural heritage while improving perceptions abroad.

In 2006, the dragon controversy began when a professor in Shanghai suggested that China relinquish the dragon as its national symbol because of its negative image in the West. Others agreed, **asserting** that young Chinese do not admire the dragon as much as older people, partly as a result of Western influences such as the Harry Potter series, which portray dragons as monsters. <B>

Regardless of such worries, the dragon remains important to most Chinese, who view it as the ancestor of their nation. Instead of abandoning the dragon, another professor recommended that people begin calling it "loong," the word in Chinese character, as a way to distinguish it from the fire-breathing Western interpretation. He argued that this would emphasize the positive aspects of the Chinese dragon, which include bringing needed rains. <C> Others have advocated the adoption of a new national symbol, such as the panda or the pig, but these options are unpopular among most Chinese.

The dragon debate in China reveals its increasing importance around the world. <D> As China continues to expand, more foreigners will pay attention to what it does. The way that the Chinese deal with their dragon will determine how other people view the country for many years.

_____ **1.** What is the main idea of this article?

(A) Dragons are no longer mysterious creatures.

(B) The dragon's majestic status is still rooted in China.

(C) China 's image around the globe is changing.

(D) Interpretations about dragons reveal cultural differences.

_____ **2.** What can be the reason for **NOT** using dragons as China's national symbol?

(A) Dragons have power to control the weather.

(B) The image of the dragon is a negative in the west.

(C) Western countries exercise some influence on China.

(D) The negative image of China is proved correct.

_____ **3.** Those who recognize the significance of dragons may agree that _____.

(A) "loong" would be a better word to refer to dragons

(B) pandas enjoy more popularity than dragons

(C) the controversy over dragons are overstated

(D) positive aspects of dragons are well-received

_____ **4.** Which of the following words is most similar to the meaning of the word "**assert**" in the 2nd paragraph?

(A) Manipulate.　　(B) Declare.　　　(C) Interfere.　　　(D) Differentiate.

_____ **5.** "**The government's rejection of the dragon as a possible mascot for the 2008 Olympics in Beijing only elevated these concerns.**"

In which blank of this article can we best add the above sentence?

The Cultural Impact of TV's Friends

You could say that the TV show *Friends* made quite an impact on society. <A> During its ten-year run, the situation comedy gave audiences a peek at the day-to-day lives of six close friends, Rachel, Monica, Phoebe, Ross, Chandler and Joey. Each character had their own unique personality, which endeared them to viewers. Many people were envious of their seemingly carefree and ideal, if not quite realistic, lifestyle and wanted to **emulate** them.

Many of the show's aspects were mimicked by the public. <B> For instance, one of the character's hairstyle became very popular and was officially called "The Rachel." The frequent use of the word "so" by the characters, as an intensifier to mean "very," caused increased use of the word in this manner by the public, although this usage did not originate from the show. Many of the characters' catchphrases also became popular, such as Ross' excuse for his infidelity, "We were on a break!", Monica's emphatic "I know!", and Joey's trademark, "How *you* doin'?" <C> Many groups of friends liked to try to figure out who was which "Friend" in the group. It also became quite common to hear people use the characters' names to describe others. "He's such a Ross," might be used to describe a guy who's timid and whiny. "Don't go all Monica on me," might be a warning not to act like the obsessive-compulsive perfectionist character.

Friends was a funny and entertaining show, and it did indeed have an effect on popular culture; the increased popularity of coffee houses for example. <D> However, time goes on and things change. New styles and trends will arise, and maybe someday we'll just look back at *Friends* with a touch of nostalgia.

_____ **1.** This article focuses on _____ .
(A) the negative impact of celebrities
(B) social aspects influenced by media
(C) interesting episodes between six friends
(D) the linguistic change caused by reality show

_____ **2.** According to the article, if you describe someone as a "Ross," that means he is probably _____ .
(A) faithful and obedient to his wife
(B) fond of academic research work
(C) not brave and likes to complain
(D) fearless and demands perfection

_____ **3.** The characters in *Friends* have influenced its audience in many aspects **EXCEPT** _____ .
(A) the emergence of the word "so"
(B) the popularity of a hairstyle
(C) the increasing popularity of coffee shops
(D) the way people describe others' personalities

_____ **4.** Which word has the similar meaning of the word "**emulate**"?
(A) Replace.   (B) Imitate.   (C) Modify.   (D) Outweigh.

_____ **5.** Where can we best add the following sentence in the article?
"**Most people could identify with all of the characters and each of their many peculiar habits.**"

Ang Lee's Path to Success

After Ang Lee failed the JCEE (Joint College Entrance Examination) the second time, his parents' dream that he would someday become a professor was dashed. Most people would have thought that he had little hope for future success, but not Lee. He decided to enroll in the National Taiwan College of Arts instead, where he developed an interest in film making. After graduation, he went to the United States to continue his studies.

He met his future wife while in America, and decided to stay there after they were married. His loving wife worked to support their family, while he continued to hone his craft. His first three Asian-themed movies, *Pushing Hands*, *The Wedding Banquet*, and *Eat Drink Man Woman*, were well received and got him noticed by Hollywood. He went on to display his **versatility** as a director in a wide range of movie genres, such as the period piece *Sense and Sensibility*, the dark drama *The Ice Storm*, and *Ride with the Devil*, a western. His first real taste of success came with his martial arts classic *Crouching Tiger, Hidden Dragon*. <5> His next film, the CGI-filled *Hulk*, was a major disappointment and he thought about retiring. However, he decided to continue and took a chance with a small independent film. This "little" film was the controversial *Brokeback Mountain*. The movie was critically acclaimed and gained Ang Lee every film director's dream, the Academy Award for Best Director.

Ang Lee's success most certainly has surpassed his parents' dreams. His story is also a good example of how one can still succeed after any sort of failure or disappointment if they have the will and determination, no matter which road they take.

CGI: computer generated image

_____ **1.** Another suitable title for this article would be "_____."

(A) The Rise of an Asian Actor

(B) Capability Determines Everything

(C) Choose the Road Less Traveled by

(D) Achievement Is Dependent on Effort

_____ **2.** According to the article, from which event can we see Ang Lee's determination?

(A) His wife earned money to support his career before he succeeded.

(B) He decided to study in a college of arts after setbacks in JCEE.

(C) He let Hollywood recognize the talent and effort of Asian directors.

(D) He made attempts to sharpen his skills in directing and script writing.

_____ **3.** Which description of Lee's movies is TRUE?

(A) *Pushing Hands* deals with life of middle-age crisis in America.

(B) *Brokeback Mountain* is a successful movie with a huge budget.

(C) *Hulk*, full of fancy special effects, was not well received by the public.

(D) *Crouching Tigers, Hidden Dragons* earned him an Oscar for best director.

_____ **4.** Which of the following word is **OPPOSITE** to the word "**versatility**"?

(A) Adaptability.　　(B) Inflexibility.　　(C) Diversity.　　(D) Sensitivity.

_____ **5.** Which of the following sentences can best fit into the blank?

(A) It became the highest grossing foreign-language film ever released in the United States.

(B) Martial arts movies are an unfamiliar genre for him and the Western audience.

(C) The surprising success of the film opened the door to Hollywood for him.

(D) The critics highly favored the film, but the box office was not so impressive.

Uncoding the da Vinci Surgery System

A surgeon cuts an incision into a patient. Sanitized surgical implements invade the body. Eventually, the operation is over and the patient's incision is sewn up. The individual, who would awaken in great pain, has just experienced great trauma to the body; he or she could be facing a long, painful, recovery.

Soon, this invasive surgery could be a procedure of the past: Robotic surgery is revolutionizing the way surgeons ply their craft and eliminating the harsh effects of cold metal invading the body. <5> One is a console, away from the patient, where the surgeon is located, and the other, a robot cart with four arms, placed next to the patient. Before the operation, three tiny slits are inserted into the patient's body. An even tinier camera is placed inside one of the openings. The surgeon uses controls that look like joysticks; these tools control arms of the robot cart, which are inserted into the patient's body. As the surgeon peers into the console, he or she sees precise, three-dimensional images from inside the patient's body. Using wrist movements on the joysticks, the surgeon tells the machines what to do; the machines, faithfully imitating the surgeon's movements, do it all perfectly—more perfectly than any human could.

Doctors in around 800 hospitals worldwide are using the da Vinci Surgical System for many procedures, including surgery for cancer and heart problems. The benefits to the patients are **myriad**: shorter recuperation period, less pain, and reduced risk of infection. Most importantly, patients can more quickly go back to their normal activities and put their surgery behind them.

Today, robotic surgery is making surgery one of the gentler and more precise arms of medicine. Who could have imagined this, even a few years ago?

_____ **1.** What is the purpose of the 1st paragraph?

(A) To explain regulations in an operation room.

(B) To describe traditional surgical procedures.

(C) To analyze the stress experienced by patients.

(D) To remind readers of the importance of health.

_____ **2.** Which of the following statements about the da Vinci Surgical System is TRUE?

(A) Surgeons have to make large incisions in a patient's body.

(B) This operation may leave patients more vulnerable to infection.

(C) The robotic machines can exactly mimic surgeons' wrist movement.

(D) Before the surgery, a tiny camera has to be swallowed by patients.

_____ **3.** As used in the article, the word **"myriad"** means _____.

(A) finite   (B) innumerable   (C) mysterious   (D) triumphant

_____ **4.** What is the author's opinion on technological improvement in medical field?

(A) It is against the will of God.   (B) It needs to be reevaluated.

(C) It is beneficial to patients.   (D) It is a two-edged sword.

_____ **5.** Which sentence best fits the blank in the 2nd paragraph?

(A) The downside of robotic surgery is that more time is needed to perform surgery.

(B) The da Vinci Surgical System differs from the traditional surgery in some aspects.

(C) The major benefits of the use of robotic equipment for operations are as follows.

(D) This technique known as the da Vinci Surgical System has two main components.

Stay-at-Home-Dads: A Kindlier, Gentler Society?

Until recently, the mother-child bond was considered sacrosanct in most societies. If a mother worked too long hours, she was often criticized for caring more about her career than about her child. Conversely, fathers were relegated as distant—albeit friendly—caregivers who found satisfaction in putting a roof over their families' heads.

Times are changing. Take the case of British mechanic Neil Walkingshaw. After his wife gave birth to a son in 2000, the couple agreed: Neil should work part-time to devote more care to his son. Refused when he asked his employer for a part-time job contract, the mechanic then sued the company on grounds of sexual discrimination. When his case was settled, Walkingshaw won and took home £3,600.

This ruling tells us how much society has changed. <5> The U.S.-based organization, the National Fatherhood Initiative, has publicized research that demonstrates the importance of a father to the well-being of his children. Here are some facts:

• Children in fatherless homes are five times more likely to be living in poverty.
• Young men with no stay-at-home-dads are much more likely to land in prison than those who have fathers in their lives.
• Fatherless children are twice as likely to drop out of school.

A 2003 British survey revealed that 33% of expectant fathers would prefer to work part time in order to spend more time with their children. The same trend is occurring across the Big Pond: The U.S. has an estimated 159,000 stay-at-home dads; that's three times as many as there were a decade ago. Could these small changes **pronounce** the beginning of a kindlier, gentler society—a society that encourages fathers to be the very best ones they can be—without discrimination of any kind?

_____ **1.** In the 1st paragraph, the author introduced the topic by _____ .

(A) explaining parents' rights and responsibilities in today's society

(B) contrasting the conventional images between mothers and fathers

(C) analyzing the opinions the public have long held on child rearing

(D) criticizing the common gender stereotypes prevailed in our society

_____ **2.** We can infer from the passage that Neil Walkingshaw _____ .

(A) is an irresponsible father   (B) is willing to look after his child

(C) lost the case against his company   (D) was accused of sexual harassment

_____ **3.** Which of the following statements is **NOT** true?

(A) The absence of the father can contribute to an increase in child poverty.

(B) Households without fathers risk social problems and higher crime rates.

(C) In a 2003 survey one third of expectant fathers want to work fewer hours.

(D) There were about 53,000 stay-at-home dads in America twenty years ago.

_____ **4.** Accroding to the article, the word "**pronounce**" means _____ .

(A) to utter a particular sound   (B) to raise someone to a higher rank

(C) to become noticeable   (D) to announce formally

_____ **5.** Which sentence best fits the blank in the 3rd paragraph?

(A) Both men and women should take their parental duties more seriously.

(B) Fathers usually have little hands-on experience in actually raising a child.

(C) Increasingly, fathers are expected to play a larger role in their children's lives.

(D) The absence of a father could cause great harm to a child's mental development.

Unit 13

The Puzzle of Memory

As we age, we **fret** about memory: Are we becoming more forgetful than ever before? Are people beginning to whisper behind our backs? Memory is a complex phenomenon. How does the process of creating memories take place? What can help us recollect things more clearly?

<5> When we experience something new, the brain's immediate memory is activated. The images transformed from our sensory stimuli are sent to the hippocampus, located behind the ears, where the information is processed and stored temporarily in short-term memory. This small part of the brain organizes this information and then transfers it to the frontal lobe of the brain——the cerebral cortex——for long-term memory retrieval. Without the hippocampus, every new experience becomes a first-time wonder, only to float away like a feather in the wind.

Indeed, in the 1950s, a man now known as **"HM,"** who had been suffering from epilepsy, had his hippocampus cut out during a brain operation. Though after the surgery his seizures did go away, HM, now in his 80s, is caught in a tragic memory trap: He still thinks Harry S. Truman is President of the United States. He does not remember a person three minutes after that person has gone.

How can we improve our memory retention? Eating the right vegetables may help: Vitamin E breaks down chemicals—called free radicals—that might cause some brain damage. Hence, eating foods rich in Vitamin E such as spinach, almonds, and sunflower seeds could improve one's memory. Also, there seems to be a correlation between improved memory and the following: making an effort to keep one's brain active; reducing stress; and getting enough sleep. Perhaps the age-old adage, "eat right and sleep right," still holds good.

_____ **1.** When a person **"frets"** over something, he or she becomes _____.

    (A) anxious   (B) exhausted   (C) humorous   (D) relaxed

_____ **2.** The memory that could be recalled in the future exists in _____.

    (A) brain's immediate memory   (B) our sensory stimuli

    (C) the hippocampus   (D) the cerebral cortex

_____ **3.** Which description about **"HM"** is TRUE?

    (A) He forgets events previous to the operation.

    (B) He still suffers from epilepsy after the operation.

    (C) He cannot form new memories after the operation.

    (D) He is an enthusiastic supporter of Harry S. Truman.

_____ **4.** In order to improve our memory, what should we avoid?

    (A) A good night's sleep.   (B) Foods rich in free radicals.

    (C) Staying mentally sharp.   (D) Eating green vegetables.

_____ **5.** Which sentence best fits the blank in the 2nd paragraph?

    (A) The process by which we retrieve information or memories in our brains consists of several major stages.

    (B) Scientists are investigating how the memory is formed and why some people have extraordinary memories.

    (C) We have learned that a tiny part of the brain called the hippocampus plays a major role in memory formation.

    (D) Once the delicate and complicated organ—brain—is damaged, we are incapable of holding on to any memories.

Pluto Gets Plutoed

How do you turn the name of a planet into a verb? Just downgrade its status to a dwarf planet. That's exactly what happened to the former planet of Pluto in August 2006. <A> People thought it was so strange that astronomers suddenly decided to **demote** the planet and the word "plutoed" quickly came into use in popular culture. It means to be demoted without a good cause or reason. While "plutoed" is intended to be a humorous use of the word "Pluto," there was a lot of serious controversy surrounding changing Pluto's status.

Discovered in 1930, Pluto was known—before its status was changed—as our solar system's ninth and most remote planet from the sun. But as astronomers began discovering an increasing number of planet-like spheres about Pluto's size, scientists speculated if Pluto should actually be considered a planet. <B> After all, it is minuscule for a planet, and there are many similar objects in its surrounding area approximately the same size.

In 1992, even more space objects in Pluto's proximity were discovered in the Kuiper Belt, a band of moon-size bodies orbiting the sun. Subsequent to this find, astronomers began wondering if Pluto belonged to the Kuiper Belt, and if so, it should not be classified as a true planet. <C> But in July 2005, a celestial object larger than Pluto—a dwarf planet called Eris—was discovered orbiting the Sun between the planets Neptune and Pluto. <D> Nevertheless, this marked the end of Pluto's planet status. If Eris isn't a planet, scientists reasoned, neither is Pluto.

The story of Pluto shows that nothing can remain the same forever, even within the scientific community. As humans learn more about our surroundings, near and far, other classifications may change, too.

_____ **1.** What is the general public's attitude toward Pluto's change of status?

(A) Positive.　　　(B) Indifferent.　　　(C) Surprising.　　　(D) Unfriendly.

_____ **2.** Which word is similar to the word **"demote"**?

(A) Omit.　　　(B) Devalue.　　　(C) Terminate.　　　(D) Utilize.

_____ **3.** Why did scientists disagree on Pluto's status as a planet?

(A) It is the most remote and isolated member in the solar system.

(B) There are a great many satellites and comets in its proximity.

(C) It belonged to Kuiper Belt, which was supposed to orbit the moon.

(D) It was relatively small in comparison with the other planets.

_____ **4.** According to the article, the author may agree that _____.

(A) more new words may be coined in the future

(B) scientific facts are also subject to change

(C) Eris may eventually take the place of Pluto

(D) scientists should not cause controversy

_____ **5.** Where can we best put the following sentence?

"The media initially called it the 'tenth planet,' although there was no official consensus at the time on whether to call it a planet or not."

What Motivates You?

Motivation is the energy that pushes us to get things done, to complete formidable tasks and to strive for an explicit goal. A common definition of this driving force is "the persistence of behavior." <u><5></u>

But what prompts us to succeed? Many scientists have undertaken studies on motivation, and there are many different answers, which can be classified as social acceptance, cognitive (thinking), affective (emotional) and conative (goals) factors.

Being motivated for social acceptance can be a crucial factor in success. This approval of one's peers involves being part of a group and following the actions of people you admire. For students, **this** can mean doing things to be in the group of people you value.

Cognitive motivation involves wanting to learn more about the world around you and to solve problems. People with this type of motivation are often scientists, doctors or researchers. Good students usually have this type of motivation as well.

Affective motivation may seem like the most basic type of motivation because it involves shunning things that make you feel unpleasant and working toward things that make your life enjoyable. People with this type of motivation are seeking an overall feeling of happiness and control in their lives.

Conative motivation involves goals, personal dreams and independence. Those who are highly motivated this way usually know exactly what they want in life, as far as jobs, friends, spouses and homes, and the things they do in life directly relate to fulfilling these **objectives**.

Perhaps this information will give you an idea of what might spur you on to greater accomplishments. Understanding more about these motivations could assist you in recognizing both the paths and barriers to your personal success.

_____ **1.** In the 3rd paragraph, the word **this** in the sentence "For students, this can mean doing things to be in the group of people you value" means _____.
(A) being strongly motivated   (B) following others' opinions
(C) winning social acceptance   (D) approving peers' actions

_____ **2.** The synonym for the word "**objective**" is _____.
(A) ambition   (B) substance   (C) actual   (D) impartial

_____ **3.** If Alan is keen on new discoveries and always tries to get to the bottom of everything, what kind of motivation is most likely to drive him to succeed?
(A) Social acceptance.   (B) Cognitive motivation.
(C) Affective motivation.   (D) Conative motivation.

_____ **4.** The author used several techniques to clarify his points **EXCEPT** by

_____.

(A) offering a definition   (B) providing examples
(C) showing the classification   (D) giving personal experience

_____ **5.** Choose a sentence that best fits into the blank in the 1st paragraph.
(A) A closer look at this enables you to comprehend what can effectively stimulate you.
(B) In other words, it means repeatedly doing something to achieve personal aspirations.
(C) There are as many things that motivate people to succeed as there are people in the world.
(D) For workers, it implies trying to fit into some social class, which often involves jobs or income.

Game On

Computer gaming today is a phenomenally popular form of entertainment that spans many genres and platforms. Its appeal is primarily due to the fact that console systems and modern PCs are so versatile that there is almost a game for every person and every moment.

Gaming has influenced other parts of modern life as well. Games have been converted into movies, like the *Tomb Raider* series, or cartoons. Gamers have also altered the way we communicate with each other; for example, 1337 speak and emoticons are now in our common usage.

Some games have progressed beyond being simple pastimes, and are recognized as serious, competitive sports. <5> At any one moment in time, up to 300,000 people are playing *Counter-Strike*. For high-profile gamers, winning a prize at a major event like the World Cyber Games (WCG) means interviews, fame, sponsorship deals, product endorsements, and even salaries as high as US$1 million a year.

The stereotype of the gamer as an unattractive teenager with no friends is well and truly gone. In South Korea, for instance, professional *StarCraft* players are treated like rock stars! Top players have thousands of fans, and their games are major events that draw huge crowds and are screened on the Internet and even on dedicated television stations.

For most people, however, gaming is a social activity. Couples might go to a local Internet cafe to play their favorite game, instead of going to see a movie. Computer gaming has become **all the rage** largely because the Internet has allowed people from across the street or across the world to test their brains and reaction time against each other in new and increasingly challenging ways.

_____ **1.** Based on the article, why do some gamers take computer games so seriously?
   (A) They need a sense of satisfaction.
   (B) They want to form a social circle.
   (C) They look for fame and wealth.
   (D) They long for connection with others.

_____ **2.** What kind of impression did the public have on most computer gamers in the past?
   (A) Indifferent.   (B) Earnest.   (C) Negative.   (D) Positive.

_____ **3.** When something becomes "**all the rage**," it turns out to be _____.
   (A) addictive   (B) infuriating   (C) standardized   (D) trendy

_____ **4.** What is this article chiefly about?
   (A) How computer gaming has affected our life.
   (B) How computer games have evolved so far.
   (C) What makes computer games become so inspiring.
   (D) What leads to the success of computer industry.

_____ **5.** Which sentence best fits into the blank in the 3rd paragraph?
   (A) Owing to the low price and constant promotion, Nintendo Wii suddenly explodes in popularity.
   (B) Two examples of very different games which have reached this status are *StarCraft* and *Counter-Strike*.
   (C) *StarCraft* and *Counter-Strike* are complex war games that are played over the Internet by many teenagers.
   (D) The *StarCraft* players do weight training regularly to make sure that they are at their peak performance level.

An Attractive Man

Is an **attractive** man strong and muscular, or lithe and slim? We might think that it comes down to personal choice, but science is indicating that there are reasons why certain features are always considered alluring in a man. <u><A></u> Thicker necks, and stronger jaws and brows are also rated as charming by women, who are influenced by biology to seek out a mate with the characteristics to produce sturdy, healthy offspring.

Another study, however, conducted by researchers in Scotland and Japan revealed that many women also find a slightly feminine face engaging on a man. <u><B></u> The researchers have concluded that a man's face that possesses some womanly traits might be viewed as having a caring personality—a man who will be a good father.

However, it seems that appearance is not everything. Researchers at Aberdeen University's Face Research Laboratory have discovered that it is not only what a man looks like that is important, but what other women think of him. <u><C></u> They claimed that women regard a man as more appealing after they've seen another woman smiling at him, and less desirable after seeing a woman staring at him with an impassive face.

This is the psychology behind why some American men take out an attractive female friend, or even hire a beautiful woman to flirt with. <u><D></u> Dr. Ben Jones, of the Face Research Laboratory remarks that, "It is another example of what social creatures we are, where choices about what we wear and what cars we buy are influenced by others and are not as personal as we think."

_____ **1.** Based on the research results given in the article, which of the following is **NOT** a characteristic of an attractive man?

(A) A man who is robust and hardy.

(B) A man who is popular among women.

(C) A man with a feminine figure.

(D) A man with a considerate temperament.

_____ **2.** The author shows how men are considered to be attractive by _____.

(A) analyzing opinion polls (B) defining important terms

(C) offering scientific studies (D) comparing and contrasting

_____ **3.** According to the article, Dr. Ben Jones' words imply that _____.

(A) we human beings cannot lead an isolated life

(B) the so-called personal preference requires re-examining

(C) people are basically unwilling to accept others' advice

(D) in our society there are too many choices to choose from

_____ **4.** The following words are synonyms for the word "**attractive**" **EXCEPT**

_____.

(A) alluring (B) desirable (C) engaging (D) impassive

_____ **5.** The following sentence can be added to the article.

"**Many studies have suggested that women like a man with wide shoulders and a narrow waist, which are signs of might and health.**"

Where would it best fit in the article?

Unit 18

Thumbs Down for BlackBerry

Although BlackBerry, wireless handheld device that sends and receives emails, costs a lot of money, some users feel more pain in their thumbs than in their wallets. <u><A></u> While using the machine's tiny keyboard, many people learn that they can type faster with their thumbs instead of their fingers. As the users become addicted to sending text messages, these repetitive movements lead them to experience the discomfort of "BlackBerry Thumb."

Experts contend that the problem results from how our thumbs are designed. Unlike our fingers, which are very **nimble**, our thumbs provide stability and do not move very well. When they are used over and over again to type out countless messages, tendons and nerves can suffer damage from these so-called repetitive strain injuries. <u><B></u>

Doctors advise that self-restraint is the best way to avoid suffering from "BlackBerry Thumb." They say that messages should be kept short, and if possible, people should try to use their other fingers. <u><C></u> Others recommend remedies for the ailment. Several companies sell splints that they claim will ease the pain, whereas the Hyatt hotel chain offers business travelers a "BlackBerry Thumb Massage" for $80 that promises to soothe their overworked joints.

People who use other small electronic devices must also take care to avoid similar problems. <u><D></u> Most importantly, people must remember to avoid too many repetitive movements and to take a break as soon as the pain begins. The way that we use our modern gadgets can decide whether they make our lives easier or more difficult.

_____ **1.** Another suitable title for this article would be " _____ ."

    (A) The BlackBerry Is out of Date   (B) Flaws of Small Electronic Devices

    (C) Taking Good Care of Our Fingers   (D) Warning for Text-Sending Addicts

_____ **2.** Which of the following is the main cause of the "Blackberry Thumb"?

    (A) The physical design of our thumbs.

    (B) Wireless handheld devices cost an arm and a leg.

    (C) Long messages are preferred over shorter ones.

    (D) Repetitive movements of our ankles.

_____ **3.** The word "**nimble**" means _____ .

    (A) marginal   (B) obstinate   (C) deft   (D) static

_____ **4.** According to the article, which of the following would **NOT** be suggested by doctors as a way to avoid BlackBerry Thumb?

    (A) Use forefingers to type messages.

    (B) Shorten the length of the messages.

    (C) Stretch the overworked joints from time to time.

    (D) Limit the time spent on writing emails with BlackBerry.

_____ **5.** "**Video game controls, computer keyboards, and cell phone keypads can all cause discomfort if used excessively.**"

    Where can we best add the above sentence?

Vision Defects and Corrective Lenses

The eye is one of the most complicated organs in the human body. Besides, the cornea plays an important part in the function of the eye. Many people have normal vision, but others are born with or develop vision problems because of the cornea disorders. <A>

One common vision defect is called myopia. This occurs when the cornea is unable to flatten properly. The effect of this condition is nearsightedness. The opposite of myopia is called hypermetropia. In this case, the cornea cannot **bulge** as it should, resulting in farsightedness. Moreover, people who suffer from astigmatism have blurred vision because of an oblong-shaped cornea that causes the eye to focus on two spots at once. Besides, a problem that almost everyone will experience is nearsightedness due to presbyopia. This condition develops as people grow older and the corneas lose their elasticity. <B>

Fortunately, all these problems can be corrected with eyeglasses. People with myopia are given glasses with concave lenses, which are thinner in the middle than on the edges. Convex lenses, which are thinner on the edges than in the middle, are used to treat hypermetropia. For astigmatism, spoon-shaped lenses are designed to correct the improper shape of the cornea. Likewise, people with presbyopia can wear bifocals, which are actually two lenses in one. In bifocals the top part of the lens might be flat while wearers can look through the bottom half to focus on things that are close up. <C>

In centuries past, vision defects were untreatable and people just had to cope the best they could. But today, thanks to the corrective lenses and contacts, most vision problems are not the handicap they used to be. <D>

_____ 1. The **OPPOSITE** of the word "**bulge**" in the 2nd paragraph is _____.

(A) blur   (B) flatten   (C) occur   (D) result

_____ 2. If your eyes cannot focus on one spot, what kind of glasses do you need to wear?

(A) Concave lenses.   (B) Convex lenses.

(C) Spoon-shaped lenses.   (D) Bifocals.

_____ 3. The tone of this article is _____.

(A) biting   (B) factual   (C) ironic   (D) solemn

_____ 4. The author's primary purpose in this article is to _____.

(A) argue for the importance of taking care of one's eyes

(B) compare the causes of different types of defective vision

(C) show the crucial role glasses play in alleviating eye problems

(D) describe different types of vision problems and their treatments

_____ 5. The following sentnece can be added to the article.

"**All of these forms of eyeglasses are also made as contact lenses, which are worn directly on the eye.**"

Where would it best fit in the article?

Unit 20

Who Are Your Real Friends?

Having friends used to be about phone calls, parties, or playing sports. <A> These days, a teenager's social life has changed dramatically. A young girl 20 years ago might spend hours on the phone gossiping to her friends, but now her own adolescent daughter may go straight on the Internet.

Today you can make a new friend with the click of a button. Through the Internet, therefore, instead of having five good friends, a teenage girl nowadays can have 75 "friends" that she talks to, flirts with and confides in. <B>.

However, researchers say that communication skills are limited by this type of online activity and there are other dangers as well. <C> For example, computer game addiction is widespread among young children with some spending over 60 hours on the Internet per week. Some kids also give out personal information to strangers in chat rooms without realizing the risks involved. When a teenager is too **exhausted** to do schoolwork because of spending hours online, then it is surely time to move the computer to a more visible family area.

Nevertheless, one positive aspect of the increased usage of the Internet is that it has encouraged a new type of openness among young people. <D> They think about what they say before they type a message and in this way many have found it easier to express themselves. They also display their creative efforts in writing and music to millions of possible viewers over the Internet.

In the end, we will have to wait and see how these young people and the Internet will change the world as we know it and how we communicate with each other.

_____ **1.** In the 1st paragraph, the author arouses readers' interest by _____ .
   (A) telling a story   (B) asking a question
   (C) using a quotation   (D) showing a contrast

_____ **2.** What does the word "**exhausted**" mean in the article?
   (A) Annoyed   (B) Compelled   (C) Fatigued   (D) Inspired

_____ **3.** Which of the following is **NOT** mentioned as a negative effect of the continuous use of the Internet?
   (A) Children might indulge themselves in playing computer games.
   (B) Students might find it hard to concentrate or study hard in class.
   (C) Teenagers might become too open to new ideas or relationships.
   (D) People might be tricked into revealing too much about themselves.

_____ **4.** The author might probably agree that the influence of the Internet on the younger generation is _____ .
   (A) beneficial   (B) destructive   (C) pervasive   (D) unknown

_____ **5.** "**Online social groups have become so popular that in Britain, 60% of teenagers aged 13 to 17 years old use them daily.**"
   Where would the above sentence best fit in the article?

The Eyewitness Problem

For a long time, the police have thought that eyewitnesses to crimes are a great help in finding culprits and charging them with crimes. However, psychologists have found that the testimony of eyewitnesses can be wrong, and that outside influences can cause fake memories to evolve.

Daniel Wright, a psychologist at Sussex University, discovered that eyewitnesses sometimes create new, false memories on their own. To show this, he ran an experiment where 40 students looked at pictures showing a crime taking place. All of the students thought they were studying the same pictures, but they were actually not. <A>

The pictures told a story of two men at a pool hall. At a one point, a woman stole one man's wallet. Yet half of the group were provided with photos showing the woman was working with an **accomplice**, while the other half had her committing the crime alone. When each student was questioned after viewing the pictures, 39 out of 40 answered correctly about whether or not the woman had an accomplice.

Then the students were put into pairs and asked to discuss the events that had occurred. <B> Each of the pairs contained two students who saw different sets of pictures. When asked to answer if the woman had an accomplice, none of the pairs should have come to an agreement. However, 15 of them did. In other words, one student in the pair convinced the other student to change his or her story. <C>

Scientists say this is because our imagination may make up details to fill in visual gaps. Besides, suggestion is another powerful reason for inaccuracy. Not only can people be easily swayed by others, but we sometimes falsify memories when "helped" with leading questions. <D> Thus, next time when eyewitnesses swear they see the whole thing, are they really telling the truth?

_____ **1.** What is the purpose of Daniel Wright's experiment?

(A) To see people's different reaction to picture books.

(B) To check the police's efficiency in cracking the case.

(C) To find out how our memories are formed and stored.

(D) To examine the correctness of eyewitnesses' accounts.

_____ **2.** When you work with an "**accomplice**," you do it _____.

(A) on your own   (B) with a partner   (C) cautiously   (D) intentionally

_____ **3.** In the experiment, when the students were paired off to discuss what they had seen, how many of them changed their story?

(A) 5.   (B) 15.   (C) 20.   (D) 39.

_____ **4.** What can we conclude from the article?

(A) People are easily influenced by their peers or environment.

(B) The police should try to solve problems on their own.

(C) Human memory might turn out to be unreliable.

(D) The majority of the eyewitnesses are not honest.

_____ **5.** The following sentence can be added to the article.

"**This is how spurious memories may unknowingly be planted.**"

Where would it best fit in the article?

Unit 22

Dangerous Obsession

After seeing actress Jodie Foster in the movie *Taxi Driver*, John Hinckley Jr. knew that he was meant to be with her. <A> He first considered killing President Jimmy Carter to impress her. When Foster started classes at Yale University in 1980, Hinckley followed her there and finally decided that only **a great feat** would get her attention. On March 30, 1981, he wrote a letter to her, stating, "I've got to do something now to make you understand, in no uncertain terms, that I am doing all of this for your sake!" That afternoon, Hinckley shot President Ronald Regan and three other people. <B>

Stalkers like Hinckley represent the dark side of celebrity attachment. Although most fans mean no harm to their idols, others might harbor unhealthy obsessions. Unlike female fans who worship or emulate male idols that they are attracted to, male stalkers like Hinckley often feel an irresistible urge to protect the women they admire. <C> Hinckley believed that he had to do something significant for his imaginary relationship with Jodie Foster to become real. He tried to make Foster like him by writing her poems to demonstrate that they shared similar interests. When this did not work, he decided to assassinate the president.

Hinckley suffered from mental illness, which made his infatuation with Foster turn **detrimental**. In 1982, a jury found Hinckley not guilty by reason of insanity and confined him to a mental hospital even though many Americans did not agree with this not-guilty verdict. <D> Because of his illness, a normally harmless celebrity crush turned vicious. Hinckley's case remains an alarming example of what can happen when a celebrity attachment goes too far.

_____ **1.** In the 1st paragraph, the author draws readers' attention by using _____.

(A) an actual story   (B) a study research

(C) a famous quotation   (D) a personal experience

_____ **2.** In the 1st paragraph of this article, **"a great feat"** refers to _____.

(A) following Judie Foster to Yale   (B) writing letters to Judie Foster

(C) murdering President Carter   (D) shooting President Regan

_____ **3.** As used in the last paragraph, **"detrimental"** means _____.

(A) decent   (B) deliberate   (C) disastrous   (D) dubious

_____ **4.** We can infer from the article that _____.

(A) most Americans felt pity for John Hinckley

(B) idols might influence fans' behavior and attitude

(C) John Hinckley graduated from Yale University

(D) stalkers might want to hurt women that they admire

_____ **5.** The following sentence can be added to the article.

"They usually have active fantasy lives, imagining that they have a meaningful connection with their beloved idols."

Where would it best fit in the article?

Lance Armstrong: Le Tour de France Didn't Make Him a Winner

"Anything is possible. You can be told that you have a 90-percent chance or a 50-percent chance or a 1-percent chance, but you have to believe, and you have to fight."

That statement, uttered by cyclist Lance Armstrong, accurately reflects Armstrong's ability to believe: this Texas-born American has experienced a daunting array of setbacks and challenges in his athletic career. <A> Only through **grit**, determination, and faith was he able to become a Tour de France legend and one of the best-known athletes in the world.

In 1996, Armstrong was already a strong cycling contender—as an amateur he had won both the US and World Championships. Later, as a cycling pro on Team Motorola, he clinched the Tour DuPont. When he was diagnosed with testicular cancer in 1996, the athlete was determined to fight the disease, even though doctors weren't optimistic about his chances of recovery. <B> Within a year Armstrong was diagnosed as clear of cancer. He won a few important races. He also established the Lance Armstrong Foundation, which promotes cancer research and helps people who have cancer.

Then he tackled le Tour de France. This race is the diva of the cycling world. It takes 22 days to complete on an often-mountainous trail that spans more than 3,000 km—1,864+ miles. Lance and his teammates won that race in 1999. But there were more bad times to come: In 2000, while training in France, Armstrong was hit by a car. <C> Incredibly, this athlete won the Tour de France every year, seven years in a row, from 1999 to 2005. No other athlete has ever accomplished such a feat.

In his autobiography, *It's Not about the Bike*, Armstrong credited his mother with his tenacity. <D> She always told him to turn every obstacle into an opportunity. And that is just what he has done.

_____ **1.** The quote in the beginning of the article stands for _____.

(A) a reflection made by Armstrong's contemporaries

(B) a legend created by Armstrong's peers

(C) a motto Armstrong has lived up to

(D) a kingdom Armstrong has ruled

_____ **2.** What does the word **"grit"** mean in the article?

(A) Maintenance.　(B) Narrative.　　(C) Oppression.　　(D) Perseverance.

_____ **3.** Which of the following statements is TRUE about Lance Armstrong?

(A) He was born in France.

(B) He suffered from lung cancer.

(C) He owes his success much to his mother.

(D) Even as an amateur, he won the Tour DuPont.

_____ **4.** What can we infer from the article?

(A) Armstrong quit le Tour de France in 2006 because of a car accident.

(B) To finish le Tour de France, participants have to cycle across mountains.

(C) Lance Armstrong Foundation has helped people to achieve incredible feats.

(D) In his autobiography, Armstrong revealed that he once wanted to give up cycling and run his own business.

_____ **5.** The following sentence can be added to the article.

"He spent months recovering from a broken bone in his back."

Where would it best fit in the article?

Sneezing in Summer and Gagging on Plums

Every summer, Monica suffers from hay fever because she is allergic to the pollen in the air. As the flowers are popping up, her nose fills up and she sneezes constantly. During this time, she cannot eat cantaloupes and plums—fruits she normally loves. If she tries, her mouth itches and she gags. Monica discovered that she was experiencing allergic "cross-reactivity": The pollen in the flowers has chemical properties in common with certain fruits. <5>

Many of us think that we are allergic to lobster, or peanuts or have an intolerance for milk. But many people who are allergic to one particular food will be allergic to an entire family of related foods. Plants contain a complex mixture of chemical components, and these can be found in a number of plants. Hence, people allergic to pumpkin may react negatively to squash, cucumbers, and watermelon. Those who are allergic to carrots may wish to **eschew** other members of the carrot family, including parsley, celery, and dill.

A recent survey showed that 19% of Taiwanese have some sort of food allergy. The main food culprits are chicken, shellfish, milk, mangoes, peanuts, and eggs. Allergic reactions can vary, ranging from a mild itching in the throat and skin to a full-blown anaphylactic attack—an inability to breathe and a sharp drop in the blood pressure that could become fatal.

However, the British Nutrition Foundation says that only a fraction of those who complain of food allergies actually have a serious condition. The Foundation concludes that fewer than 1% of adults worldwide have a serious food allergy, and that fewer than 2% have a food intolerance. Perhaps, claiming to have a food allergy is "in" right now. But if you think you're allergic to pumpkins—well, stay away from cucumbers, too.

_____ **1.** In the 1st paragraph, the author used Monica's story to _____.

(A) instruct us how to choose wholesome food

(B) demonstrate how severe allergies can be

(C) explain what allergic cross-reactivity is

(D) entertain the readers with an anecdote

_____ **2.** What does the word "**eschew**" in the 2nd paragraph mean?

(A) Consume.　　　(B) Embrace.　　　(C) Shun.　　　(D) Trim.

_____ **3.** Which of the following allergic symptoms is **NOT** mentioned in the article?

(A) A high fever.　　　　　　　(B) Skin irritation.

(C) A fit of sneezing.　　　　　(D) Breathing difficulties.

_____ **4.** Which of the following statements is TRUE about food allergies?

(A) About one-fifth people in Taiwan suffer from food allergies.

(B) Food allergies usually develop into severe complications.

(C) Food allergies threaten quite a few people's life.

(D) Only fruits and plants will trigger food allergies.

_____ **5.** Which of the following sentence would best fit in the blank in the 1st paragraph?

(A) Therefore, if you want to avoid itching or gagging, you should stay away from plants and flowers.

(B) Thus, if a person reacts negatively to the pollen, his body will reject those pieces of fruit as well.

(C) To strengthen your immune system, you should get yourself exposed to these chemical properties.

(D) However, such food intolerance occurs most frequently in summer and can be cured with a few shots.

Unit 25

The Bittersweet Truth about Sugar

We're all getting fatter, and Americans are leading the way. Here are some sobering statistics: a staggering 64% of Americans are overweight, as are a third of U.S. children. <5> We all can cite reasons for this epidemic: too much fast food, too much sedentary living, too many carbohydrates, etc.

However, a little-known substance, called high fructose corn syrup (HFCS), is playing a major role in thickening the waistlines of Americans. Twenty-five years ago, foods and soft drinks were sweetened with simple cane sugar or beet sugar. Today, almost half the sugar Americans consume is in the form of HFCS. Take a can of sweetened soda for example. It has the equivalent of thirteen teaspoons of sugar! Health experts advise that no more than ten to twelve teaspoonfuls of sugar should be consumed daily. Nevertheless, Americans **gulp down** three times that amount, most of which comes from soft drinks!

Here's more bad news: "Fructose Can Lead to Overeating." When you eat carbohydrates made up of glucose, the pancreas produces insulin and the fat cells produce a hormone called leptin. These two substances inform your brain when you've had enough. When you consume fructose, your body doesn't produce those two substances——so you'll keep stuffing yourself. The more fructose you eat, the more fat is spewed out into your bloodstream. Hence, consuming HFCS-laced foods is equivalent to eating a high-fat meal.

Before you consume an innocuous-looking can of soda, take a close look at the ingredients. If you see "fructose" on the label, you may wish to reconsider.

_____ **1.** What is the main purpose of this article?

(A) To discuss how obesity can be controlled.

(B) To point out the problems with HFCS.

(C) To inform us the importance of HFCS.

(D) To clarify some myths about dieting.

_____ **2.** According to the article, approximately how many teaspoonfuls of sugar do Americans take every day?

(A) 10.　　　　　(B) 13.　　　　　(C) 25.　　　　　(D) 35.

_____ **3.** Why do we tend to overeat when we consume too much fructose? That's because _____ .

(A) no insulin and leptin will be produced to suppress our appetite

(B) the more fructose we eat, the more carbohydrates we want to eat

(C) more fat cells will be produced and they will grow bigger quickly

(D) the pancreas and fat cells will be stimulated and people will feel hungrier

_____ **4.** What does the phrase **"gulp down"** in the 2nd paragraph mean?

(A) Maintain.　　　(B) Retrieve.　　　(C) Swallow.　　　(D) Vomit.

_____ **5.** Which sentence would best fit in the blank in the 1st paragraph?

(A) Instead, researchers are trying to find a way to stop the situation from deteriorating.

(B) On the whole, Americans consume much more junk food than people in other countries.

(C) Indeed, the Center for Disease Control states that obesity is now the number one killer in America.

(D) As a result, the authorities concerned should take action to fight against this discrimination.

And They Live Happily Ever After...

Clichés generally get a bad reputation. It's because they are expressions so overused that they reveal no personality on the user's part, or rather, his lack of personality. But let's face it: there are many situations in life where it is hard to be original or honest. <u><A></u> "Congratulations! May you two be blessed with many years of happiness!" is the obvious remark at a wedding even if you have serious doubts about the couple's compatibility. At a funeral, isn't "My condolences. At least he is at peace now," much better than, "So, how much money will you inherit?" You see, although clichés can be insincere and superficial, they are safe and **unprovocative**.

Although clichés sound universal, many actually reflect a particular society's values. <u><B></u> American business life—capitalistic and competitive in nature—is full of sporting expressions. You might be thrown *a curve ball* in an interview. You have to make *home runs* in business. The current command to *think outside the box*—be unconventional—is so overused that eventually, thinking within the box will be unusual instead.

The world of art, music and films has also contributed. <u><C></u> Does *love* really *mean you never have to say sorry*? *Do gentlemen* really *prefer blondes*? Is your sweetheart *the sunshine of your life*? The clichéd themes and characterizations of novels and movies—the lonely cowboy, the poor but handsome hero who gets the rich girl, the mafia boss who suffers—provide comfort and familiarity in our real but unpredictable world.

So clichés have many uses—they help us when we are at a loss for words, they entertain and amuse and they bind us as a community. <u><D></u> Does anyone not at some point or another hope to *live happily ever after*?

_____ **1.** If something is "**provocative**," it makes people feel _____ .

    (A) concerned   (B) delighted   (C) entertained   (D) offended

_____ **2.** The clichés related to sporting expressions in the article exemplify

_____ .

    (A) the innovative characteristic in American society

    (B) the aggressive aspect of American business life

    (C) the popularity of baseball in the United States

    (D) the universality of clichés across the world

_____ **3.** This article was most likely written by someone who believed that clichés

_____ .

    (A) might not be genuine but indispensable

    (B) inhibit one's originality and creativity

    (C) make people become shallow thinkers

    (D) stop people from expressing themselves

_____ **4.** What is the purpose of the article?

    (A) To elaborate the origins of clichés.

    (B) To explain why people use clichés.

    (C) To urge people to stop using clichés.

    (D) To show the cultural aspects of clichés.

_____ **5.** The following sentence can be added to the article.

    "**And in many ways, they also express our deepest desire.**"

    Where would it best fit in the article?

Olive Oil: The "New" California Wine

"What do you smell?" she asked.

I leaned over and sniffed the bottle in her hands.

"Floral," I said. Her face creased. Clearly, I had more to learn.

What do you think the two people are discussing—wine? Guess again—it's olive oil. Indeed, good olive oil can be as complex to the tongue as is good wine. It can taste grassy or peppery. It can remind you of apples, nuts or chocolates. Increasingly, Americans with sophisticated palates are clamoring for the very best olive oil, and they're getting it. <5>

It's no coincidence that California—the state renowned for its wine industry—is leading the parade in olive oil production. California has a Mediterranean climate that lends itself both to grape and olive production, and olives are now flourishing in the wine-producing regions of Napa, Sonoma, and Mendocino counties.

Just like their counterparts in Europe, California oil producers are learning the tricks of the trade: They know that the best oils come from hand-picked olives and must be pressed immediately. Besides, the best oil should be "cold-pressed" since heat can have a negative impact on the taste.

As more Americans are aware of healthy eating, they have discovered Mediterranean cooking—featuring fresh vegetables, fish, and meat—**fits the bill** perfectly. This cuisine demands the highest quality olive oil, and Americans are becoming adept learners regarding the intricacies of selecting the correct oil. One rule of thumb for using high-end olive oil: Use it for drizzling over prepared food while the cheaper oils can be used to cook the food. Thinking of having grilled eggplant? Salad greens? A perfectly done steak? Make sure you pick the appropriate oil and have fun exploring the exciting new world of "liquid gold." *Bon appetite!*

_____ **1.** What is the best title for the article?

(A) Tricks of the Olive Oil Trade.　　(B) The History of Olive Oil.

(C) Mad about Olive Oil.　　(D) The Mediterranean Diet.

_____ **2.** Based on the article, why is olive oil gaining popularity among Americans?

(A) Because the taste of olive oil can be as delicate as that of wine.

(B) Because the olive oil industry is booming in California.

(C) Because Americans are becoming more health-conscious.

(D) Because instead of wine, Americans start to use olive oil to cook.

_____ **3.** When something **"fits the bill,"** it is _____ .

(A) a real bargain　　(B) what you want

(C) exotic and tasty　　(D) within your budget

_____ **4.** Which of the following statements is **NOT** true?

(A) To produce the best olive oil, olives should be gathered manually.

(B) There are a lot of vineyards in Napa, Sonoma, and Mendocino counties.

(C) When deep frying the food, cooks would suggest using cheaper olive oils.

(D) Olives should be stored for years and then boiled before they are pressed.

_____ **5.** Which sentence best fits in the blank in the article?

(A) In the past decade, the gourmet olive oil business has been booming in the Hollywood State.

(B) This substance is produced in the Mediterranean region, such as Italy, Spain and Portugal.

(C) To fully enjoy it, you have to know how to differentiate between a fruity olive oil and a spicy oil.

(D) If you pick the olives too soon, the oil will be bitter; if you pick the olives a bit late, it will lack flavor.

How Successful Advertising Campaigns Work

How do you make a product usually purchased by women attractive to men? How do you position a little music player as a stylish "must-have" for the younger generation? The ads must appeal, on a profound cultural level, to the targeted buyers. The images, colors, and music must be geared specifically towards their tastes.

<5>

In the 1920s and 1930s, Marlboro Cigarettes appealed mostly to women. "Mild as May," trumpeted the Marlboro slogan. However, in the late 1950s, Marlboro went through an image overhaul. The introduction of the rugged Marlboro Man in both print and TV was aimed at male users. The new commercials depicted a cowboy atop a horse. As he does manly outdoor things, he puffs on a cigarette; stirring music plays in the background. The ads worked—by 1957, men were buying them **in droves**. The American cowboy perfectly represented American masculine freedom.

In 2003, Apple launched a world-wide campaign, aimed at young people, to promote its new iPod Mini music player: Against bright backgrounds, silhouetted figures whirled to music, clutching their iPods. Viewers heard hip-hop, techno, and garage rock—music for today's youth. Apple chose to place ads in environments in which young people would congregate. Hence, in London you can see their ads in Virgin (Music) Megastores, subway stations, and bus shelters. In Montreal, the iPod silhouettes were plastered over the McGill (University) subway terminal. Advertisers from the 1950s would have been astonished at this strategy: Fifty years ago, the main advertising mediums were only print and television.

So while today's ad campaigns are vastly different—and more multilayered—than those of past decades, ads must reach us emotionally. As Bob Garfield of *Ad Age* has written, "[Ads] have touched us, understood us, [and] reflected our lives."[1]

[1]http://adage.com/century/campaigns.html

_____ **1.** To attract male users, Marlboro Cigarettes included several features in its new commercials **EXCEPT** _____.

(A) cowboys galloping   (B) music from westerns

(C) men doing household chores   (D) background from American West

_____ **2.** The phrase "**in droves**" in the 2nd paragraph refers to _____.

(A) a crowd of people   (B) a sense of direction

(C) a round of applause   (D) a state of excitement

_____ **3.** In the article, why did the author mention the places like Virgin Megastores or McGill subway terminal?

(A) To demonstrate the influence of globalization on ad campaigns.

(B) To exemplify the cultural diversity in big cities around the world.

(C) To illustrate the places where young people like to gather together.

(D) To explain why they are important landmarks in different countries.

_____ **4.** Based on the article, what is the most important factor advertisers have to take into consideration?

(A) Gender difference.   (B) Market orientation.

(C) International focus.   (D) Economic climate.

_____ **5.** Which sentence would best fit in the blank in the article?

(A) To win their heart, advertisers have to conduct a full-scale market research to find out their customers' preference and comments on their products.

(B) Successful ad campaigns, such as Marlboro Cigarettes and today's iPod, have become less sophisticated, but more time-consuming than those before.

(C) Other than tackling different challenges and addressing the needs of the real users, advertisers today have to understand consumers' basic rights.

(D) Two ad campaigns—Marlboro Cigarettes and iPod—demonstrate respectively how advertisers from different decades have done this successfully.

Bullies: From Schoolyard to Cyberspace

A recent survey taken by British schoolchildren showed that 10 percent of them had sent a threatening email or text message to another student. While school bullies have tormented kids for years, this new kind of cruelty, called "cyberbullying," takes being mean to a new and disturbing level.

The most prevalent problem with cyberbullying is that it does not stop at school. In fact, some cyberbullies send a majority of their mean-spirited messages through email, chat rooms, text messaging or blogs, 24 hours a day, seven days a week. <A> For students bearing the burden of this behavior, there is no escape, even when away from school.

Cyberbullying can include simple taunts, cruel observations about someone's appearance, and even death threats. No matter how severe it is, victims feel terrible about the cyberbullying. Sadly, some kids are driven to suicide by the bullying, while others withdraw from friends and family and even ask if they can change schools or relocate. <B>

Getting cyberbullying to stop takes **fortitude** by kids, parents, school officials, or even the police. While stopping simple taunting may just take a phone call to the bully's family by parents or school officials, the police must get involved in tracking down bullies who make threats of killing someone or seriously hurting them. <C> And for the schools' parts, they should take steps to prevent cyberbullying through student education and new anti-bullying rules.

<D> It is crucial that students and their parents remember that cyberbullying can be stopped by taking action and contacting the proper authorities. Serious threats need police attention to bring the perpetrators to justice, and the more minor incidents need school involvement to rectify the problem.

_____ **1.** Cyberbullying is different from other types of bullying for the following reasons
EXCEPT it _____ .
(A) can happen anytime, anywhere
(B) can happen without the presence of the bullies
(C) often includes many life-threatening messages
(D) tortures the victims mentally rather than physically

_____ **2.** According to this article, which of the following is CORRECT to stop
cyberbullying?
(A) Parents should get involved once their children are cyberbullied.
(B) Schools must reveal the identities of the bullies and relocate the victims.
(C) The police should be contacted whenever vicious messages are received.
(D) Students should be taught not to fret about simple taunts about appearance.

_____ **3.** How does the author develop the article?
(A) By citing different examples.
(B) By presenting a problem and some solutions.
(C) By describing a process.
(D) By clarifying some misconceptions.

_____ **4.** The word **"fortitude"** means _____ .
(A) a firm and determined attitude   (B) a ceaseless and strong passion
(C) the willingness to sacrifice   (D) an act of sudden impulse

_____ **5.** Where can we best add the following sentence?
"These reactions illustrate just how bad the problem can be."

Will Global Warming Cause Worldwide Political Conflicts?

There is no doubt that the Earth is in a period of global warming, as scientists have predicted an increasing number of floods, rising sea levels, droughts and other weather-related disasters over the next few decades. <A>

For countries with **temperate** climates, the effects of global warming will probably not be as severe as for countries closer to the equator, such as those in South America and Africa. These predicted effects have the strong possibility of causing political conflicts, particularly between "rich" and "poor" countries. <B>

These conflicts may arise from the release of CO_2, which traps energy and pollution within the atmosphere, heating the planet. Many "rich" countries— particularly those in the northern hemisphere—produce a much larger amount of CO_2 than "poor" countries. <C> This makes "poor" countries resentful of the polluting "rich" countries.

Desertification—where land turns to desert—is one result of global warming and a cause of political conflict. The Darfur region of Sudan, for example, has experienced a political and ecological disaster from global warming. More than 200,000 people have died from this conflict which was partially caused by the land slowly turning to desert.

Rising sea levels, the opposite of desertification, caused by melting glaciers may force millions of people from low-lying countries like Bangladesh to move to higher land, sparking political conflicts as these refugees migrate to other countries.

<D> These two examples highlight how worldwide climate changes caused by global warming can potentially cause political conflicts and wars throughout the world, as millions of people look for new homes to escape rising sea levels or desertification.

_____ **1.** Why are rich countries responsible for global warming and the subsequent conflicts? Because they _____ .
(A) do not help the poor countries to cope with the desertification
(B) do not regulate the number of vehicles and light bulbs
(C) have the lion's share in the emission of CO_2 in the atmosphere
(D) refuse to sign a contract dealing with the refugee problem

_____ **2.** We can replace the word "**temperate**" with _____ .
(A) arid   (B) tropical   (C) moderate   (D) continental

_____ **3.** To demonstrate the political conflicts brought about by global warming, the author cites the examples of _____ .
(A) hot weather and famine
(B) uneven distribution of resources
(C) desertification and devastating tsunami
(D) natural disasters and the refugee problem

_____ **4.** We can infer from the 4th paragraph that _____ .
(A) the Darfur region of Sudan suffered from political chaos
(B) Sudan may soon have wars with other neighboring countries
(C) Sudan may have to accommodate refugees from low-lying countries
(D) all the land in the Darfur region of Sudan is no longer fertile because of desertification

_____ **5.** Where can we best put the following sentence in the article?
"**However, the poorer countries will suffer more from global warming though they are not causing it.**"

Forget the Sting: Wasps Recruited for Explosive Detection

Dogs have been used for years to detect drugs or explosives in aircraft luggage. <5> The new bomb-sniffing system, called the "Wasp Hound," being developed for terrorism-prevention agencies, uses small, non-stinging wasps to find explosives hidden at airports and border crossings.

The "Wasp Hound" uses five these half-inch-long wasps in a plastic tube with a screen at one end and a camera at the other. The screen allows air to enter the tube, and the camera connects to a laptop computer, where the wasps' behavior can be monitored. When the wasps smell a chemical they've been trained to find, they fly to the screen end of the tube, which indicates they smell explosives in the **vicinity**.

Biological engineers train the wasps to react to smells by consistently providing sugar water at the same place in the tube every time the wasps are exposed to explosives. Through this process, they learn that the smell of explosives leads to a sweet meal. This "classical conditioning" training, made famous by Pavlov's dogs, is effective for all animals, including humans. In fact, bees have also been trained in this manner to detect landmines and other explosives.

The advantage of wasps over dogs is that wasps are inexpensive, easy to feed and take care of, and can be trained in just a few minutes, as opposed to the months it takes to train a dog for the same mission. Moreover, wasps also have a better sense of smell.

With such advances in bioengineering, someday unusual insects and animals may fill jobs once appropriate for only humans and dogs. And perhaps within ten years, we will see airport police sporting tubes of wasps to find drugs and explosives instead of dogs on leashes.

_____ **1.** The word "**vicinity**" in the 2nd paragraph is closest in meaning to

_____ .

(A) the terminal   (B) the windscreen

(C) the underground   (D) the neighborhood

_____ **2.** When using the "Wasp Hound," the police need to carry some special

equipment **EXCEPT** _____ .

(A) a tube   (B) a leash   (C) a camera   (D) a laptop

_____ **3.** Based on the article, if you want to train an animal to perform a certain trick,

what should you prepare?

(A) Tubes.   (B) Rewards.   (C) Chemicals.   (D) Explosives.

_____ **4.** The 4th paragraph explains _____ .

(A) the use of wasps for explosive detection

(B) the training of wasps for terroism prevention

(C) the strengths of using wasps over dogs

(D) the advances in bioengineering

_____ **5.** Which sentence would best fit the blank in the 1st paragraph?

(A) Dogs can be used to detect dangerous chemicals in the subway tunnel as
well.

(B) Dogs, however, are sometimes unable to carry out such difficult tasks
successfully.

(C) Also, the changes of the wasps' flying activity indicate the location of the
explosives.

(D) But scientists have recruited a new animal—wasps—to search for these
hidden materials.

Catch-22: From Fiction to Real Life

When we're forced to make a choice between two unpleasant outcomes, the U.S. novelist Joseph Heller gave us a short and wonderful description for this dilemma: a catch-22. In his novel *Catch-22*, there is a fictional air force rule (Catch-22) that wartime air force pilots must face: if a pilot continues flying dangerous combat missions without asking to be relieved of this life-threatening duty, he must be insane. But if he asks his superiors for permission not to fly these missions, he would be sane, and therefore must carry on flying. <A>

The word "catch," means a hidden problem or something within a situation that is undesirable and must be overcome. <B> For example, you could say you got a great new job with a high salary, but there's a catch: the job is on the night shift. This means that there is the bad (the catch) to go along with the good (a high-paying job).

A catch-22 is different, though, because there is no positive outcome. Here's an example of a catch-22: Not exercising is bad for your health, but if you exercise in a city with a lot of air pollution, that's bad for your health, too. So, you can see that no matter what you choose and do in a catch-22 situation, you lose. <C>

Heller's novel was an important satire on the organizations behind the war, and made fun of the ridiculous ideas and crazy language used by **bureaucracies** in an effort to control people's thoughts and actions. <D> The fictional catch-22 exemplified Heller's thoughts on the war, and he must be pleased to see the phrase "catch-22" come into common usage in fewer than 10 years after the book was published.

_____ **1.** What does the 1st paragraph intend to tell the reader?

(A) The situation where the "catch -22" can be used.

(B) The author's criticism of the American army.

(C) The self-contradictory nature of a "catch -22" situation.

(D) The contrast between the original and the present usage of the "catch -22."

_____ **2.** "Catch -22" was first coined as a phrase for _____.

(A) a vicious circle   (B) an insane pilot

(C) a win-win situation   (D) a fictional regulation of the air force

_____ **3.** Which of the following statements is TRUE?

(A) A high-paying job with a disadvantage of long commute has a "catch."

(B) Heller did not approve of the cruelty and nationalism brought by war.

(C) In a catch-22 situation, people try in vain to outsmart those in power.

(D) *Catch-22* is a novel and biting satire on the system of the election.

_____ **4.** What does the word **"bureaucracies"** possibly mean?

(A) Weapons that can cause mass destruction.

(B) Citizens who are in favor of censorship.

(C) People employed to run government organizations.

(D) Hypocrites who cater to the need of the authorities.

_____ **5.** Where can we best add the following sentence?

"Scattered around the novel are dialogues and themes manifesting Heller's hatred of war."

And You Thought Sugar Was Bad for You!

Read any health-related news headlines and you'll see stories on how too much sugar, caffeine and artificial sweeteners in colas and sodas is bad for you. But did you know that when Atlanta, Georgia pharmacist John Pemberton invented his sweet-tasting drink, Coca-cola, one of its ingredients was cocaine, now a highly illegal drug? <A>

In the early days of Coca-Cola, Pemberton was actually trying to develop a "health drink," based on Europe's successful cocawine (a blend of wine and cocaine). Instead of producing a thirst-quenching drink, he used cocaine and kola nuts in this new product for their stimulating effect. <B> It was found in myriad over-the-counter products, such as throat lozenges—for sore throats—and other pain remedies.

By 1904, however, the government was growing worried about companies using cocaine in their products, so the Coca-Cola Company and other companies were forced to remove all traces of the drug from their products. This didn't stop Coca-Cola's success as a popular drink, though, for it continued to have lots of caffeine, from which Coca-Cola drinkers would still get an energy "boost." <C> Though the United States government tried to force the Coca-Cola Company to exclude caffeine in its drinks, the company ultimately **prevailed**, allowing for other products to include caffeine as well.

Today, Coca-Cola, or "Coke," as it's often referred to, has grown to be the most widely recognized product brand in the world. <D> And with very minor changes, it is still made with the same basic recipe as it was more than 100 years ago—minus the cocaine!

_____ **1.** Which one of the following is **NOT** discussed in this article?

(A) The danger and side effect of using cocaine in Coca-Cola.

(B) The original ingredients included in the early version of Coca-Cola.

(C) The changes in the recipes of Coca-Cola during the past century.

(D) The reasons why Pemberton chose certain ingredients for his product.

_____ **2.** According to the article, what do cocaine, kola nuts and caffeine have in common? They can _____.

(A) relieve the pain   (B) enrich the flavor

(C) renew one's vitality   (D) all be banned by the government

_____ **3.** How is Coca-Cola different from the health drink invented in the early days?

(A) It contains more sugar and artificial sweeteners.

(B) Its ingredients do not include the illegal drug any more.

(C) It emphasizes more about the effect to quench one's thirst.

(D) It is still popular more because of its flavor than because of its effect.

_____ **4.** The word "**prevail**" is closest in meaning to _____.

(A) consent   (B) compensate   (C) intervene   (D) triumph

_____ **5.** Where can we best add the following sentence in the article?

"**Back then, cocaine was considered a new miracle drug good for dulling pain and giving energy.**"

Don't Put Those Comic Books Away

In the past, comic books had a bad reputation at most schools. Teachers banned them from their classrooms, and many schools forbade students from reading them on school grounds. However, a new program called the "Comic Book Project" is not only bringing comics into school, but it is also spurring students on to read, write, and illustrate them—at school! <A>

"The Comic Book Project" began in 2001 as an after-school club at an elementary school. It was started by Michael Blitz, an educator from Columbia University who was convinced that the arts could be utilized to promote learning. In particular, Blitz maintained that comic books could help to boost literacy in schools, especially when students created their own comic books. <B>

"The Comic Book Project" initially drew in students who liked the visual arts, but the importance of good writing soon became clear to those taking part in the club. The students, for example, could draw pictures of the scenes in their comics, but they also had to come up with dialogues for their characters. <C> As time went on, and the students had to write, revise, and edit their stories over an extended period, their writing and reading skills blossomed. And since they were always on the lookout for new ideas and inspiration, many students in the club began to read more—not only comic books, but also traditional fiction, such as novels and short stories.

Based on the success of this first program, "the Comic Book Project" is now being used by 45 other schools in New York and in other cities around the United States. <D> So, in the future, thanks to this innovative program, comic books may no longer be **outlawed** in schools, but instead welcomed as valuable learning tools.

_____ **1.** What would be another suitable title for the article?

(A) The Comic Book Project Founder—Michael Blitz

(B) The Influence of Comic Books on Teenagers

(C) How to Improve Students' Reading Ability

(D) Promoting Literacy through Comic Books

_____ **2.** Students in this project began to read traditional fiction because they were

_____ .

(A) instructed to adapt traditional novels and stories into comic books

(B) learning how to make an outline for comics through reading novels

(C) required to read traditional fiction before creating their own comics

(D) searching for creative and stimulating material for their own comics

_____ **3.** Which of the following statement is TRUE?

(A) Through this project, Blitz intends to raise our awareness of visual arts.

(B) This project has been proved successful and innovative around the world.

(C) Blitz believed that comic books could become a great teaching resource.

(D) This project was integrated into part of the curriculum at primary school.

_____ **4.** When something is **outlawed**, it becomes _____ .

(A) illegal   (B) immortal   (C) invaluable   (D) irrelevant

_____ **5.** "**Students were instructed on how to write out the ideas for their stories and outline the plots.**"

Where would the above sentence best fit in the article?

Modeling Industry Today: All About the New

Twiggy. Jean Shrimpton.[1] In the 1960s, you couldn't open a fashion magazine without seeing these women gracing the pages over and over again. Back then, the fashion industry demanded a few megastars who would both sizzle on the page and immediately sell the product well. These individuals—almost all women—were treated like royalty wherever they went. <A> However, this is not the case anymore. The information-and-media-saturated young people of today demand a constant new influx of different images. Why would they want to see the same person over and over again? Too boring.

The Internet plays a huge role in this transformation of the modeling industry. Today's young people see many more images than their counterparts of a generation ago. <B> Being white, blond, and blue-eyed is no longer a **prerequisite** for being considered a knockout. People are more readily accepting individuals with different hues and features. In fact, the person who does not have perfectly even features is often preferred over the one with the more symmetrical face. However, a model who is on top of the world today can become a "has-been" in just a few seasons.

Increasingly, celebrities are stepping into the footsteps previously trod by supermodels. Today's famous athletes and superstars hawk goods ranging from watches, cereal to telephone networks. <C> But if that superstar no longer commands international adulation, his or her marketability vanishes, as do the high-paying commissions.

There is good news in all this: You no longer have to be perfection personified in order to become a successful model. But there is bad news: <D> Even if you get your lucky break, don't expect to stay on top of the world for very long. There will always be someone newer to replace you.

---

[1]Twiggy and Jean Shrimpton were two "supermodels" (before that term became popular) of the 1960s. They both shared delicate, elfin features and exceedingly thin physiques.

_____ **1.** The author of this article may agree that _____ .

    (A) successful models today can't be thin and blond

    (B) teenagers like to imitate the behavior and style of the supermodels

    (C) stars appearing in advertisements for commercial products may change from time to time

    (D) the popularity of Twiggy and Jean Shrimpton foresees today's trend in modeling industry

_____ **2.** Which of the following words is closest to the word "**prerequisite**"?

    (A) Reference.   (B) Condition.   (C) Alternative.   (D) Projection.

_____ **3.** According to the article, what has transformed the modeling industry?

    (A) The Internet and the youngsters.

    (B) The baby-boomers in the 1960s.

    (C) The sudden emergence of megastars.

    (D) The celebrities and paparazzi.

_____ **4.** Who may be more likely to become a huge hit in today's modeling world?

    (A) Someone with a friendly smile.

    (B) Someone possessing exotic facial features.

    (C) Someone who can sell all sorts of goods.

    (D) Someone with perfect a body shape and a modern look.

_____ **5.** Where can we best put the following sentence?

    "**They become bored more easily, and demand constant visual variety.**"

Unit 36

Woe Is Jan. 24

"**H**appy New Year!" Get ready to be depressed.

A psychologist in Great Britain has declared Jan. 24 as the gloomiest day on the calendar. By three weeks into a new year, he says, the cheery afterglow of Christmas has vanished, leaving behind only a stack of bills. New Year's resolutions—all about how dieting, exercise and stopping smoking are going to make you a fabulous person—are already history. And to make Britons' lives that much bleaker, the weather is relentlessly terrible.

Winter in Great Britain is no picnic in general, says Dr. Cliff Arnall, a professor at the University of Cardiff in Wales. "SAD," or "Seasonal Affective Disorder," is **rampant**. SAD is a depressed condition linked to a lack of light, and it is a rarity among people who live in sunny climes. But in Britain, where winters are notoriously cloudy and dark, about a third of the population suffers from the appropriately named SAD. A small percentage can't even function without treatment.

So Dr. Arnall had a whole SAD season's worth of candidates for his worst day of the year. He came up with Jan. 24 as his winner—or perhaps, loser—through a formula that took into account seven factors including weather, time since Christmas, failure to keep resolutions, level of debt, monthly income, low motivation, and the need to take action. Arnall produced the equation for a travel company that wanted to know when people were most likely to want to escape Britain on vacation.

Of course, any formula simplifies real-life situations, but other mental health experts have agreed in principle with Arnall's depressing findings. Perhaps for his next project, though, the professor literally could lighten up and tell us what day is the happiest of the year. <5>

_____ **1.** How does the author begin the article?

(A) Using a contrast.   (B) Giving an example.

(C) Sharing an experience.   (D) By quoting a famous line.

_____ **2.** Based on the article, Dr. Arnall considers January 24 to be the gloomiest day of the year for many reasons **EXCEPT** that _____ .

(A) people are to pay the Christmas bill

(B) the weather is getting more unbearable

(C) people are making their New Year resolutions

(D) the pleasant Christmas atmosphere disappears

_____ **3.** The meaning of the word "**rampant**" is similar to _____ .

(A) controversial   (B) infamous   (C) unpredictable   (D) widespread

_____ **4.** Why did Dr. Cliff Arnall create the formula?

(A) To relieve people of their mental stress.

(B) To arouse the public's health awareness.

(C) To assist doctors in diagnosing the disorder.

(D) To help the travel agency run their business.

_____ **5.** Which sentence would best fit the blank in the last paragraph?

(A) It might turn out to be another daunting task for him.

(B) It's a safe bet that it wouldn't fall any time in winter.

(C) Doctors would feel discouraged by his new discovery.

(D) Patients would be glad to learn the good news from him.

Emails Can Make Cowards of Us

To: Mary@hotmail.com
From: peter@yahoo.com
Subject: GOOD-BYE!
Mary,
We had fun, but let's not see each other anymore, OK?
I've found someone new.
Peter

Can you imagine going through your email and finding this message from the person you *thought* was your affectionate boyfriend? Email is not a very appropriate way to tell somebody "good-bye" when the other person is not expecting it. <u><A></u> They're letting email do the job for them.

When somebody reads an email you have sent, he or she will be reading your message without you. That person cannot pick up accurate verbal or emotional cues from your message, no matter how many smiley faces or "LOL's" you use. So when you use email— be sensitive to the needs of others. <u><B></u> Think about this scenario: your best friend has deeply offended you and you're furious. You could send him or her an ill-tempered message stating how awful he/she is, or you could give that person a nasty write-up on MySpace for all the world to see. But is that really the best way to resolve the issue? <u><C></u> You may feel better in the short term, but this type of **malicious** act says more about *your* weaknesses than it does about the other person's.

If you wish to break up with a boy—or a girlfriend, try not to do it the way Peter did. If Peter has found someone new, he should communicate that directly to Mary. Speaking face to face is the best, but talking to the person on the telephone can be acceptable. Sure, **it** is going to be a lot tougher in these ways, but such action shows courage and—most importantly—sensitivity to the other individual directly. <u><D></u> Don't let email make a coward out of you.

_____ **1.** What is the main purpose of this article?

(A) To describe how to improve one's EQ.

(B) To explain the etiquette of breaking up.

(C) To inform the reader how to use email.

(D) To find who are the least brave people.

_____ **2.** The word "**malicious**" in the 2nd paragraph means _____.

(A) charitable   (B) heroic   (C) spiteful   (D) voluntary

_____ **3.** The word "**it**" in the last paragraph refers to _____.

(A) sending emails   (B) talking in person

(C) calling the person   (D) ending a relationship

_____ **4.** According to the article, which of the following statements is CORRECT?

(A) It is thoughtful to use email to break up with a close friend.

(B) Sending cruel messages just exposes one's own shortcomings.

(C) Emoticons help introverted people express their true feelings.

(D) Breaking up face to face would usually inflict serious damage.

_____ **5.** "**Increasingly, however, individuals are no longer communicating complex emotions face to face.**"

Where would the above sentence best fit in the article?

Unit 38

American Idol or Object of Ridicule

In the early days of television, many TV shows were created to fill the emerging markets. Among them were game shows and talent shows that offered ordinary people a chance to be on TV to win money or prizes by demonstrating their knowledge or talent. As TV audiences grew over the years, these types of programs became more and more popular. There were locally produced shows that put common folk on the air, but there were others that featured well-known celebrities. From the infatuation with celebrities and their public and private lives, the past years have given birth to what is known as the "Reality Show."

Reality shows are all **encompassing**. Some have people do incredibly dangerous stunts or disgusting feats to win money. Some shows involve has-been celebrities living in a closed space with others in what is supposed to be a "real" environment so that audiences can watch and enjoy their interactions. It has been said that some of the dialogues and actions in these shows are scripted or changed for "ratings value."

One of the worst offenders is probably *American Idol*, which is known for its unwritten policy of putting on people without any ounce of talent, only to have them mocked by the so-called judges in front of a national, and maybe even a global, audience. <5> There is no denying that *American Idol* has produced its stars. However, if truth is to be known, the point of shows like *American Idol* is to humiliate, and have people watch while others suffer shame and tears in their failure. Unfortunately, many people love to watch these types of shows and the ratings have never been greater. Some psychologists say that people enjoy watching the failures of others to cover for their own failures in life.

So does "Reality TV Show" really present reality?

_____ **1.** The word "**encompassing**" in the 2nd paragraph means _____ .
   (A) including a wide range of subjects
   (B) originating from different sources
   (C) providing all kinds of opportunities
   (D) directing towards a certain audience

_____ **2.** People enjoy watching reality shows for many reasons **EXCEPT** that

   _____ .

   (A) they love to laugh at other people's failures
   (B) they want to know famous people's private lives
   (C) they enjoy the reality presented on TV programs
   (D) they can see ordinary people perform difficult tasks

_____ **3.** Which of the following statements is TRUE about *American Idol*?
   (A) It is broadcast only across America.
   (B) The ratings of *American Idol* are not satisfactory.
   (C) Psychologists also take part in it.
   (D) Its purpose is to embarrass participants.

_____ **4.** The article was most likely written by someone who _____ .
   (A) despises the purposes of reality shows
   (B) advocates the production reality shows
   (C) feels entertained by watching reality shows
   (D) appreciates the celebrities' contribution to reality shows

_____ **5.** Which of the following can be added to the blank in the 3rd paragraph?
   (A) Variety shows and sitcoms are also widely enjoyed across the country.
   (B) It adds to the entertainment value for a contestant to be publicly ridiculed on
       stage.
   (C) It is ironic that the show is also scripted or carefully edited to boost ratings.
   (D) Participants are encouraged to act in order to create some dramatic effects.

Eco-Chic

Not too long ago in Taiwan, thousands of people queued up for hours and were willing to pay an outrageous price to obtain a canvas bag that had an environmentally-friendly slogan printed on it. For most of these people, the environment wasn't really their main concern. If it was, they could have bought other similar bags at much lower prices with less **hassle** or could get them free from government agencies. The main reason was that the bag was the must-have item at that time.

Most people today are aware of the need to protect the environment. Most people do their part: recycling, reducing and reusing what they can. However, the sad thing is that many only do so when it is convenient for them, when someone is watching or when it is fashionable.

One good example is hybrid cars. They have been available for many years, but have been generally ignored by the public. People continued to buy and drive gas-guzzling and high-polluting SUVs. It wasn't until many Hollywood celebrities started driving hybrids that sales of these cars started to increase. <5> Another example is the promotion of using recycled material for clothing so as not to waste precious resources anymore. Consumers feel that they are on board to save the world while simply doing their holiday shopping. However, one shocking phenomenon is the sale of "green dollars," which a person can buy so that they can continue to pollute and use up natural resources; the proceeds from **these sales** supposedly go to private or non-governmental organization to continue research on environmental protection.

Environmental awareness has improved greatly in the past few years. However, the amount of waste, pollution and natural resources consumed increases each year. The only way to save the environment is to be conscious of it all of the time, not only when it is convenient or in style.

_____ **1.** According to the article, which one is **WRONG**?

(A) Celebrities play an important part in promoting the sale of SUVs.

(B) Environmental protection is being commercialized to some extent.

(C) Being environmentally-friendly is not as easy as just buying related products.

(D) Lots of people may spend enormous amounts of time and money buying products for the purpose of fashion.

_____ **2.** Which of the following has similar meaning to the word "**hassle**?"

(A) Credibility.   (B) Difficulty.

(C) Stimulus.   (D) Recommendation.

_____ **3.** In the 3rd paragraph, **these sales** refer to the sales of _____ .

(A) resources   (B) clothing

(C) recycled material   (D) green dollars

_____ **4.** What is the author's tone in this article?

(A) Encouraging.   (B) Cynical.   (C) Critical.   (D) Taunting.

_____ **5.** Which of the following can be best put in the blank?

(A) Many celebrities prefer the comfort and safety of SUVs.

(B) "Green" clothing has caught on with Europe for some time.

(C) More celebrities are becoming environmentally-conscious.

(D) The reason was that it was now "in" to have one of these cars.

ADVANCED READING 1

Idiot or Savant?

There is a notion in the professional world that if a person possesses numerous advanced degrees, then that person is undeniably very intelligent. However, a person that has a Ph.D. or an MBA could have graduated at the bottom of their class and just barely **made it through**. The word "*savant*" is borrowed from the French language. It describes a person with natural and superior intelligence; a born genius. Leonardo da Vinci was a noted *savant*. He was a polymath, a person with skills and knowledge in many areas, from art to engineering. And he was mostly self-taught.

People that are naturally-gifted usually don't realize it. They may have a talent for solving puzzles or breaking codes that can surprise people. When they attend institutions of higher learning, they may get bored with the curriculum because they already know what is being taught. Most usually drop out, not because they failed or had financial problems, but just because they think it is a waste of their time. <5> Some are called idiots for giving up their chance; however, most don't really care about that little piece of paper. They would rather go on and do their own thing. Some succeed; some don't. But when they do, they are usually very, very successful.

The founders of Google and Steve Jobs, the founder of Apple, were all anti-establishment. They went out and did their own thing, and have become very successful. The biggest success story would have to be Bill Gates. He dropped out of Harvard and started to do his own thing by starting up a company in his parents' garage. His company is now called Microsoft and he is one of the richest persons in the world. Idiot or *savant*?

_____ **1.** What is this article mainly about?

    (A) Successful persons usually arise from a modest background.

    (B) Naturally-gifted people may not exhibit great performance at school.

    (C) Academic performance can determine one's capability in some fields.

    (D) Self-taught persons are wrongly regarded as intelligent geniuses.

_____ **2.** What does the phrase "**make it through**" possibly mean?

    (A) Succeed after a series of obstacles.

    (B) Overcome difficulties with ease.

    (C) Narrowly escape from a danger.

    (D) Tackle a problem with efficiency.

_____ **3.** The author cites the example of Leonardo da Vinci to _____.

    (A) help explain the meaning of a word

    (B) elaborate on the importance of self-reliance

    (C) illustrate how much a man of capability can accomplish

    (D) compare a born genius with hard-working common people

_____ **4.** What can be inferred from this passage?

    (A) Leonardo da Vinci must have had intelligent parents.

    (B) Bill Gates may not have succeeded if he had not dropped out of Harvard.

    (C) Steve Jobs may have felt dissatisfied with fixed and rigid educational system.

    (D) Anti-establishment people are more likely to succeed in technology.

_____ **5.** Which of the following sentences can be best put in the blank?

    (A) They prefer home schooling to traditional education in raising a genius.

    (B) It may take some time for school teachers to get acquainted with these unusual students.

    (C) Some feel that these institutions of higher learning are too close minded and don't allow free thinking.

    (D) Those misfits often encounter difficulties in personal relationships when they start to work with others in the society.

Designing for Women

After the Industrial Revolution and mass production of goods for the public began, product design was mostly bland and utilitarian. As competition increased, more attention was paid to product design and marketing. At the time, men were the breadwinners and decision makers, so most of the design and marketing were geared towards them. After World War II, more women entered the workforce and became wage earners. Realizing that they had a new market, the manufacturer began to make products that appealed to women. <A> Over time, many companies found that they had to design products specifically for women if they wanted to remain competitive. **Their needs** and desires had to be considered. This meant compactness, ease of use and style. The types of products ranged from automobiles, computers and other electronic goods. <B> The marketing style of products has also been changed to appeal to more women.

In the electronics industry, for instance, products are being designed to accommodate smaller hands, shorter finger reach, portability in handbags, and other factors, such as longer finger nails. <C> Cell phones today come in a myriad of colors instead of the ubiquitous black and silver of the past. They also come in different styles and with different features to suit all tastes. For example, some cell phones with built-in digital cameras have their automatic focus set at arms length as it was observed that many young women liked to take pictures of themselves with a friend. Even the video game industry, which used to cater to teenage boys and young men, is taking female gamers more seriously as recent studies have revealed that women make up 43% of present gamers. Video and computer game developers are designing adventure and role-playing games with female protagonists that they hope will appeal to female gamers. <D> The women's market is very **lucrative**. Women, being more fashion-conscious than men, are more likely to change their cell phones, digital cameras or other items more often in order to stay in line with the current style. Who knows? Maybe in the future when you go into an electronics store, there will be a "his" and "hers" section.

_____ **1.** According to the article, when designing for women, producers must bear the
following in mind **EXCEPT** _____ .
(A) their stature   (B) easy operation
(C) style   (D) all-in-one function

_____ **2.** In the 1st paragraph, the phrase **"their needs"** refer to the needs of

_____ .
(A) companies   (B) designers   (C) women   (D) wage earners

_____ **3.** The word **"lucrative"** possibly means _____ .
(A) unpredictable   (B) profitable   (C) sluggish   (D) dynamic

_____ **4.** According to the article, which of the following is **WRONG**?
(A) Women account for almost half of the population playing video games.
(B) After the Second World War, companies started to pay attention to
marketing.
(C) Men are not so much influenced by color and design of a product as women.
(D) Women tend to change their electronic products more frequently than men.

_____ **5.** Where can we best put the following sentence?
**"However, these were usually the same products that came in pink or
pastel colors with cutesy names."**

Feeding Baby Right

Breastfeeding babies used to be common before women joined the workforce and formula milk was invented. During the 70s, when women's liberation became a big thing and employment opportunities increased, many women started using the bottle on their babies instead. Some women have even decided against breastfeeding, thinking it will affect their figures. <A>

The World Health Organization (WHO) estimated that 1 million babies die or fall ill every year from **diarrhea** picked up from unhygienic bottle feeding or from formula milk powder mixed with unsafe water. <B> Experts stress that breastfeeding, especially just after birth, is necessary for the baby's survival. A newborn's immature immune system cannot protect him or her from countless bacteria, germs and other invaders. While it is hard to find the exact nature of human milk, there are many special substances in it that are uniquely designed to protect the baby. <C> Moreover, as a report published in the *Singapore Medical Journal* explains, a mother's human milk changes over time to meet the different phases of baby sucking, e.g. foremilk and hindmilk. Infant formula unfortunately can only provide a 'rigid' menu to the infant. This is not physiological. Therefore, breastfeeding or human milk is still the best gift for infants.

Besides, breastfeeding involves a lot of holding, cuddling and eye-contact and is great for bonding. <D> Women who breastfeed have half the risk of developing breast cancer than those women who don't. Full-time breastfeeding can also burn as much as 250 calories a day, so it's a way to help Mom lose pregnancy weight.

Because breast milk really is the ideal food for infants, the UN (United Nations) has recommended that mothers who can breastfeed their babies nurse for the first six months of their infant's life. If you cannot do full-time breastfeeding, you should at least consider part-time feeding.

_____ **1.** What is this article mainly about?

    (A) The pros and cons of breastfeeding.

    (B) The procedures of breastfeeding.

    (C) Comparison between breast milk and formula milk.

    (D) Benefits for mothers and infants from breastfeeding.

_____ **2.** Women are not willing to breastfeed their babies for the following reasons **EXCEPT** that _____.

    (A) women want to enter the workforce

    (B) preparing instant formula milk takes less time

    (C) breastfeeding may prevent a woman from staying fit

    (D) feminism liberates women from household violence

_____ **3.** What does the word "**diarrhea**" possibly mean?

    (A) A head injury.   (B) A chronic illness.

    (C) A stomach discomfort.   (D) A malfunction in genes.

_____ **4.** According to the article, which of the following is CORRECT?

    (A) Every year one million babies in the world are not breastfed.

    (B) Women are less likely to get breast cancer if they do breastfeeding.

    (C) Breastfeeding helps improve the relationship between the couples.

    (D) Instant milk is not nutritious because it contains artificial hormones.

_____ **5.** Where can we best put the following sentence?

    "**Human milk contains living cells, hormones and enzymes whose molecular structure can't be reproduced in infant formula.**"

Round-the-World Plastic Surgery

In today's global marketplace, people scour the world for the best deals in anything. Some of the most sought-after bargains involve plastic surgery. Most of us yearn to become beautiful, and many of us will traverse the globe to become so—but only for the best price.

People from developed countries such as the US , the UK , and Japan are travelling to countries such as Thailand, Malaysia, Hungary, and the Czech Republic. First they bask in the warm sun and laze on the beaches. <u><5></u> This "healthcare tourism" package industry is booming, involving thousands of patients and healthcare providers worldwide.

For example, Beautiful Beings is a UK-based agency that arranges for British clients to visit the Czech Republic for surgery. In one year this company sent more than 200 British citizens to Prague. The entire package included week-long accommodations, a local guide, and a liposuction procedure. The cost? US$3,000, or £1,700. A person in London would pay double that price.

There are drawbacks. While the surgeon may speak English, there's a good chance the nurses and other health care providers may not. If the patient experiences complications once he or she has returned home, how does that individual receive immediate treatment? Surgery is dangerous; travelling around the globe to be treated by a doctor you do not know is risky at best.

Taiwan, too, is slowly entering the healthcare tourism industry. This country is well known for offering LASIK laser eye surgery at reasonable prices—eye surgery in Taiwan can cost US$1,000, which is cheaper than the prices offered in almost any other country. Patients in Taiwan, too, can be assured of first-class medical conditions.

The desire to become transformed will often **overtake** any fears of the risks involved in overseas plastic surgery. No doubt the medical tourism industry will only grow in the years to come.

_____ **1.** According to the article, the tour package provided by Beautiful Beings does **NOT** include _____ .

(A) accommodation arrangements   (B) after-surgery consultation

(C) a local tour guide   (D) plastic surgery

_____ **2.** What can we infer from this article?

(A) The main reason for having cosmetic surgery overseas is the expertise of the surgeons.

(B) Medical tourism will only falter because more and more people are aware of the unknown risk.

(C) Some countries in South Asia and East Europe offer plastic surgeries at better prices than developed countries.

(D) Taiwan may soon lower the price of laser eye surgery to compete with other countries.

_____ **3.** According to the article, why is overseas cosmetic surgery risky?

(A) The medical procedure is not the same as that in one's country.

(B) There might be some misunderstanding due to the language barrier.

(C) The doctors may ask for more money in return for better treatment.

(D) The medical condition provided there may be unhygienic and awful.

_____ **4.** The phrase _____ can be used to replace the word "**overtake**".

(A) take heed of   (B) give priority to

(C) come to terms with   (D) take precedence over

_____ **5.** Which of the following sentences can be best put in the blank?

(A) What follows is a thorough check-up to determine the condition of the donor.

(B) Patients are warned of taking holidays overseas for cosmetic surgery.

(C) They can go over their recovery period better this way.

(D) Then they submit to the surgeon's knife.

Were the Lights on in Ancient Egypt?

Many people have **speculated** on how ancient civilizations were able to create monuments that still stand to this day. Take the Egyptian pyramids for example. They had the manpower, an understanding of engineering, but how did they light the project? This has baffled scientists for ages. <5> Some say that special shafts built into the pyramids channeled light inside and was reflected to where it was needed.

However, discovery of an ancient battery, now best known as the "Baghdad Battery," proves that the ancients had knowledge of the power of electricity. It was a crude design. It consisted of a clay pot with iron and copper rods tightly sealed to the pot, which contained a slightly acidic solution. It produced only a minuscule amount of electricity and would have required hundreds hooked up in series to have any effect. There were also no signs of the existence of any sort of device that could have been used for the battery to create light, until the discovery of rock carvings that resemble an ancient light bulb, now known as the Dendera light. So it is possible that the Egyptians may have had a working light source. Its design was copied many years later, and it worked. However, no other proof that **they** ever existed was found.

Some experts continue to insist that the Egyptians had electrical lighting during the construction of the pyramids as there were hardly any traces of soot on the walls or ceiling of the tunnels and passageways that would indicate the use of torches or oil lamps.

It might also be possible that the Egyptians had assistance from extraterrestrials. And that, whoever they were, they took their tools with them when they were finished.

_____ **1.** Which subject is discussed in the article?

(A) The lighting facilities used in the Egyptian pyramids.

(B) Many mysteries surrounding the ancient Egyptian civilization.

(C) Theories and discoveries about the lighting in ancient Egypt.

(D) How the ingenuity of ancient civilization sheds light on the modern technology.

_____ **2.** Which of the following words has the closest meaning to "**speculate**" in the 1st paragraph?

(A) Guess.   (B) Narrate.   (C) Loathe.   (D) Suspect.

_____ **3.** What does the pronoun "**they**" in the 2nd paragraph refer to?

(A) Carving.   (B) Light sources.   (C) Egyptians.   (D) Designs.

_____ **4.** According to the article, which of the following is TRUE?

(A) Egyptian's knowledge of electricity has yet to be proved.

(B) Egyptians may have carved their discoveries and ideas on the rock.

(C) No trace of soot in the pyramids indicates that Egyptians used oil lamps.

(D) The Baghdad Battery explains how Egyptians produced enough light.

_____ **5.** Which of the following sentences can be best put in the blank?

(A) Some suggest that Egyptians built pyramids from the inside out, so light was not a big issue.

(B) Some say they must have received either divine or extraterrestrial assistance.

(C) Some argue there were also no signs of the existence of any sort of light emitting devices in pyramids.

(D) Some dismiss the theory that Egyptians produced their pyramids alone.

Unit 45

Crossing Cultural Borders

- "*When my Chinese student asked me how much money I made, I was shocked. Even though we Germans are direct, money talk is just too intrusive. Now I realize that it's just a matter of small talk for them, a way to show interest and even friendliness.*" Maria Schmidt, German teacher.
- "*The Germans are really aggressive. When they shake your hands, they squeeze it hard enough to hurt.*" Christine Lim, Singaporean sales executive.
- "*My Japanese friend is a little strange. She doesn't talk much, but she makes a lot of humming and nasal noises in a conversation.*" Reinhold Krieger, German accountant.

<A> Every country has its own way of looking at physicality, language and human relationships. In the examples above, some communication blip has occurred because one party has not understood the other. For instance, Japanese speech patterns tend to be **deliberate**, with a lot of turn-taking. The hmms and ahs indicate that they are listening and the silences in between are actually meant for formulating a thoughtful response. But to a voluble Italian or chatty, used-to-instant-response American, you can imagine that such a conversational pattern could be a little disturbing.

<B> In today's world, where many companies are multinational and cross-border business a daily routine, cultural miscommunications can have serious impact. For instance, the Germans consider a strong handshake a sign of confidence. If your grip is less than firm in a job interview, you might as well see yourself out of the room.

<C> There's a real need to understand the values and philosophies underlying someone's culture. You often hear about Asian versus Western values, about how respectful Asians are of group and hierarchy and how competitive and individualistic Americans can be. Neither is inherently good or bad. And clichés and stereotypes can be misleading. Also, there are always individual quirks. Generalizations are useful only because they provide a framework in which we can start co-operating. Use them wisely and always with an open mind——that is the key to good communication skills. <D>

_____ **1.** What is the main idea of this article?

(A) Misunderstanding often results from ignorance and prejudice.

(B) Certain cultural taboos should be avoided for fear of misunderstanding.

(C) Different styles of communication can be explained in the context of cultural difference.

(D) Each culture has its own merit but should try to learn as much from other cultures as possible.

_____ **2.** The three quotations at the beginning of the article indicate that _____.

(A) Chinese tend to talk more straightforward than Germans

(B) Germans' handshakes are firmer than expected for foreigners

(C) Germans avoid any personal topic in a conversation

(D) the Japanese language has a lot of nasal sounds

_____ **3.** Which of the following sentences is **WRONG**?

(A) Western values place more emphasis on individualism.

(B) Chinese and Americans hold different opinions about hierarchy.

(C) Americans are prone to give prompt response in the course of a conversation.

(D) Japanese often use silence as a means to show their disagreement.

_____ **4.** The word _____ has the **OPPOSITE** meaning to the word "**deliberate**."

(A) impulsive   (B) ingenious   (C) willful   (D) intentional

_____ **5.** Where can we best put the following sentence?

"**Cultural sensitivity, however, is not just a list of dos and don'ts.**"

True Love: A Short Course

Poets and greeting card companies do great business writing about eternal love, but a Cornell University professor says being in love forever and ever is a myth. The reality, says Prof. Cindy Hazan, is that romantic love runs its course in 18 to 30 months.

Hazan interviewed 5,000 people from 37 cultures and subjected couples to medical testing for a study she did about love. She found that during the courtship, three chemicals —dopamine, oxytocin and phenyl ethylamine—combine in the brain to produce the intense feeling we label "love." Hazan also discovered that men are affected by these chemicals more quickly and more profoundly than women.

However, for both sexes, Hazan found that the action of the chemicals was powerful, if **transitory**. "Love" lasted only long enough for couples to court, mate and perhaps produce an offspring. Then, the chemicals lost their potency, and the excited sensations of "love" disappeared. <5>

Once the thrill is gone, Hazan says some people look for a new partner. For example, actress Gwyneth Paltrow believed actor Brad Pitt was the man of her dreams, but around the 30-month mark in their affair, she left him. She admitted that Pitt hadn't changed, but she just felt differently about him. Other couples stay together largely out of habit. One woman, who had been married 54 years, said that the sweaty-palms feeling she had about her husband had disappeared after a couple of years, and that other ties made their relationship worth keeping.

In *A Midsummer Night's Dream*, Shakespeare observed, "The course of true love never did run smooth." What would the playwright have thought if he knew that the course of true love ran ever so briefly, too?

_____ **1.** What is the main idea of this article?

(A) True love is a phrase created by card companies to lure consumers.

(B) It is not love that can keep a relationship going on smoothly.

(C) Chemicals inside our head may affect the way we behave and feel.

(D) Scientific research suggests that passion does not last eternally.

_____ **2.** According to Hazan's studies, we can find the facts **EXCEPT** "_____".

(A) Lovers are influenced by dopamine, oxytocin and phenyl ethylamine

(B) During the course of love, women tend to react more strongly to the effect of the chemicals than men

(C) Once the effect of the chemicals wanes, some people continue with their relationship not completely out of love

(D) It may be hard for anyone to experience the strong sensation after more than 30 months of a relationship

_____ **3.** What does the word "**transitory**" mean?

(A) Stable.　　　　(B) Elusive.　　　　(C) Formidable.　　　(D) Fleeting.

_____ **4.** According to the last paragraph, what do we find in Shakespeare's play?

(A) True love is something worth fighting for.

(B) Lovers often act on a sudden impulse of passion.

(C) Experiencing obstacles is unavoidable in the course of true love.

(D) The course of true love burns itself out in a certain period of time.

_____ **5.** Which one of the following sentences can be best put in the blank?

(A) Love appears to be a biological mechanism that helps the human race survive.

(B) But even the most ardent romantics develop a tolerance to the effects of these chemicals.

(C) People who need these chemicals could become serial romantics, who are always genuinely in love.

(D) Most men fall in love more quickly and easily than women.

Mom's Wisdom

It was a tough day. Stranded in the rain with a leaking umbrella and a headache, I stepped onto the pedestrian crossing. Suddenly, a Mercedes flashed by, drenching us in a spray of rain. Without thinking, I **let out some colourful expletives**.

His tiny hand still clasped in mine, my son looked up at me earnestly and said, "You shouldn't use words like those, Mommy. You should say, 'Oh, my goodness' or something like that."

Believe it or not, I had gone into motherhood with the best of intentions. <A> After all, I was given the chance to mold another human being. My son would have the nation-building intelligence and courage of Nelson Mandela. <B>

But it's a very tough job being good. I'd read all the parenting literature. Take nutrition. Yes, juniors should eat healthily but I rather like junk food and sweets myself. Bedtime? Be disciplined and consistent as sleep is important. The reason I was having a horrible day was because I'd stayed up watching television the night before. I could of course tell my son to do just what I say rather than what I do. But they say personal example is everything. <C> So I drag my son through the park (nature) when I really want to go shopping. I pat cats and dogs (love animals), all the time suppressing my fear of furry creatures. Thank goodness my son hasn't asked for a pet.

Being a wise parent is like acting, and not even real actors get it right all the time! <D> So right now, I'm pinning all my hopes in his genes and pray that my child will become a decent individual in spite of me. After all, didn't Nelson Mandela grow up in an unjust, chaotic environment, with lots of badly-behaving adults?

_____ **1.** According to the article, we can know that the author is _____ .
   (A) a desperate mother with a misbehaved child
   (B) a devoted mother who enjoys parenthood greatly
   (C) a learning mother who finds the difficulty in raising her child
   (D) a struggling mother trying to strike a balance between career and
        motherhood

_____ **2.** When the author says she **"let out some colourful expletives,"** it means she
   _____ .

   (A) lectured   (B) swore   (C) snapped   (D) taunted

_____ **3.** What can be inferred from the 4th paragraph?
   (A) The mother tried to abide by all the rules regardless of her own preference.
   (B) The mother won't buy her son a pet for her fear of flurry little animals.
   (C) Sacrificing herself for the well-being of the children is definitely worthwhile.
   (D) Nutrition, being close to nature, and love for animal are more important than
        the mother has thought.

_____ **4.** Why does the author mention Mandela again in the last paragraph?
   Because she wants to _____ .
   (A) show how she was influenced by him
   (B) show how she would mold her child
   (C) relieve herself from the sense of guilt
   (D) compare the similarity between Mandela and her son

_____ **5.** Where can we put the following sentence?
   **"And I was going to become a much better person in the process as
   well."**

LOHAS = "Happy Life": A Worldwide Trend for the Good of the Planet?

LOHAS is an acronym for "Lifestyles of Health and Sustainability." <u><A></u> Hence, individuals within the LOHAS universe prefer organic food and renewable energy sources, investing in socially conscious corporations, and introducing medical practices other than Western medicine. <u><B></u> Below is a brief overview of the expanding LOHAS universe.

Sustainable Economy. LOHAS-committed companies and organizations will ensure that what they do will be ecological, cost-effective, and will benefit the maximum number of people possible. Companies that decrease carbon emissions or support micro lending to people in Third-World countries are standard-bearers within the LOHAS universe.

Healthy Living. The organic, natural food sector historically has garnered **the lion's share of** the LOHAS market. Organic food sales in the US exceed US$40 billion a year. While organic food now constitutes one to two percent of food sales in the US, experts predict that the percentage will rise to five to ten percent.

Alternative Healthcare. This category includes medical treatments that are not part of the "scientific," hospital-based healthcare system, such as acupuncture, herbal remedies, reflexology, and massage. Research has revealed that these alternatives can actually save money; they can keep individuals healthier longer.

Personal Development. Highly stressed individuals today are looking for peace and quiet. Americans are flocking to organizations that offer contemplation and meditation. Yoga devotees now number in the millions, with people worldwide attending yoga classes.

Many LOHAS-branded products are now being introduced to Taiwan. <u><C></u> With a high economic growth and industrial pollution for years, it is no surprise that the Taiwanese, too, are developing a concern for the environment and for healthy lifestyles. The government is working on a major recycling initiative and enforcing energy-efficient policies for businesses and the public. <u><D></u>

In Chinese, the literal translation of LOHAS means "happy life." Taiwanese are now seeking more earth-friendly solutions in order to keep us——and our planet——happier.

_____ **1.** Which of the following does **NOT** belong to the LOHAS universe?

(A) Taking some meditation classes for inner peace.

(B) Dedicating oneself to the environmental protection.

(C) Working as a SOHO and traveling abroad whenever possible.

(D) Supporting companies that give financial aid to poorer countries.

_____ **2.** According to the article, which of the following can contribute to sustainable economy?

(A) Economical and efficient manufacturing.

(B) Traditional Eastern herbal therapy and practice.

(C) A tax cut for companies that produce less exhaust.

(D) Ban on globalization and the import of foreign produce.

_____ **3.** If a product has **the lion's share of the market**, it _____ .

(A) is the original prototype

(B) accounts for the largest percentage

(C) has no equals in terms of quality

(D) is the one and only product of this kind

_____ **4.** How is the trend of LOHAS developing in Taiwan now?

(A) People in Taiwan are not so keen in taking part in this trend.

(B) A lot of LOHAS-related products have already caught on in Taiwan.

(C) The government in Taiwan is among the first countries to initiate this activity.

(D) The concept of LOHAS is appealing to Taiwanese because it conforms to the traditional Chinese philosophy.

_____ **5.** Where can we best put the following sentence?

"LOHAS consumers and companies are committed to saving the environment, effecting peace worldwide, and seeing social justice being done."

Unit 49

Winning Handicap: Matthias Berg

He is a lawyer actively involved in local politics, a champion sportsman who has won 14 gold medals, 9 silvers and 6 bronzes in field athletics and alpine skiing in World, European, and Paralympics championships. <A> A passionate horn player, he performs 25 concerts a year, has released three CDs and has just completed a concert tour of Japan . Yet these are just his interests. His main job is heading a government department with 400 employees.

You would think that this must be another self-satisfied overachiever. <B> But his achievements are astounding indeed considering that Matthias was a "thalidomide baby."

"Thalidomide" was a drug developed by the German pharmaceutical company Grünenthal. It was sold mainly to pregnant women to combat morning sickness and to help them sleep. It was released before adequate safety tests were conducted. 10,000 babies in the late fifties to early sixties were born with severe **malformations**. Matthias' mother took only one tablet but the damage was done. Her baby was born with flipper-like arms so short that they reach just his armpits.

Matthias remembers the difficulties of his childhood. <C> "I had three things against me—I was short-armed, red-haired and my accent was different. It wasn't always easy, not being invited to dates or birthday parties and so on. But I am no victim." The teasings of childhood were soothed by close family support. <D> "We helped him choose his instrument. We thought the horn was the best for him because he needed only three fingers for the valves of the horn," said his mother, a musician herself. Asked if his accomplishments were a compensation for his handicap, the 45 year-old father replied with a grin, "Oh no, I think I would have done all these things if I had been 'normal' too. Discipline is just the fight against my natural laziness."

If there were a personality contest as well, Matthias Berg would surely take another gold medal.

_____ **1.** Matthias showed interest in the following subjects **EXCEPT** _____.

    (A) conducting a concert   (B) legal practice

    (C) field athletics and skiing   (D) recording his music

_____ **2.** In the 3rd paragraph, the **OPPOSITE** word for "**malformation**" would be

    _____ .

    (A) deformity   (B) normality   (C) hospitality   (D) immunity

_____ **3.** Which of the following is **NOT** true?

    (A) Matthias was discriminated for his accent and strange figure.

    (B) Matthias set out to fulfil many achievements as a tribute to his mother.

    (C) It stands to reason that the effect of Thalidomide was so tremendous that even a small dosage can cause great damage.

    (D) Thalidomide babies refer to infants born with disabilities because their mothers took Thalidomide during pregnancy.

_____ **4.** What is the author's opinion about Matthias Berg?

    (A) The author is intimidated by Berg's talents.

    (B) The author shows great sympathy for Berg.

    (C) The author thinks highly of Berg's personality.

    (D) The author does not state his personal judgment about Berg.

_____ **5.** Where can we best put the following sentence?

    "**Yet in truth, Matthias Berg is a very pleasant fellow, bespectacled and dimpled with an easy smile.**"

Puppies Behind Bars

Dogs have long been used to help people with disabilities, particularly the blind. Unfortunately, it takes about two years and $25,000 to properly train a dog for this purpose. But in 1997, Gloria Gilbert Stoga established the nonprofit organization, "Puppies Behind Bars," so that people in prison, with plenty of time on their hands, could do most of the training on a volunteer basis.

Many people were nervous about this program at first, especially for the safety of the dogs in correctional facilities. To ease concerns, "Puppies Behind Bars" does not let prisoners guilty of vicious crimes work with any animals. Furthermore, inmates wishing to participate must endure a thorough interview process so that residents with violent tendencies can be **weeded out**.

Once in the program, prisoners must attend bi-weekly training sessions. They spend the rest of the time just living with their puppies and teaching them basic skills such as toileting, sitting and standing on command, and simply walking in crowded areas without getting confused. After sixteen months, the inmates turn their dogs over to professional dog handlers for the final five months of training.

Judy Goldman was one of the first recipients of a "Puppies Behind Bars" graduate. She was so impressed that she visited the prison where the dog was raised to thank the trainers. "They're so proud, and they well should be," she says, "**They** do an excellent job."

Perhaps the greatest beneficiaries of the program are the inmates. <u><5></u> Most importantly, they receive the unconditional love that only a puppy can provide. Prisoner Roosevelt Lewis says of his dog, "Joshua has given me back my peace of mind."

It seems that "Puppies Behind Bars" is giving everyone involved a new "leash on life."

_____ **1.** What is mainly discussed in this article?

(A) Dogs that help janitors to monitor the inmates.

(B) A program that has benefited both prisoners and the disabled.

(C) An organization dedicated to the welfare of stray or abused dogs.

(D) Volunteers that are chosen to assist the invalid and the prisoners.

_____ **2.** To participate in the program, inmates must do the following **EXCEPT**

_____ .

(A) go thorough an interview

(B) attend the training class every other week

(C) live with the dogs until they are given to the recipients

(D) teach their dogs basic skills such as following the command

_____ **3.** If someone is **weeded out**, that means he/she is _____ .

(A) discriminated   (B) rescued   (C) detained   (D) eliminated

_____ **4.** What does "**They**" in the 4th paragraph refer to?

(A) Puppies.   (B) Recipients.   (C) Inmates.   (D) Trainees.

_____ **5.** Which of the following can be best put in the blank?

(A) While training the animals, they learn patience and responsibility.

(B) The physically-challenged can benefit from this program as well.

(C) Trained properly, every prisoner can contribute to the society in this way.

(D) Inmates can take time to reflect upon their sins before returning to the society.

01. CABCA		**26.** DBABD	
02. BDDBA		**27.** CCBDA	
03. DBBAA		**28.** CACBD	
04. DBACC		**29.** CABAB	
05. BCACC		**30.** CCDAC	
06. BCDDC		**31.** DBBCD	
07. ACBCD		**32.** CDACD	
08. DBABB		**33.** ACBDB	
09. BCABC		**34.** DDCAC	
10. DBCBA		**35.** CBABB	
11. BCBCD		**36.** ACDDB	
12. BBDDC		**37.** BCDBA	
13. ADCBC		**38.** ACDAB	
14. CBDBD		**39.** ABDCD	
15. CABDB		**40.** BAACC	
16. CCDAB		**41.** DCBBA	
17. CCBDA		**42.** DDCBC	
18. DACCD		**43.** BCBDD	
19. BCBDC		**44.** CABBA	
20. DCCDB		**45.** CBDAC	
21. DBBCD		**46.** DBDCA	
22. ADCBC		**47.** CBACB	
23. CDCBC		**48.** CABBA	
24. CCAAB		**49.** ABBCB	
25. BDACC		**50.** BCDCA	

閱讀經典文學時光之旅：英國篇

宋美瑋　編著

閱讀經典文學時光之旅：美國篇

陳彰範　編著

1. 精選八篇經典英美文學作品，囊括各類議題，如性別平等、人權、海洋教育等。
2. 獨家收錄故事背景的知識補充、原文講解。
3. 附精闢賞析、文章中譯及電子朗讀音檔，自學也能輕鬆讀懂文學作品。
4. 可搭配108課綱英文多元選修課程及加深加廣選修課程。

Reading Power 系列

★ 108課綱、全民英檢中／中高級適用

Advanced

精選閱讀

翻譯與解析

王郁惠、鄭翔嬬　編著

Main Idea

Details

Vocabulary in Context

Structure

Reference

Inference

三民書局

01 智慧設計：重新包裝的神造說？
Intelligent Design: Creationism Repackaged?

翻譯

　　在人類歷史早期，人們認為一切難以解釋的自然現象或其他事物，都出自諸神的安排。**古文明崇拜諸多不同的神，這些神高興時會帶來好運，人類做錯事也會加以懲罰。**或根據聖經記載，全能的上帝創造了宇宙萬物，也包括人類。

　　幾個世紀以來，幾乎所有人都一直相信，上帝創造了地球萬物。許多早期的科學家得以更了解我們這世界，敢於提出「不是只有上帝」的論調。然而，一心想捍衛「上帝存在」思想的宗教團體，往往將這些人貼上女巫、巫師，或是**異端**的標籤。以科學角度看待事物的人，和那些堅持上帝成就萬事萬物的神造說信奉者，彼此論戰達數個世紀之久。科學最終獲得勝利，演化理論廣為世人所接受。

　　為了不被擊垮，神造說信奉者想出了「智慧設計」的說法。這理論有點複雜，基本上是主張：科學或許能證明某些事情，但在找不到合理解釋時，那就一定是上帝的傑作。有些智慧設計的追隨者甚至更進一步，將超自然的存在和高智商的外星人一併納入。科學界通常對這見解置之不理。智慧設計直到最近才成為一項議題，因為該見解的支持者極力想在學校推動成為一個學科。反對的人認為，將純科學和宗教或超自然現象混淆是不對的，而且認為，這就好比將天文學和占星術混為一談。

　　論戰仍在持續中。隨著科學和技術的進步，或許有朝一日，我們所有尚未解決的問題都將獲得解答，從而證明神造說和智慧設計都是錯的。不過，或許只要向科學界提出「請證明上帝不存在」的質疑，智慧設計的信奉者就能發出最後反敗為勝的一擊。

解析

1. 這篇文章主要是在分析(C)所謂智慧設計理論(Intelligent Design) 所引發的爭議，此為最完整說明作者的目的。根據文章，智慧設計理論的內容和之前所提到的神造說理論(creationsim) 很雷同，並不是全新的理論，故(B)不正確。本文重點不是提出理論或說明討論的過程，故(A) (D)為非。

2. 從前句及當句可推論出，被認為是異端邪說者 (heretics)，可能不相信世界萬物的誕生只靠神的力量，和 witches, sorcerers 一樣不被傳統基督教的支持者所接受，故選(A)。

3. 從第三段最後可得知(B)**智慧設計理論的支持者，希望它被列入學校課程**。文中並無提到科學家支持智慧設計理論，故(A)為非。從第三段開頭可得知，智慧設計理論是承認科學可以解釋一些現象，故(C)不正確。(D)在本文中並未提到。

4. 從最後一句可顯示出，作者認為(C)**智慧設計理論可能最後還是會佔上風**，因為科學可能很難證明上帝不存在。

5. 此句主要是說明古代文明對神的認知，最適合放在第一段，故選(A)。第二段主要是說明科學對神的質疑，第三段主要是說明智慧設計理論的內容和引起的爭議，第四段主要是作者對這議題可能發展的看法。

翻譯

　　你知道有種小孩，膽小又不愛運動。那種很不擅長運動的小孩。那種樹木在深夜摩擦著他家房子，就會哭著找媽媽的小孩。那種看了有關蛇類的電視節目後，接下來幾個禮拜都會作惡夢的小孩。但這個小可憐蟲卻用故事來減輕自己的恐懼。那些深夜的樹木，讓他編寫出令人意想不到的故事，構思了一個又一個天馬行空的故事。

　　這人是誰？正是身兼電影導演與製作人的史蒂芬·史匹柏。

　　年輕時候的史匹柏很愛嚇自己，也愛嚇別人。他把他的幾個妹妹她們鎖到有塑膠骷髏頭的衣櫃裡面去，再把燈關掉，骷髏頭便詭異地亮起來。想當然爾，妹妹們會放聲尖叫起來。史匹柏的《法櫃奇兵》系列，還有電影《世界大戰》中，充滿了讓觀眾震慄、驚嚇的鏡頭。

　　史匹柏受到許多其他未必是可怕的經驗所影響。四歲時，年幼的史匹柏會和父親一起觀賞流星，一看就是幾個鐘頭。他的電影《第三類接觸》，就是在紀念他與父親這項深具意義的經驗。本身信奉猶太教的史匹柏，深受德國人奧斯卡·辛德勒的勇氣所感召，此人從二次世界大戰的集中營，救出一千一百位猶太人，使他們免於喪命。史匹柏因拍攝此鉅作《辛德勒名單》，榮獲一九九三年奧斯卡金像獎最佳導演獎。

　　一個小孩會變成什麼樣的大人，你永遠看不出來。史匹柏就是最好的例子。這個膽小的孩子，長大後就變成一個製作讓世人著迷，也改變世界生活的大人。

解析

1. 此為文章主旨題，前三段主要說明史匹柏小時候容易受驚嚇和長大後喜歡嚇人的經驗，造就他在電影上能成功地展現恐怖的場景，而第四段則用另外兩個例子 (和父親一同觀星及身為猶太人的經歷) 說明他人生經驗如何影響他電影的取材，故選(B)。(C)的敘述太籠統，而文中並未提到(A)(D)。

2. 此為文章的細節題，文章第四段後半部提及《辛德勒名單》以二次世界大戰猶太人集中營為故事背景，講述辛德勒的故事。

3. 本題考的是細節的部分，(A)從第一段知道史匹柏並不擅長於體育；(B)從第三段知道史匹柏有姊妹，並不是家中唯一的小孩；(C)史匹柏在一九九三年贏得的是奧斯卡最佳導演獎而非演員獎；(D)選項敘述正確。

4. 從此句的上下文中可知此處文意上有一轉折，上段提到史匹柏的電影讓人覺得spellbound and frightened，但他的電影未必都是這樣，因此可推測 go bump in the night 含有類似的意思，故選(B)。

5. 此句放在(A)的位置，前面敘述史匹柏小時候十分容易受到驚嚇，之後正好說明 Speilberg 如何透過說故事的方式減輕自己的恐懼。(B)的位置應舉例說明史匹柏捉弄他人的方法，(C)的位置則舉出其他的例子說明史匹柏的經驗是如何影響他的電影，(D)的位置屬於結論句，應總結全文，故不適合。

---

eerily adv. 恐怖的　　spellbound adj. 著迷的　　things that go bump in the night　夜裡可怕的聲響

practicing adj. 虔誠的　　enthrall vt. 迷住　　alleviate vt. 減輕，減緩

能真心喜歡芭蕾嗎 ?? 是有可能……
CAN One Enjoy Ballet?? Just Maybe...

翻譯

　　在大多數人得知，連舉世聞名的俄國作家安東·契訶夫曾說：「我完全不懂芭蕾舞」時，都覺得鬆了一口氣。**事實上，很多人對這種舞蹈也有類似的看法。**他們承認浮現腦海的就是：熟練、敏捷的舞者在空中跳躍，做出極為固定的動作。服裝看上去多半過時。還有就是，怎會有這種用腳尖在跳的舞蹈?!

　　但這偏見真能說得過去嗎？若有人說：「看交際舞你會不會怕？」答案大概千篇一律：「當然不會！」我們都欣賞探戈舞的熱力四射，或是華爾滋的一派優雅。那為什麼芭蕾舞會帶給我們大多數人這樣的反感呢？它只不過是另一種的舞蹈啊！造成文化上有這樣的看法，部分是根源於芭蕾舞的歷史。毫無疑問的，芭蕾舞是上流社會的藝術形態。從文藝復興時代金碧輝煌的義大利宮廷，到十八世紀雄偉氣派的法國皇宮，芭蕾舞一直以來獲得皇室與權貴的資助與喜愛。芭蕾舞漸漸變成一種少數人能理解及欣賞的藝術。

　　試著用不同的角度來看待芭蕾舞。男、女舞者用身體做出令人難以置信的動作，帶有力量、平衡與情感。芭蕾舞女主角在越步時一躍而起，看似能與地心引力相抗衡。多年來令人驚訝的苦功與訓練，造就了舞者能像體操選手一般毫不費力地旋轉、高舉和跳躍的好身手。所以動作制式化或者故事情節太過時又如何呢？每個人都能欣賞其中的技巧。不妨去看一場表演，坐定位，讓音樂和典雅將你包圍。

> 註：jetè 芭蕾舞的動作，一腳向前，另一腳向後伸展的跳躍動作，稱為「越步」。

解析

1. 由上下文可知此處文意上有一轉折，上句提到我們都欣賞探戈的活力或華爾茲的優雅，因此可猜出 antipathy 和 admire 意思相反，故選(D)。

2. 本題考文章細節，第一段提及芭蕾舞的 stylized moves 和 antiquated costumes，第二段提到 ballet's history，最後一段提到芭蕾的 old fashioned plots，故引起人們對芭蕾的偏見有(A)(C)(D)，故選(B)。

3. 作者的意見出現在第三段，鼓勵讀者放鬆，好好欣賞芭蕾力與美的表現，故選(B)。(A)為事實並非作者的看法，(C)(D)文中未提及。

4. 本題為文章主旨題，前兩段主要說明芭蕾令人覺得難以欣賞的原因，但第三段則希望讀者以不同的角度去欣賞這種舞蹈，故選(A)。(B)只是文中的一個細節，文中並未提到(C)(D)。

5. 此句放在(A)的位置，由 in fact 所引導的句子，在文意上除了有承接上文也含有補充說明的作用，此處正好承接前句契柯夫對芭蕾的觀點，接著說明一般大眾和對芭蕾 (this dance form) 也有相似的看法。陳述一般大眾的意見主要出現在第一段，(B)(C)的位置是討論芭蕾的歷史，而(D)出現的段落是作者在講希望讀者如何欣賞芭蕾，均不適合此句。

---

envision　vt.　想像　　　instill　vt.　注入灌輸　　　antipathy　n.　厭惡反感　　　Renaissance　n.　文藝復興時期

poise　n.　平衡、姿勢　　jeté　n.　越步　　　defy　vt.　違抗

04 人類生存的關鍵
Key to Our Survival?

　　牙籤常被視為理所當然的物品，日常生活中不需要的小東西，有時卻又**不可或缺**。牙籤幾乎不花什麼錢，但在你真正需要的時候，卻算得上無價。除此之外，沒有人可確認誰發明了牙籤。牙籤也可能是最早用於牙齒保健的工具，可能在人類物種生存中扮演了重要的角色。

　　歷史記錄中最早使用的牙籤是某種木質器物，可追溯到西元前五百年到西元七百年的某個時間點，當時牙籤是佛教和尚例行清潔儀式的一部分。這個習慣之後由貴族所採用，然後隨著牙齒保健的重要性受重視，漸漸流傳到一般大眾的生活。人們在意是否擁有乾淨健康的牙齒，這促成了牙科的創新發明，譬如牙刷和牙線。

　　研究早期人類牙齒的人類學家發現，靠近牙齒根部有弧形的溝槽，他們認為這是由某種用於清潔牙齒的工具所造成的。**看起來是我們人類早期的祖先，可能使用了容易取得且立即可用的草根來清潔齒縫。**更為近期的研究，在已變為化石的牙齒上也發現類似的溝槽，甚至可以追溯到一百八十萬年以前！

　　這些研究已經促使許多人認定，牙籤是我們存活的關鍵，重要性與火等事物相當。原因在於：如果我們某位史前的祖先，真的對有一小塊食物塞在他牙縫，覺得沒什麼大不了而且他又不夠聰明，找不到東西把食物挑出來的話，他的牙齒就會蛀的蛀、掉的掉。沒了牙齒，他就無法進食。要是他不能進食，他就小命不保了，而要是他小命不保，我們今天也不會在這裡了。

1. 本文主要是介紹牙籤在考古上的發現及其應用對人類健康的重要性，故選(D)。文章中並無提到是誰發明了牙線 (dental floss)，故(B)為錯誤。

2. 從第三段可得知，考古學家在古代人類牙齒底部發現的(B)**弧形溝槽 (curved grooves)**，證明了古代人類有使用某種清潔牙齒的工具。

3. 本題選錯誤的選項，從第二段第一句，可得知歷史文件上 (historical records) 有記錄了古代佛教和尚用工具清潔牙齒來做為某種儀式，因此(A)不正確。從第二段可推論出 (B) (C)，最後一段說明了潔牙工具的重要性，可推論出(D)。

4. 從 "**but** at times it is indispensable" 可得知與上一句語意 (a trivial thing that you can do without in your daily life) 相反，所以 indispensable 和 do without 詞意應是相對的，所以應為(C) **vital**「不可或缺，重要的」之意。

5. 本句應放在古代人類如何清潔牙齒的段落，故選(C)。(A)位置應放牙籤的介紹。(B)選項應放佛教徒潔牙的宗教儀式。(D)選項應放潔牙對人體健康的重要性。

indispensable adj. 不可或缺的	hygiene n. 衛生	dental floss n. 牙線
anthropologist n. 人類學家	fossilized adj. 化石化的	sanitary adj. 衛生的
disposable adj. 可丟棄的	lethal adj. 致命的	

翻譯

　　「五呎 N 吋」指的是什麼？這是一般成年人的身高。事實上，並未有個確切的數字，但統計資料顯示，平均落在五呎和六呎 (153 公分～183 公分) 之間。假如你的身高略高或略低於這個範圍，也算是正常的，除非你的身高跟這範圍比起來，相差百分之二十以上。許多東西，例如傢俱和門，通常都是配合平均高度的人所設計。身高太高或太低很可能受到他人嘲弄，或是不太容易找到合身的衣服，但是也可能有好處，特別是在籃球、賽馬或是賽車等運動方面。

　　不過，是什麼決定一個人的身高呢？**生物學家指出，遺傳和環境是兩項決定性的因素。**研究人員指稱，一個人遺傳自父母的基因，占百分之六十到八十，而一個人居住的環境和生活水準，以及成長時的營養水平，占百分之二十到四十。就歷史角度而言，西方國家的人民一直以來都比亞洲人高，但隨著生活水準及營養水平的改善，某些亞洲國家的人民正快速迎頭趕上西方各國。舉例來說，根據最新統計，在美國，男性平均是五呎十吋 (178 公分)，而美國女性平均是五呎四吋半 (164 公分)；在臺灣，男人和女人的平均身高，分別是五呎七吋半 (171 公分) 和五呎二又四分之三吋 (159 公分)。

　　研究還顯示，隨著愈來愈多國家更進一步的發展之後，人類的身高也逐漸增加。但研究也揭露了西方世界一項奇特的趨勢——歐洲的平均身高在增加當中，而美國的實際上卻在減少當中。部分的人，特別是歐洲人推論，那是因為美國人對垃圾食物偏愛到無法自拔，這只會讓他們變得更胖，而不是更高。

解析

1. 本題是考作者如何在文章中帶出主題，作者在第一段中先藉由提出一個問題，然後(B)**解釋說明一個名詞的意義**，帶出主題為身高，然後再闡述有那些因素影響身高，及世界各地的身高變化。

2. 根據最後一段第一句，世界各國隨著經濟環境的改善，身高也跟著增加，因此可推論出 (C)。

3. obsession 根據語意，應是指美國人「**熱愛，著迷**」於垃圾食品之意，才使得他們越來越胖。故選(A)。

4. 根據第三段提到的數據，台灣女性平均身高 (159 cm) 比美國女性平均身高 (164 cm) 少五公分，故(C)為正確選項。文章並未提到(A)(D)選項。(B)選項應改為 genes，才是決定身高最重要的因素。

5. 此格應為整段的主題句，說明影響身高的因素，由下文可得知，決定身高的兩個主要因素是(C)**基因和環境**。

average-sized adj. 一般尺寸的	auto racing n. 賽車	mature vt. 成熟
counterpart n. 相對應的事物	respectively adv. 各自地	obsession n. 著迷

06 名字又有何干？
WHAT'S IN A NAME?

翻譯

名字又有何干？玫瑰不叫玫瑰，亦無損其芬芳。——《羅密歐與茱麗葉》第二幕，第二景

按照莎士比亞這段話，我們的名字無法定義我們是怎樣的人。但確實可用以分辨我們是誰，並跟著我們一輩子。因此，父母在替小孩命名時都格外的小心。

通常替男生取些能傳達力量與傳統感覺的名字。二〇〇五年，全美人氣最高的前十個男生名當中，有九個來自聖經。而且，長子繼承父親全名的情況還滿普遍的，以此用來傳承家族力量及傳統。

二〇〇五年排名前十的女生名當中，只有五個是從聖經來的，因為女生名和男生名不同，通常選擇考量是美感與情感。女生名要流行起來，其中的一個方式是透過電影和藝術。二〇〇五年人氣排名第三的名字——麥迪遜，在一九八四年電影《美人魚》某個角色使用此名之前，其實是聞所未聞的。二〇〇五年人氣排名第五的「奧莉薇亞」，最早是出現在莎翁的喜劇《第十二夜》。

在黑人族群中，有些父母親替孩子命名時，會從他們的非洲傳統中汲取長處。名字可能是從非洲語言中，表示國王、皇后、強壯、美麗等諸如此類的字裡頭選出來。但有時候，黑人父母會將非洲字和音節合在一起，創造獨特的新字。

因此，名字或許不能定義我們是怎樣的人，卻常常是人們得知我們的第一件事，也是人們記得的最後一件事。這也難怪我們希望靠我們的名字帶來力量、美感與榮耀。

解析

1. 本題要選出適當的標題，考的是文章的主旨，第一段的最後一句 (parents take special care when naming their children) 即點出主題，而後三段分別就父母如何為男孩、女孩取名以及黑人如何為小孩取名做說明，故選(B)。
2. 此為文章細節題，第二段提及父母在為男孩取名時會特別注重家族的傳承 (a sense of strength and tradition)，因此長子常和父親同名，故選(C)。
3. 文章第一句先解釋引文的意思 (our names do not define who we are)，不過在 but 一字之後作者提出另一種看法 they (= our names) certainly identify us and follow us throughout our lives，所以作者認為名字有其重要性，並非只是一種符號故選(D)。
4. 由下句黑人會從他們原用的非洲語言中找出一些和國王、皇后、強壯和美麗等相關字替小孩命名，可推測 heritage 一字有「從以前傳承下來」的涵義，故選(D)。
5. 此句放在(C)的位置，Madison 為女子名，文章第三段在說明父母如何為女孩命名，放在此處也正好為前句「女孩子的名字有時會受到電影影響」舉出實例；(A)的位置應為引言，(B)的位置應舉出常見出自於聖經的男子名，而(D)的位置應舉出黑人用哪些能代表非洲文化的字來為孩子命名。

heritage n. 傳統　syllable n. 音節　quotation n. 引言　virtually adv. 事實上

翻譯

因為許多工作和學校課程都要求在期限內完成，人們在工作上難免有所延遲。甚至有個字是形容欠缺把事情做完的動力——「拖延」。而且，雖然有些人可能會嘲笑其他人拖延，但拖延可能造成很深的憂慮與絕望。

心理專家相信導致拖延的原因不是腦部受傷的問題就是心理方面有障礙。造成拖延的生理因素或許在於，某部分專司工作安排的人腦，可能受到損傷，或是無法發揮正常功能。精神上，也就是心理上造成拖延的問題可能包括：自尊低落、多多少少感覺到事情會不對勁，或是心情沮喪，讓人從而感到悲傷與無助，連帶使人很難把事情做完。

拖延者有兩種類型：擔心無法完成的，還有對於拖延還是無動於衷的。第一種類型的人，對於無法完成工作，可能有很多的負面情緒；過於輕鬆的拖延者，對於沒做完的事情通常不擔心。

雖然長時間的拖延可能一發不可收拾，所幸，有一些方法可以改正一個人的拖延行為。了解你拖延的原因，是停止此種行為的第一步。另一個有用的方法，是將你的工作排出先後順序，並密切注意時間管理。設定目標，並且保證達成這些目標，也是一個避免拖延，提高工作與課業生產力的方法。

不論一個人拖延的理由是什麼，他或她應試著向諮商師請教，了解造成他們拖延的原因可能是什麼，以及如何加以克服。

解析

1. 文章中提到 it (= procrastination) can cause profound distress and despair，從語意與生活經驗可推測 distress 和 despair 意思相近，故選(A) anxiety。

2. 此為文章細節題，第二段提到導致拖延的原因有身體 (brain problem) 和心裡 (low self-esteem, mental depression) 兩個層面，文中未提及(C)。

3. (A)第二段提到有一類的拖延者對於未完成的工作仍舊可以保持鎮定；(C)第四段提到停止拖延的第一步為瞭解拖延的原因；(D)諮商師可以幫助人們找出拖延的原因。而從第一段最後一句可得知(B)為正確。

4. 第二段提到拖延的原因，這是屬於(A) cause and effect；第三段提到拖延者的區分類型，屬於(D) classification and division；第四段提到解決的方法，屬於(B) problem and solution。而並沒有使用(C) **Compare and Contrast**。

5. 此句在說明有一些方法可以改變長期拖延的行為，放在(D)的位置，正好作第四段 (解決拖延方法) 的主題句。

procrastination n. 延遲	procrastinate vi. 拖延	distress n. 憂慮	despair n. 絕望
prioritize vt. 依重要排列	productivity n. 生產率	contempt n. 輕蔑	ecstasy n. 狂喜
serenity n. 寧靜	malfunction n. 故障	torment n. 折磨	chronic adj. 長期的

龍該退位了嗎？
Exit the Dragon?

翻譯

　　幾千年來，龍在中華文化中扮演了重要且對人有益的角色。在中國，龍具有正面的象徵，帶來和平和繁榮。然而，有些官員害怕國家的形象在西方會受損，因為龍在西方被視為邪惡的。這已造成中國內部討論，怎樣才能在增進國外的觀感的同時，又能保存國家的文化遺產。

　　關於「龍」的爭論於二〇〇六年展開，當時上海有位教授建議，中國應摒棄龍這個國家象徵，因為龍在西方帶有負面形象。其他人表示贊同，聲稱中國的年輕人不像老一輩這麼崇敬龍，這有一部分是受到西方的影響，例如《哈利波特》系列小說將龍描繪成怪物。而二〇〇八年北京奧運的吉祥物中，龍也遭到政府否決，這更加深了這方面的關注。

　　儘管有這方面的擔憂，龍對大多數中國人來說依然重要，視其為民族的祖先。另一位教授不但沒有背棄龍，反而建議人們開始用中文字裡的 loong 來稱呼，以區分西方噴火龍的詮釋。他的論點認為，此舉能彰顯中國的龍的正面形象，包括降下及時雨。也有人倡議採用新的國家象徵，像是熊貓或豬，但這些選擇不為多數中國人所接受。

　　龍在中國引發的爭論，顯示該國在全球與日俱增的影響力。中國繼續擴張的同時，更多外國人會留意它的所做所為，中國人處理龍的作法，將決定其他人往後許多年會如何看待這個國家。

解析

1. 本篇文章主要是探討，(D)東西方文化對龍的不同詮釋，引起一些中國內部的討論是否該繼續用龍來代表中國，但大致而言，龍還是具有崇高的地位。
2. 從第二段的描述可得知，不贊成使用龍當中國象徵物的人認為，(B)龍在西方世界中帶有負面印象，且年輕人並不尊崇龍。而(A)是描述龍的正面形象；(C)(D)本文並沒提到。
3. 從第三段的說明可得知，支持(A) "**loong**" 來翻譯「龍」的人認為這樣可以加強龍的正面印象，和西方對於龍的負面印象有所區隔。
4. 根據上下文，assert 這裡應該是(B)「宣稱，堅稱」之意。
5. 此句應該放在段落中有說明對龍做為中國象徵的疑慮，故最適合放在(B)。而(A)位置為用以說明龍的傳統形象與中國政府的顧慮的差異。(C)位置依上文可以進一步舉例龍的正面形象。(D)則是用來敘述龍在中國引發的爭論之考量因素。

prosperity n. 繁榮	perception n. 觀感	controversy n. 爭議	relinquish vt. 放棄
assert vt. 堅稱	distinguish vt. 區分	fire-breathing adj. 噴火的	advocate vt. 提倡
manipulate vt. 操控	interfere vi 介入	differentiate vi.; vt. 區別	

翻譯

　　電視劇《六人行》可說對社會帶來相當大的衝擊。在這部情境喜劇播放的十年間，觀眾得以一窺六位親密友人的日常生活，包括瑞秋、莫妮卡、菲比、羅斯、錢德勒、喬伊。每個角色都具有自身獨特的性格，深受觀眾喜愛。他們的生活方式就算不是很符合實際生活，但看起來自在又完美，許多人羨慕之餘，也想仿效他們。

　　該劇在許多方面受到大眾的模仿。舉例來說，其中一個角色的髮型大受歡迎，正式的說法就稱之為「瑞秋式髮型」。角色間經常使用 so 這個字眼，是用來表示「非常……」的強調用語，雖然這用法不是從該劇才開始的，卻也造成一般大眾更加頻繁地以這種方式使用該字。劇中人物的許多口頭禪也流行起來，像羅斯不忠的時候所用的藉口：「我們那時處於分手狀態！」莫妮卡加強語氣的「我知道！」還有喬伊的招牌問句：「嘿，你好嗎？」等等。**大多數人都能認同所有的角色以及他們眾多的獨特習性。**許多朋友之間也會試著分出同群朋友當中，分別是誰像六人行中的哪一位。聽到有人用劇中角色來形容其他人的情形，也變得相當普遍，「他簡直就跟羅斯一樣。」，有可能是用來形容一個既膽小又愛抱怨的男性。「你不要像莫妮卡那樣對我。」，可能是告誡對方，不要像這個偏執又強迫的角色一樣要求完美。

　　《六人行》是個有趣的娛樂節目，而它確實影響了流行文化，咖啡廳更受歡迎便是一例。然而，時光流逝，事物跟著改變，新的流行時尚會興起，也許有朝一日，我們在回顧《六人行》時，只留下一絲懷舊之情吧。

解析

1. 本篇文章主要是介紹，熱門電視影集「六人行」(B)**對社會及文化方面的影響**，包括語彙的使用、咖啡店的盛行。

2. 由第二段 "He's such a Ross," might be used to describe a guy who's timid and whiny." 可得知，Ross 應是代表(C)**膽怯愛抱怨的人物**。

3. 本題是選這部影集沒有影響下列那一個層面，由第二段 "...although this usage did not originate from the show." 此句可得知，正確為 (A) **"so" 的使用並非起源於這部影集**。而(B)選項可在第二段中第一個例子中找到。(C)在第三段第一句中；(D)則是在第二段最後三句。

4. 本文第一段的最後一句帶出第二段的主題，因此可由 "Many of the show's aspects were mimicked by the public." 推論出 emulate 應是 (B)**「模仿」**之意。

5. 本句最適合放在描述影集角色個性的段落，故選第二段的(C)**人們可以認同這些角色，及他們各自特殊的性格**。

---

endear vt. 使喜愛　　emulate vt. 模仿　　mimic vt. 摸擬　　intensifier n. 強調語句

catchphrase n. 流行語　　infidelity n. 不忠實　　whiny adj. (whine vi.) 哭哭啼啼的

obsessive-compulsive adj. 偏執又強迫的　　perfectionist n. 完美主義者　　nostalgia n. 懷舊

翻譯

　　李安第二次大學聯考失利之後，他父母親寄望他有朝一日成為教授的夢想破碎了。大多數人可能會認為，他未來成功的機會渺茫，但李安可不這麼認為。他決定轉而就讀國立台灣藝術學院，在那裡他培養了拍攝電影的興趣。畢業後，他前往美國繼續他的學業。

　　他在美國時遇到未來的妻子，兩人婚後他決定留在當地。他心愛的妻子工作來撫養家庭，而他繼續磨練他的技巧。他最早的三部亞洲主題的電影：《推手》、《喜宴》、《飲食男女》，接受度都很高，讓他受到好萊塢的注意。他繼續在各式電影題材中展現他導演方面的長才，像是時代劇《理性與感性》；黑暗劇《冰風暴》；以及西洋片《與魔鬼共騎》。他第一次真正嚐到成功的滋味，是在武俠經典大片《臥虎藏龍》時。該片創下美國影史上外語片最賣座的紀錄。他接下來的電影是充滿電腦動畫的《綠巨人浩克》，是個很大的挫敗，讓他考慮退出影壇。然而他決定繼續下去，冒險嘗試小型獨立製片。這部「小」電影，即是充滿爭議的《斷背山》。該片大受讚揚，並為李安贏得一座奧斯卡最佳導演獎，這是每位電影導演的夢想。

　　李安的成就必然已超越他父母的期望。他的故事也是個良好的典範，說明一個人不管決定走哪一條路，在受到任何失敗或沮喪後，若還保有意志力和決心，他依舊能夠成功。

解析

1. 本篇文章主要是說明導演李安在決定投入導演事業一路上的困難及努力，因此最適合的答案為(D)。

2. 在本篇文章中可表現出李安決心的事情，是(B)他在聯考失敗後不氣餒，而去攻讀藝術學校。有此決定才會有之後的發展。

3. 由第三段 "His next film, the CGI-filled *Hulk*, was a major disappointment" 可推論出(C)。(A)的錯誤在於推手是處理亞洲不是美國的主題。從對斷臂山的描述 "a little film"，可知它並不是大製作，故(B)不對。(D)選項臥虎藏龍並不是讓他贏得最佳導演的電影，所以不正確。

4. 從下文中 "in a wide range of movie genres" 可推論出 "versatility" 應是「多才多藝之意」，所以相反的字應為(B) "inflexibility"「沒有彈性變化」。

5. 本格應是描述《臥虎藏龍》的句子，從前一句可推論出這是李安第一部在西方世界成功的例子，因此票房口碑應該都很好，故選(A)。(C)選項的錯誤在於這並不是第一部讓好萊塢注意到李安的片子，而是《推手》、《喜宴》、《飲食男女》這三部片。

---

dash　vt.　破散　　hone one's craft　磨練技術　　versatility　n.　多變化　　genre　n.　類型

martial arts　n.　功夫武術　　CGI (computer generated image)　n.　電腦動畫　　acclaim　vt.　讚賞

middle-age crisis　n.　中年危機　　adaptability　n.　適應性

翻譯

　　外科醫師在病患身上劃下一刀。消毒過的外科手術工具進入體內。手術終於結束，完成縫合。病患的身體剛歷經巨大創傷，甦醒時將十分疼痛，未來也將度過漫長、痛苦的痊癒期。

　　不過很快這種侵入性的手術可能將走入歷史：機器人手術正為外科世界帶來革命性改變，將減少冷冰冰的手術工具侵入體內的負面影響。**這種稱為「達文西外科手術系統」的技術主要有兩項元素。**一是外科醫師所在地的遠端操作臺，另一是位於病患身邊、擁有四隻機械手臂的機器車。手術前會先在病患身上劃下三個微小切口，將體積更小的攝影機從切口進入體內。醫師用類似電玩搖桿的儀器操縱機器人，控制機器手臂在病患體內進行手術，醫師也能從遠端操作臺看到清晰的體內三度空間影像。透過手腕動作操控把手，醫師指揮機器人動作，機器人則精準完美地仿效醫師動作，執行比人類更精準的手術過程。

　　全球約有八百間醫療院所的醫師，今日都已在許多手術中採用達文西系統，包括癌症與心臟疾病手術。對於病患益處眾多，例如縮短術後恢復時間、減輕痛苦、降低感染風險等。最重要的是，病患生活能更快回歸正軌，將手術拋諸腦後。

　　今日，由機器人手術使得外科手術成為一門更安全、更精確的醫術。人們在幾年前有曾想過這一天會發生嗎？

解析

1. 文章第一段在描述傳統手術，從開刀、縫合到最後病患恢復的階段，正好與第二段介紹的新的手術作一個對照，故選(B)。

2. 本題考的是細節的部分，(A)從第二段可知，外科醫師只需要在病患身上開三個細長的切口；(B)從第三段可知達文西外科手術系統會降低感染的風險；(D)從第二段可知一台極小的相機會被置入於三個切口之一，而非用吞入的方式。所以正確為(C)。

3. 文章第三段在說明達文西外科手術系統的優點，冒號之後列出了種種的好處，故選(B) **innumerable**。

4. 整篇文章只提到達文西外科手術系統這種新的手術的開刀方式以及與傳統手術相比較之下新的手術的好處，故選(C)。

5. 文章第二段在說明醫師運用這種新的手術的流程，空格之後提到達文西外科手術系統要用到控制面板 (console) 和機械車 (robot cart) 這兩樣東西，故選(D)。整篇文章都沒有提到(A)達文西外科手術系統的缺點；文章雖然有大概提及傳統手術和達文西外科手術系統的不同，卻沒有條列式的敘述，故(B)選項不適合；(C)選項應出現於第三段說明達文西外科手術系統的優點。

incision n. 切割	implement n. 器具	trauma n. 創傷	invasive adj. 侵入性的
console n. 控制面板	joystick n. 搖桿	myriad adj. 無數的	recuperation n. 恢復
regulation n. 規定			

家庭主夫：友善溫和社會之始？
Stay-at-Home-Dads: A Kindlier, Gentler Society?

翻譯

一直以來，母子聯繫在多數社會都是神聖不可侵犯的價值。若母親長時間工作，常會遭批評重職場而輕家庭。反觀，父親儘管較為疏離卻是和藹的，也是要照顧家庭，被賦予擔負家庭生計的責任。

不過時代在改變。以英國技工尼爾‧沃金蕭為例。他的妻子於西元二千年生子之後，夫妻兩人協議尼爾應改為兼職工作，多多照顧親生兒子。當他要求雇主改為兼職合約被拒之後，尼爾便控告公司性別歧視。最後尼爾勝訴，獲得三千六百英鎊的賠償金。

這項判例告訴我們社會已大大轉變。**社會愈來愈期待父親在孩子的生活中扮演更多角色。**美國組織「全國父親計畫」公布的研究指出，父親對孩童的幸福確有其重要性。以下為部分數據：

‧ 在無父親家庭成長的孩子，生活貧困機率是平常的五倍。

‧ 相對於擁有父親陪伴的年輕人，沒有父親相伴的年輕男性入獄機率較高。

‧ 無父親的孩童輟學機率是平常的兩倍。

一份英國於二〇〇三年的民調指出，即將成為父親的男性之中有百分之三十三的人希望改為兼職工作，以增加陪伴兒女的時間。這項趨勢也蔓延至大西洋的另一岸。據估計，全美各地共有十五萬九千多名家庭主父，較十年前成長了三倍。這些微小變化是否代表社會將變得更溫和、更友善，同時鼓勵父親扮演好自己的角色，而不再有任何歧視？

解析

1. 文章第一段描述在傳統價值觀中，母親和父親分別所應該扮演的角色，故選(B)。

2. 本題考的是細節的部分，從第二段的敘述可推測尼爾‧沃金蕭願意花時間照顧小孩，因此應該是位負責任的父親，應該為(B)**會願意當保母**；(C)在那場官司中尼爾‧沃金蕭勝訴，還得到三千六百英磅；(D)是尼爾‧沃金蕭控告他的公司性別歧視，而非他被告性騷擾。

3. 本題考的也是細節的部分，(A)(B)的敘述出現在第三段，(C)的內容出現於最後一段第一句，(D)在最後一段有提及，但選項**敘述應該將二十年前改為十年前 (a decade)。**

4. pronounce 在此並非是一般較常見的意思：「發音」，從上下文猜測此字在此有「**宣告**」或「**顯示**」等含意，故選(D)。

5. 第三段一開始透過尼爾‧沃金蕭一案的判決，說明**社會對父親的價值觀已慢慢在改變**，父親不再只是要賺錢養家，在教養子女上也該付出更多的心力，故選(C)，亦可承接接下來的研究報告中所指出的父親對小孩的身心發展具有一定的重要性。整篇文章在強調父親角色的改變，故(A)的敘述不適合；而文章沒有提到(B)父親沒有育兒經驗；(D)選項較適合做「全國父親計畫」這個機構研究報告的結論。

sacrosanct adj. 神聖不可侵犯的	conversely adv. 相反地	relegate vt. 貶抑
albeit conj. 雖然	initiative n. 行動	Big Pond n. 大西洋
pronounce vt. 正式宣佈	prevail vt. 普遍存在	

翻譯

隨著年齡增長，我們開始為自己的記憶感到焦慮：我們是否比以往更健忘？人們是否開始在我們背後竊竊私語？記憶是種錯綜複雜的現象。記憶創造的過程又是如何？有什麼能幫助我們更清楚地回想？

我們已知，腦部稱為「海馬體」的一小部位主導記憶形成。當我們歷經新事物時，腦部會出現立即記憶。由感官刺激轉化而成的影像被傳送至位於耳後的海馬體，經過處理後暫存於短期記憶中。海馬體組織資訊後，移轉至腦前葉的大腦皮質供長期記憶。若無海馬體，所有新體驗都會變成初次驚奇，卻只會像風中羽毛般消逝。

事實上，一九五〇年代時，一名罹患癲癇的男子 HM 在腦部手術中切除海馬體。雖然術後癲癇症狀不再發作，但現在年逾八十的 HM，卻深陷記憶的困境之中：他仍認為杜魯門是現任的美國總統。而任何人只要離開三分鐘，他便忘得一乾二淨。

我們該如何改善記憶力？正確地攝取蔬菜也許有幫助：維他命 E 能分解一種稱為自由基的化學物質，該物質會損害腦部。因此食用富含維他命 E 的蔬菜，例如菠菜、杏仁、葵花籽等便能夠提升記憶力。除此之外，改善記憶力與以下事物也有關聯：儘量增加腦部活動、減輕壓力和睡眠充足等。也許老人家們常說的「飲食與睡眠正常」仍是改善記憶力的不二法則。

解析

1. 當我們變得健忘或有人在我們背後竊竊私語時，我們應該是會「焦慮不安」，故選(A)。

2. 本題考的是細節的部分，從第二段的敘述可知：暫存在「海馬體」的短期記憶會被傳送到**腦前葉「大腦皮質」**的部份成為長期記憶，以供日後去回想，故選(D)。

3. 本題考的也是細節的部分，主要針對第三段的內容：(A) HM 仍記得手術前所發生的事，但由於切除大腦中海馬體的部份，所以手術後發生的事馬上就忘記了；(B)手術後 HM 就不再受癲癇發作之苦；(D)文中未提及，只提到在 HM 動手術前，在位的總統是杜魯門。故正確選項為(C)。

4. 本題考的也是細節的部分，主要針對第四段的內容：文章中提到要多吃富含維他命 E 的食物，因為維他命 E 會破壞自由基，而這種物質會造成腦部傷害，故要避免**富含自由基物質的食物**，故選(B)。

5. 此空格需放入第二段的主題句，此段在說明**記憶形成的過程**，同時從此段的最後一句可知，在這過程中**海馬體扮演很重要的角色**，故選(C)。第二段沒有提到(A)「檢索」(retrieve) 資訊或記憶的步驟；而(B)句的後半部，「為何有人記憶過人」也是文章沒提及的；(D)選項較適合放在此段結尾，可用來強調大腦內部構造精密，一旦受損便會影響記憶的形成。

---

fret vi. 煩惱	stimuli n. 刺激	hippocampus n. 海馬體	frontal lobe n. 腦前葉
cerebral cortex n. 大腦皮質	retrieval n. 重獲	retention n. 記憶力
free radical n. 自由基	spinach n. 波菜	correlation n. 關聯性	adage n. 格言

冥王星「被冥王星了」
Pluto Gets Plutoed

翻譯

　　要如何將一顆行星的名字轉化為動詞？只要將行星降級為矮行星即可。這正是冥王星這顆前行星在二〇〇六年八月所遭受的命運。人們都覺得很奇怪，天文學家竟突然決定將冥王星降級，也讓「被冥王星」(plutoed) 這個字迅速被運用於流行文化之中。這個詞語意指無來由地遭到降級。該語詞是幽了「冥王星」這個字一默，不過事實上，改變冥王星地位一事仍有諸多爭議。

　　冥王星發現於一九三〇年，在它遭到降級之前，原本是太陽系第九大行星，也是距離太陽最遙遠的行星。但由於天文學家發現愈來愈多行星狀的天體大小與冥王星相仿，讓科學家懷疑是否該繼續將冥王星列為行星。畢竟以行星而言，冥王星體積太小，而且鄰近區域還有許多體積相似的星球。

　　一九九二年時，在一條繞行太陽、大小與月球近似的科伊伯帶，發現了更多與冥王星相去不遠的星球。由於這項發現，天文學家開始思索冥王星是否也隸屬於科伊伯帶之中，倘若如此，冥王星就不該被列為行星。然而二〇〇五年七月在海王星與冥王星之間，發現另一顆體積大於冥王星、同樣繞行太陽的矮行星，名為「厄里斯星」。**媒體原本稱之為第十行星，不過當時官方尚無共識決定它是否為行星。但這已使冥王星不再具備行星地位。科學家認為，若厄里斯星並非行星，冥王星當然也不是。**

　　冥王星事件證明沒有事物能恆常不變，就算在科學界亦然。隨著人類對周遭遠近環境的認識更深，其他分類標準也可能改變。

解析

1. 從第一段中的 "People thought it was so strange that astronomers suddenly decided to **demote** the planet" 此句中的 strange 可推論出一般民眾對 Pluto 地位突然的改變，是 (C)驚訝的。

2. 根據第一段上下文推論，"demote" 應該為 (B)「降級」之意。

3. 第二段和第三段主要是探討科學家對冥王星地位的爭論。從 "After all, it is miniscule for a planet" 可得知冥王星無法被一致同意定義為行星，理由主要是 (D)它大小的問題。(A)(B)並不影響它被定義為行星。(C)選項中 Kuiper Belt 應該是環繞著太陽而運行。

4. 全文中從最後一段第一句 "The story of Pluto shows that nothing can remain the same forever, even within the scientific community." 此句可推論出作者認為 (B)即使是科學發現，也可能會有更改的時候。

5. 由 "tenth planet" 可得知，本句應該出現的段落，應該介紹說明在九大行星之外另外新出現的行星 (Eris)，故選 (D)。而 (A)位置應該是進一步說明冥王星的事件。(B)位置出現的段落則是要討論定義行星的條件。(C)位置為敘述冥王星是否列為行星的爭議。

---

demote vt. 使降級	sphere n. 天體	speculate vt. 推測	minuscule adj. 極微小的
proximity n. 鄰近	Kuiper Belt 科伊伯帶	orbit vt. 繞行軌道	celestial adj. 天空的
Neptune n. 海王星	classification n. 分類	consensus n. 共識	

翻譯

　　動機是種能量，是推動我們做完許多事、完成艱鉅的任務與達成明確的目標。一般對這種動力的定義是「行為之持續」。換言之，動機代表反覆做某件事以達成個人抱負。

　　但什麼能激勵我們成功？許多科學家針對動機進行研究，也有許多不同答案，其中可歸類為社會認可、認知（思考）、情感（情緒）與欲求（目標）。

　　期望獲得社會接受是成功的關鍵因素。同儕間的認同包括成為團體的一部分，以及仿效你景仰的人的行為。對學生而言，這代表努力以躋身自己所重視的團體。

　　認知動機則包括更了解自己身處的世界與解決問題。擁有這種動機的人通常是科學家、醫生或研究人員。好學生通常也擁有此類動機。

　　情感動機似乎是最基本的動機類型，因為這包括閃避帶來不快的事物、擁抱讓生活更愉快的事物。擁有這類動機的人，都希望生活獲得整體的幸福與掌控權。

　　欲求動機包括目標、個人夢想與自我獨立。強烈地受此類動機所驅使的人，通常十分明瞭自己人生所求，例如工作、朋友、伴侶、家庭等，他們生活中行為都與達成這些目標有直接的關係。

　　或許以上這些資訊，可以讓你更明白哪種因素能激勵自己獲得更大成就。更深入了解這些動機，也能幫助你認知個人成功的途徑與阻礙。

解析

1. 此題考的是指涉詞 (reference)，從上下文中，可知 this 指的是前一句中的 this approval of one's peers，也是此段第一句中所提到的 social acceptance，故選 (C)。

2. 從 fulfilling these objectives 這詞組中，可先判定 objective 一字在這做「名詞」使用，故不可能選 (C) 或 (D)。再從上文的提示中可知 objective 指的應該是 **what they want in life**，故選 (A)。

3. 此題考的是推論，從題幹的敘述可知 Alan 的求知慾很強，且凡事喜歡打破沙鍋問到底，和第四段所提到的 "**Cognitive motivation involves wanting to learn more about the world around you and to solve problems.**" 不謀而合，故選 (B)。

4. 文中第一段 (A) 先定義什麼是「動機」，第二段接著指出可將動機 (C) 分類，第三到第六段則分別解釋並 (B) 舉例說明這四類的人會為哪些原因而努力，文中沒有提到 (D)。

5. (B) 句正好承接第一段對動機的定義；(A) 句乍看之下似乎合理，但若選此句則第二段開頭的疑問句應該刪除，若文章要放入 (A) 句，較佳的位置是放在第二段最後的部份；(C) 句是針對動機此主題所做的一般性敘述 (general description)，較適合放在第二段或最後一段；(D) 句較適合放在第三段作舉例說明。

---

formidable　adj.　難以克服的　　explicit　adj.　明確的　　persistence　n.　持續　　cognitive　adj.　認知的

conative　adj.　意志的　　　　　shun　vt.　閃避　　　　　spur　vt.　鼓舞

16 熱門電玩
Game On

翻譯

　　今日，電玩是極受歡迎的娛樂現象，跨越多種娛樂類別與平台。其主要吸引力在於遊樂器與現代個人電腦種類之繁多，幾乎每個人、每個時刻都能找到適合的遊戲。

　　電玩也影響現代生活的其它層面。電玩遊戲常被改編成電影，如《古墓奇兵》系列電影或卡通。玩家也改變人們溝通的習慣，例如網路駭客語言或表情符號今日都已十分普遍。

　　有些遊戲已發展到超越了單純的消遣，而成為嚴肅且競爭激烈的運動。《星海爭霸》與《CS》這兩套截然不同的遊戲，都已具備極高的地位。最多同時有三十萬人參與 CS 遊戲。對想出鋒頭的玩家來說，若能在世界電玩大賽等大型賽事勝出，便有訪問、名氣、贊助合約、產品代言等活動隨後而至，年薪甚至高達一百萬美元。

　　一般人對電腦遊戲玩家的刻板印象，總是些沒有朋友的平凡青少年，但現已徹底改觀。例如在南韓，「星海爭霸」遊戲專業玩家所受的禮遇有如搖滾巨星！頂級玩家有數千名支持者，各種競賽也備受重視，總能吸引大批人潮，也在網路上播出，甚至還有專屬電視台轉播。

　　但對多數人而言，玩遊戲是種社交活動。與其看電影，情侶們反而會到附近的網咖玩他們喜愛的遊戲。電腦遊戲之所以風行全世界，主要因為網際網路讓身處於不同地區、國家的人們，從新的且愈加困難的方式之中，彼此鬥智，考驗自己的腦力與反應速度。

解析

1. 本題考的是細節的部分，答案在第三段的最後一句，在電玩大賽中得名，隨之而來的是**名利雙收**，故選(C)。

2. 從第四段的第一句可知，以前電玩者給人的刻版印象是 an unattractive teenager with no friends 的負面印象，故選(C)。

3. 從此段的前兩句的例子可知，打電動已經取代了看電影成為時下**流行且受歡迎**的社交活動，故選(D)。

4. 本題考的是文章的主旨，前兩段主要說明電玩不僅成為受歡迎的娛樂之一，也**影響到我們生活**的其他層面 (像是電影和溝通方式)，第三、四段更提到電玩已被視為一項嚴肅的運動，同時電玩者更是備受禮遇，最後一段則說明電玩儼然成為一種社交活動，故選(A)。(C)只是最後一段的一個細節，文中並未提到(B)(D)。

5. 文章第三段在說明有些電玩已演變成為一項**嚴肅且競爭激烈的運動**，空格處正好可舉例說明，故選(B)，敘述中的 **this status** 正好和此觀點相呼應。(A)句較適合出現在解釋為什麼近來電玩大受歡迎的段落；(C)句應該出現在說明戰爭遊戲或線上遊戲的段落；(D)句應出現在說明電玩者是多麼重視比賽的段落。

span vt. 橫跨	console n. 主機	1337 speak(Leetspeak) 網路駭客語言
emoticon n. 表情符號	high-profile adj. 高知名度的	sponsorship deal n. 贊助合約
endorsement n. 代言 (背書)	be all the rage 非常受歡迎	infuriating adj. 使人憤怒的

一個有魅力的男性究竟該是健壯或是精瘦呢？我們或許認為這是歸結於個人好惡選擇，但科學研究顯示，某些特質之所以總是成為男性吸引人之處，是有其原因。**許多研究指出，女性喜好肩寬腰窄的男性，而認為這兩種特質是力量與健康的象徵**。較粗的脖子、較有線條的下巴及較濃密的眉毛也頗受女性青睞，因為女性受生物學影響，都希望尋找具有繁衍強壯健康後代特質的伴侶。

然而蘇格蘭與日本研究人員進行的另一項研究卻指出，許多女性也喜歡臉部具女性柔和特質的男性。研究者總結是，男性臉部若具備女性特徵，外界通常相信他較有愛心，能成為個好父親。

但似乎外貌並非一切，亞伯丁大學臉部研究實驗室的人員發現，重要的不只是男性的外表，其他女性對男性的觀感也一樣重要。他們宣稱女性若發現其他女生向某位男性微笑以對，會認為該名男性更具魅力；反觀若其他女性冷漠對待某位男性，女性也會對他興趣缺缺。

基於這種心理，有些美國男性會刻意與極具魅力的女性同行，甚至花錢聘請美麗女子與他打情罵俏。臉部研究實驗室的班·瓊斯博士指出：「這個例子再度證明人是社會性動物，無論是穿什麼衣服、購買何種汽車，這些決定都受到他人影響，並非想像中只是種個人選擇。」

1. 本題考的是文章細節，第一段提到女性喜歡強壯和健康的男子 (might and health)，第二段提到女性喜歡會照顧他人的男子 (caring personality)，第三段提到女性喜歡受女生歡迎的男子 (what other women think of him)，(C) 選項應改為 a man with a feminine face。

2. 文章中不斷**引用科學研究調查** (包含來自蘇格蘭、日本和亞伯丁大學實驗室的研究) 和專家學者 (如班·瓊斯) 的說法，來證明哪種類型的男子較具吸引力，故選(C)。

3. 最後一段中提及班·瓊斯認為看似個人的偏好 (personal preference) 有時其實是也是受到他人影響所做出的決定，因此(B)**所謂「個人的偏好」的概念是需要再檢視的**。

4. 文章中出現了許多 attractive 的同義字，除了 alluring、engaging、desirable 還有 charming、appealing。而 an **impassive** face 正好與此句子前半出現的 smiling 相對，故可推測(D)此字並未含有 attractive 之意。

5. 此句在描述的是女性喜歡體格強壯的男子，放在(A)的位置，正好接下一句：「較有男子氣概長相的男性也較具有吸引力」。(B)的位置應說明男性具有哪些較女性化臉龐的特質反而較有吸引力；(C)的位置應說明為何其他女性對某位男性的看法也是影響女性挑選男性的原因；(D)的位置應說明為何美國男子會找年輕的女子作陪的原因。

lithe adj. 輕盈的	sturdy adj. 健壯的	feminine adj. 女性的
engaging adj. 吸引人的	impassive adj. 面無表情的	flirt vt. 調情
robust adj. 強壯有活力的	hardy adj. 刻苦耐勞的	temperament n. 氣質

翻譯

　　黑莓機這種無線手持裝置能夠收發電子郵件，雖然價格昂貴，但對部分使用者而言，姆指承受的痛苦比荷包更大。在使用黑莓機的小鍵盤時，許多人認為自己用姆指輸入文字訊息的速度比其他指頭更快。由於用戶愈來愈習慣發訊息，反覆操作也讓他們感受到「黑莓姆指」症狀的不適。

　　專家指出，這種問題源於姆指的構造與其他手指不同；相對於其他指頭動作靈活，姆指以穩定為重，活動較不靈活。當人們反覆使用姆指鍵入訊息，肌腱與神經可能會造成所謂的重覆性傷害。

　　醫師建議，自制便是避免「黑莓姆指」最佳方式。他們認為訊息應盡量簡短，若可能也應使用其他手指輸入訊息。其他人則提供治療症狀的方式。數間公司推出宣稱可舒緩疼痛的夾板；凱悅連鎖飯店提供商務旅客要價 80 美元的按摩服務，宣稱可舒緩過度使用的關節。

　　使用其他小型電子設備的人們，也必須注意避免相同的症狀。**若過度使用電玩搖控器、電腦鍵盤與手機鍵盤，都會造成不適**。最重要的是，人們切記要防止太多重覆活動，並在疼痛發生時盡快休息。我們使用各種現代裝置的方式，將決定這些工具讓我們的生活更方便，或是更不便。

解析

1. 本篇文章主要是說明，喜歡用掌上型電子設備傳收發電子郵件或簡訊的人，手指可能產生的問題及醫生建議的使用方法，並不是探討電子產品的缺陷，故選(D)。

2. 根據第二段第一句及其下文說明，黑莓拇指會出現的原因主要和拇指的構造很有關係，如加上經常性的傳簡訊的動作，就會受傷，故選(A)。

3. 由此句 "Unlike our fingers, which are very **nimble**, our thumbs provide stability and do not move very well." 可推論出 "nimble" 和 "stability, do not move very well" 應是相反的字意，故選(C)。

4. 從第三段中醫師的建議可推論出(A)(B)(D)，文章中並無提到醫師建議要伸展關節，所以選(C)。

5. 此句最適合放在(D)，承接說明還有那一些電子儀器會造成同樣的問題。(A)應解釋為何使用電子儀器會造成疼痛。(B)應說明拇指疼痛的原因。(C)應說明如何避免黑莓拇指。

handheld adj. 手持的	discomfort n. 不舒適	nimble adj. 靈敏的	tendon n. 腱
repetitive strain injuries n. 重複性傷害	self-restraint n. 自我節制	ailment n. 小病	
splint n. 夾板	soothe vt. 紓解	obstinate adj. 固執的	deft adj. 靈巧的

翻譯

　　眼睛是人體最複雜的器官之一。除此之外，角膜在眼睛功能上扮演了重要的角色。許多人的視力是正常，不過也有很多人因為角膜病變而使先天或後天出現視力問題。

　　一種普遍的視力缺陷稱為近視。這源於角膜無法正常調整屈光度，而造成只看得清楚近處事物。與近視相反的稱為遠視。因為角膜無法正常屈光，所以只看得清楚遠處事物。此外視力散光者常眼前一片模糊，因為呈橢圓形的角膜造成視線同時聚焦於兩處。另一項幾乎人人會經歷的近視現象稱為老花眼。隨著年齡增長，角膜逐漸失去彈性，便會出現老花眼。

　　所幸眼鏡能夠改善上述一切問題。近視者可戴上中間薄、外圍厚的凹透鏡。中間厚、外圍薄的凸透鏡則用以改善遠視。對散光者而言，配戴湯匙狀的鏡片是設計來矯正形狀不正常的角膜。有老花眼症狀的人可戴上雙光眼鏡，將兩種鏡片合而為一。雙光眼鏡上半部為平光鏡片，配戴者可利用下半部鏡片閱讀距離較近的事物。以上這些鏡片也都已製為隱形眼鏡，可直接配戴於眼鏡上。

　　數百年前，視力缺陷無法治療，人們只能盡力調適。但今日拜矯正鏡片與隱形眼鏡之賜，多數視力問題所造成的障礙已不若以往。

解析

1. 文章中提到遠視這種眼疾和近視正好相反，後者是角膜無法變平 (flatten)，因此可知 bulge (凸起；上下文語意為屈光) 的相反詞正是 (B) **flatten**。

2. 本題考的是細節的部分，第二段提及若有散光這種問題，眼睛會無法對焦，第三段提到這類病患需**戴湯匙形狀的眼鏡**來矯正眼角膜的形狀，故選 (C)。

3. 本篇文章在說明常見的視力問題，第二段先解釋造成各種視力問題的原因，第三段則說明要如何解決這些問題，都是**事實性的陳述**，故選 (B)。

4. 本題考的是文章的主旨，從第一段介紹眼睛的視力缺陷，第二段說明各類視力的問題，以及第三段的提供矯正的方法，故選 (D)。(B)選項只涵蓋了第二段的重點，而 (C) 選項則是只提及第三段的重點，文中並未提到視力保健的重要，故不選 (A)。

5. 此句在說明**上述這些不同情況的眼鏡也有做成隱形眼鏡**，文章只有第三段提到眼鏡，故只能放在 (C) 的位置。

myopia n. 近視	cornea n. 角膜	hypermetropia n. 遠視	astigmatism n. 散光
oblong-shaped adj. 橢圓形的		presbyopia n. 老花眼	elasticity n. 彈性
concave adj. 凹面的		convex adj. 凸面的	bifocals n. 雙光眼鏡

誰是真朋友？
Who Are Your Real Friends?

翻譯

　　從前交朋友多是打電話、開派對或一同運動。但今日青少年的社會生活已大幅改觀。二十年前的青少女會花好幾個小時打電話與朋友聊八卦，但現在她正值青春期的女兒則可能直接上網。

　　現在人們只要按下一個按鈕，就能交到新朋友。因此，透過網路，今日的青少女不像她們母親過去只有五個好朋友，可能有高達七十五名「朋友」可以聊天、打情罵俏與吐露心聲。網路社群團體現已在英國廣受歡迎，以致於十三歲至十七歲的青少年有六成每日使用網路。

　　然而，研究人員指出，這種網路活動限制人們的溝通技巧，且存在其他危險。例如，電玩成癮的現象讓年幼的兒童，每週甚至耗費六十個小時在電玩上。有些孩子也會在聊天室中將個人資訊洩露給陌生人，不了解其中的危險性。當青少年因耗費許多時間上網，以致於無心顧及課業，這時就該將電腦移至家人可看到的區域。

　　不過，時常使用網路也有正面意義，它鼓勵年輕人透過新的管道敞開胸懷。在鍵入訊息前先思考，也有助於提升表達能力。而且在數百萬網路潛在讀者面前寫作或作曲，也能展現年輕人的創意。

　　最後，我們還得繼續觀察，究竟年輕人與網路將如何改變我們所知的世界，以及如何改變彼此溝通的方式。

解析

1. 第一段提到二十年前的小女生和二十年後她的女兒的社交生活是截然不同的，用以比較前者是講電話而後者上網的這二種差異，故選(D)。

2. 此題從下文及經驗可推測，青少年花太多時間上網，會因為太累而無法專心上課，故選(C)。

3. 本題考的是細節的部分，文章的第三段提到上網的壞處及負面影響，包括(A)電玩成癮、(B)太累無法專心上課和(D)洩漏個人資料，但並未提及(C)對新想法或人際關係變得開放。

4. 文章中分別有提到網路的好處 (第四段) 與壞處 (第三段)，但在結尾處作者採取較不明確 (中立) 的態度，認為還需要更多的時間才能知道網路所造成的影響，故選(D)。

5. 此句利用數據在說明網路社群受歡迎的程度，放在(B)的位置正好承接上文：透過網路可以輕鬆交友。(A)的位置在說明以前和現在交友方式的改變，(C)在說明網路潛藏的危機，(D)說明網路讓年輕人展現創意，均不適合。

confide vi. (向某人) 傾訴	addiction n. 沉迷	compelled adj. 強迫的
fatigued adj. 疲倦的	indulge vt./vi 沉溺	pervasive adj. 普遍的

翻譯

有很長一段時間，警方認為目擊證人非常有助於找出真正犯罪者，以及對他們提出控告。然而心理學家發現，目擊證人的證詞可能有誤，而外在影響力也可能導致虛假記憶產生。

薩塞克斯大學心理學家丹尼爾・萊特發現，目擊證人有時會自己創造出新而虛假的記憶。為了證明此論點，他進行一項實驗，讓四十名學生看幾張顯示一項犯罪正在發生的照片。所有學生都以為他們看的照片一樣，但實際上並非如此。

照片呈現兩名男子在撞球間內。在某個時間點上，一名女子偷了其中一名男子的皮夾。不過，提供給半數學生看的照片顯示該名女子和一名**共犯**一起行動，而給另外一半學生的照片則顯示她單獨作案。看完照片後，每名學生都接受詢問，四十名學生中有三十九名都正確回答出「這名女性是否有共犯」。

隨後學生被分成兩人一組，討論事情發生經過。每組都是由看了不同照片的兩名學生組成。當被問及是否這名女子有共犯時，每組照理說都不應有統一答案。然而，有十五組得出統一答案。換句話說，同組的一名學生說服另一名學生改變他或她的說法。

科學家表示，會出現這種情況，是因為想像力會捏造出一些細節，以串起不連貫的視覺訊息。除此之外，他人建議也是影響正確性的另一項有力因素。人們不只可能輕易被他人所動搖，而且在受到具有引導性的問題「協助」之下，有時也會扭曲記憶。**正因如此，偽造的記憶可能不受察覺地被植入腦中。**所以下次，當目擊證人發誓他們看到整件事發生的經過時，他們所言真是事實真相嗎？

解析

1. 文章的第二段第一句明確地指出該實驗的目的 Daniel Wright discovered that eyewitnesses sometimes create new, false memories on their own，因此他做了以下的實驗來證明，故選(D)。

2. 轉折詞 while(然而) 透露出語意的前後對比，後半句說到該名女子是獨自犯案，而前半句卻指出該名女子是和共犯 (accomplice) 共同**犯案**，故選(B)。

3. 本題考的是細節的部分，答案在第四段，有 15 對的人有共同答案，也就是有 15 個人被同組的另一人說服而更改答案，故選(B)。

4. 本題考的是推論的能力，(A)選項前半部似乎合理，但文中並未提及環境的影響；文中只提到目擊者證詞的正確性有時是有待商榷的，但並未提到(B)警方應自己辦案；從丹尼爾・萊特的實驗和最後一段可推論出(C)，從文章中作者暗示目擊者的證詞有時**不可信賴**，是因為記憶力的問題而非目擊者不誠實，故無法推論出(D)的敘述。

5. 此句放在(D)的位置，此敘述**在說明錯誤的記憶是如何被植入的 (how memories may be planted)**，因此之前的句子應提出可能造成這樣結果的方法，最後一段正好提到想像力和他人建議會影響記憶；(A)(B)(C)的位置都在說明丹尼爾・萊特的實驗目的與方式故不適合。

culprit n. 罪犯　　testimony n. 證詞　　pool hall n. 撞球間　　accomplice n. 共犯

22 *危險的執迷*
Dangerous Obsession

翻譯

在看到女星茱蒂‧福斯特在電影《計程車司機》中的演出後，小約翰‧辛克利就認為他是她的真命天子。起初，他考慮刺殺卡特總統來獲得她的注意。當福斯特在一九八〇年開始到耶魯大學上課時，辛克利跟蹤她到那裡，最後決定只有進行一項壯舉才能獲得她的注意。一九八一年三月三十日，他寫了一封信給她，表示「現在我必須做一件事，讓妳明白瞭解到，我都是為了妳才這麼做！」那天下午，辛克利向雷根總統和其他三人開槍射擊。

像辛克利這類跟蹤狂，代表著愛慕名人這種行為的黑暗面。雖然大多數影迷都無意傷害自己的偶像，還是有人可能抱持不健康的執迷心態。不像女影迷會崇拜或效法喜愛的男性偶像，像辛克利這類男跟蹤狂，常會感到一種無法抗拒的衝動，要保護他們愛慕的女性。**他們通常會有很強的幻想行為，想像自己跟成為他們深愛的偶像有深刻關係。**辛克利相信，他必須做出某種激烈舉動，才能讓自己和福斯特的幻想關係成為真。為了讓福斯特喜歡他，他試著寫詩給她，以展示他們有共通興趣。在這個舉動未發生效果時，他決定去行刺總統。

辛克利飽受心理疾病之苦，使他對福斯特的迷戀轉而變得有害。一九八二年，陪審團以精神失常的理由判決辛克利無罪，並將他監禁在一所精神病院中，雖然許多美國人並不認同這項判決。因為他的疾病，使得正常情況下無害的名人崇拜行為變得危險。辛克利的案例成了個實例，這告訴我們若崇拜名人過了頭，可能會有怎樣的後果。

解析

1. 文章第一段以一個發生在茱蒂‧福斯特身上的**真實故事**開頭，故選(A)。
2. 小約翰‧辛克利企圖要以一驚人之舉引起茱蒂‧福斯特的注意，從第一段的最後一句可知辛克利打算(D)暗殺雷根總統。
3. 從上文中可知辛克利對福斯特的迷戀最後造成**不好**的結果，選項中(C)含有負面的意思。
4. 本題考的是推論的能力，選(B)是因為第二段提到有時粉絲會崇拜、仿效偶像，甚至想要保護他們的偶像，故可推論**偶像會影響粉絲的行為**；第三段提到大多數的美國人不同意辛克利無罪的判決，因此推論他們並不同情辛克利，所以(A)不對；文中只有提到辛克利因為福斯特在耶魯大學讀書而尾隨她到那，但並未提及辛克利畢業於耶魯大學，故無法選(C)；至於(D)，文中提到的是跟蹤者是想要保護他們崇拜的女性而非傷害她們。
5. 此句出現複數代名詞 they，而第一段在講述發生在茱蒂‧福斯特和小約翰‧辛克利之間的事，故(A)和(B)這兩個位置都不適合；放在(C)的位置，不僅讓代名詞 they 有所指涉 (male stalkers)，同時透過接下來的例子 (his imaginary relationship with Jodie Foster) 也正好說明何謂 imagining that they have a meaningful connection with their beloved idols；若放在(D)的位置，they 就成了 most Americans 的代名詞，而且語意也不對。

feat n. 事蹟	stalker n. 跟蹤犯	celebrity attachment n. 名人依戀
irresistible adj. 無法抗拒的	assassinate vt. 刺殺	infatuation n. 迷戀
detrimental adj. 有害的	verdict n. 判決　deliberate adj. 謹慎小心的	dubious adj. 存疑的

翻譯

「任何事都有可能。你會聽到自己有九成勝算，或五成勝算，或百分之一的勝算，但你都得相信，而且必須努力奮鬥。」

這些話出自於自行車手藍斯・阿姆斯壯，準確反映出阿姆斯壯保有信心的能力：這位出生於德州的美國人，運動生涯中曾經歷一連串足以令人灰心喪志的挫折。正是透過堅毅、決心和信念，他才能成為環法自由車賽的傳奇人物，以及世界上最家喻戶曉的運動員之一。

一九九六年，阿姆斯壯已經是一名優秀的自行車賽車手——業餘時代他就贏得過美國和世界盃自行車賽冠軍。不久後，他以摩托羅拉車隊職業自行車手的身份，摘下杜邦大賽冠軍。當他在一九九六年被診斷出罹患睪丸癌時，這名運動員決心要對抗癌症，即使醫生對他從癌症中復原的機率並不樂觀。在不到一年後，阿姆斯壯就被診斷已經從癌症中康復。他贏得幾項重要賽事。此外也成立藍斯・阿姆斯壯基金會，鼓勵癌症研究並幫助癌症患者。

然後他奪下了環法自行車賽冠軍。這項賽事是自行車界最受矚目的重頭戲。比賽要花 22 天完成，賽道大多是崎嶇山路，全長超過三千公里——等於一千八百六十四英哩。藍斯和他的車隊隊友贏得一九九九年那場比賽。但還有更多難關等著他：在西元二千年間，阿姆斯壯在法國訓練時被一輛車撞到。**他花了好幾個月才從背部骨折的傷勢中復原。**令人難以置信的是，從一九九九到二〇〇五年，這位運動員連續七年，每年都贏得環法自由車賽。從來沒有其他運動員完成過如此壯舉。

在自傳《重返豔陽下》中，阿姆斯壯表示自己之所以能夠不屈不撓，要感謝母親。她總是告訴他，要將每道阻礙轉化成一次機會。而他只是這麼做而已。

解析

1. 引言之後的第一段第一句就提到 That statement, ...accurately reflects Armstrong's ability to believe.，由此可知這個引言就是阿**姆斯壯的座右銘**，故選(C)。

2. 從 grit 之後出現的字，包括 determination 和 faith，可推測出這一串字都傳達出正面、積極的意思，同時因為這些要素，阿姆斯壯才能創造環法自由車賽的傳奇且成為家喻戶曉的運動家，故選(D)**perseverance**。

3. 本題考的是細節的部分，最後一段提及阿姆斯壯**將自己的堅毅歸功於母親**，故選(C)；第一段有提到阿姆斯壯是德洲出生的美國人，所以(A)不正確；第二段提到阿姆斯壯被診斷出有睪丸癌，而非(B)選項中的肺癌；第二段還提到阿姆斯壯參加杜邦大賽時已經是職業選手了，故(D)也不對。

4. 本題考的是推論的能力，第三段提到環法自由車賽的比賽路程是 an often-mountainous trail，故可推測出參賽者必須(B)**橫跨重山**；文章並未提及(A)(C)(D)。

5. 此句放在(C)的位置，前一句正好提及阿姆斯壯發生了車禍，因此接著說他**花了幾個月的時間背部骨折漸漸復原**後，才能參加環法自由車賽；(A)的位置在敘述阿姆斯壯的信念使他克服困難成為傳奇人物，不適合放置細節的部分在此；(B)的前面提到醫生認為阿姆斯壯戰勝癌症的機會不大，但此敘述提到的是骨折的恢復，並無相關；(D)的位置在強調阿姆斯壯堅毅不拔的精神，不適合置入此句。

daunting adj. 嚇人的	array n. 一系列	setback n. 挫折	grit n. 勇氣與毅力
contender n. 競爭者	amateur n. 業餘愛好者	tenacity n. 不屈不撓	

24 在夏天打噴嚏和被梅子噎住
Sneezing in Summer and Gagging on Plums

每年夏天，蒙妮卡都飽受花粉症之苦，因為她對空氣中的花粉過敏。隨著花朵盛開，她的鼻子會阻塞，使她不斷打噴嚏。這段期間，她不能吃一向愛吃的香瓜和梅子。如果她要吃，嘴巴就會發癢並使她噎住。蒙妮卡發現，自己正經歷到過敏的「交叉反應」——花朵中的花粉跟某些水果具有相同化學成分。**因此，若一個人對花粉有過敏反應，他的身體也會排斥這些水果。**

許多人認為自己對龍蝦或花生過敏，或者對牛奶有不適反應。但很多對某種食物過敏的人，通常會對屬於同類的相關食物全都過敏。植物含有複雜的化學成分組合，而這些成分也存在於許多植物中。因此對南瓜敏感的人，可能對南瓜屬植物、黃瓜和西瓜也都有排斥反應。對胡蘿蔔過敏的人，最好也避開其他胡蘿蔔類成員，包括荷蘭芹、芹菜和蒔蘿。

最近一項研究顯示，百分之十九的台灣人有某種食物過敏症。主要引起過敏的食物包括雞肉、貝類、牛奶、芒果、花生和蛋。過敏反應相當多樣，從喉嚨和皮膚的輕微發癢，到激烈過敏發作都有可能——呼吸困難和血壓驟降，可能引發生命危險。

然而，英國營養基金會指出，這些抱怨自己有食物過敏的人中，只有一小部分實際上情況嚴重。基金會作出結論，認為全球患有嚴重食物過敏的成人低於百分之一，而有食物不適反應的成人則低於百分之二。也許，聲稱自己有食物過敏在如今很「入時」。但如果你覺得自己對南瓜過敏，那麼，勸你最好也別吃黃瓜。

1. 在第一段的地方作者先提到夏天時蒙妮卡會對花粉過敏，這個時候她不能吃像香瓜和梅子這些平時她喜歡的食物，否則就會出現過敏的症狀，這種狀況就是**所謂的「過敏的交叉反應」**，故選(C)。

2. 此段先說明對某一種食物過敏的人，也會對這食物相關的家族過敏，接著舉出兩個例子做進一步的闡述，所以可以推知，對胡蘿蔔過敏的人，也應**避免**胡蘿蔔這個家族的相關食物，選(C)。

3. 本題考的是細節的部分，第三段提到過敏常出現的症狀輕者是喉嚨、皮膚搔癢，嚴重的會呼吸困難、血壓突然驟降 (anaphylactic attack)。同時也應注意第一段作者也透過花粉熱的例子提到，過敏的症狀還有鼻塞、打噴嚏等。但文中沒有提到(A)。

4. 本題考的也是細節的部分，文中提到**百分之十九的台灣人會出現食物過敏的狀況**，相當於**五分之一**，故選(A)；(B)錯在只有一小部分對食物過敏的人會出現嚴重的症狀；(C)選項中的敘述 quite a few 意思是「相當多」，故不對；除了水果和植物之外，第三段也提到雞肉、貝類、牛奶、雞蛋也會引起過敏，故(D)也不對。

5. 文章第一段利用故事說明何謂「過敏的交叉反應」，因此最後一句也應該緊扣這個主題，所以選(B)；(A)選項中提到要避免過敏症狀，就不要碰觸花和植物，這樣的敘述太過籠統，也未針對「過敏的交叉反應」做說明。文中並未提到增強免疫系統的方法，也沒有提到治療過敏的方法，故(C)(D)選項不適合。

gag vt. 塞住	pollen n. 花粉	hay fever n. 花粉症	cantaloupe n. 香瓜
itch vi. 發癢	property n. 成分	component n. 成分	squash n. 南瓜屬植物
eschew vt. 避免	parsley n. 荷蘭芹	celery n. 芹菜	dill n. 蒔蘿

25 甜而苦，有關糖的事實
The Bittersweet Truth about Sugar

翻譯

　　我們都越來越胖，而且美國人正一路領先。以下是幾項讓人警覺的統計數字：美國人之中，有驚人的百分之六十四體重過重，兒童則有三分之一是過重的。**確實，疾病控制中心表示，如今肥胖是美國人的頭號殺手。**我們都可以舉出這種流行疾病的原因：吃太多速食、太常久坐不動的生活習慣、攝取太多碳水化合物等等。

　　但有一項鮮為人知的物質，名為高果糖玉米糖漿 (HFCS)，在美國人腰圍不斷增大的情況中扮演了主要角色。二十五年前，食物和飲料都是以簡單的蔗糖或甜菜糖來添加甜味。如今，美國人所攝取的糖份中，幾乎有半數都是高果糖玉米糖漿。以一罐有糖汽水為例，裡面所含糖份等於十三茶匙砂糖！健康專家建議，每人一天不應攝取超過十到十二茶匙量的糖份。儘管如此，美國人還是大口吞下了三倍之多，其中大部分都來自飲料！

　　以下這項消息更糟：「果糖可能導致暴食。」當你吃下由葡萄糖構成的碳水化合物時，胰腺會產生胰島素，脂肪細胞會產生一種叫做瘦體素的荷爾蒙。若已吃了足夠食物，這兩種物質會通知腦部。當你攝取果糖時，身體不會產生這兩種物質，因此你會繼續把東西塞進肚子裡。吃越多果糖，就會有越多脂肪湧入血液中。因此，攝取加了高果糖玉米糖漿的食物，等於吃下一份高脂肪餐點。

　　在你喝下一罐看起來無害的汽水之前，看一看成分表吧。如果你看到上面有「果糖」這個字，也許會想再考慮一下。

解析

1. 本題考的是文章主旨，第一段點出主題「肥胖的問題愈來愈嚴重」，第二段提出攝取過量的 HFCS 是造成肥胖的主因之一，第三段進一步提出果糖會導致飲食過量 (overeating)，最後一段則提醒讀者要小心不要攝取過量的糖分，故選(B)。(A)(D)的敘述太過於籠統，因為文章只有針對攝取過量的糖分作探討；(C) HFCS 是危險的，不是重要的。

2. 本題考的是文章細節，第二段最後提及美國人每日攝取的糖分是健康標準 (十到十二茶匙) 的三倍，相當於三十到三十六茶匙，故選(D) 35。

3. 本題考的也是細節的部分，答案在第三段。由於在攝取果糖時，身體不會產生胰島素和瘦體素來提醒身體已有飽足感，因此會導致飲食過量，故選(A)。

4. 從上一句中，可推測 gulp down(吞嚥) 一詞有 consume(吃/喝食物) 之意，故選(C) **swallow**。

5. 文章第一段在說明肥胖的問題愈來愈嚴重，此問題在美國更是日益惡化，空格前提到一些統計數據，說明此問題在美國的嚴重性，故選(C)提出更多的數據說明肥胖的恐怖：**肥胖問題是美國的頭號殺手**。選項(A)中 instead，宜改為 thus/therefore 較為合理。文章中雖然有提到 junk food 的問題，但在此應更清楚地點出垃圾食物和美國人肥胖之間的關聯，或者是直接提出事實證據，故(B)選項不適合。(D)選項中 discrimination 這個用字不恰當，宜改為 problem。

staggering adj. 驚人的	epidemic n. 傳染病	sedentary adj. 坐著的	carbohydrate n. 碳水化合物
fructose n. 果糖	waistline n. 腰圍	beet n. 甜菜	glucose n. 葡萄糖
pancreas n. 胰線	insulin n. 胰島素	leptin n. 瘦體素	innocuous adj. 無害的

翻譯

　　陳腔爛調通常都評價不佳。因為它們是一些被過度濫用的表達方式，已經顯示不出使用者的個性，或者應當說，顯示該人缺乏個性。不過，讓我們面對這項事實：在生命中許多情境下，很難保持原創性或誠實。「恭喜！祝你們百年好合！」這是婚禮中顯然該致上的賀詞，就算你十分懷疑這對夫妻是否適合彼此。在葬禮中，「請節哀順變。至少他現在安息了。」總比「所以呢，你會繼承多少遺產？」好得多。由此可見，雖然陳腔爛調可能不夠真誠而且膚淺，但它們很保險而且不具挑釁意味。

　　雖然陳腔爛調聽起來很普遍，實際上有相當多反映出特定社會價值。美國商業界──本質上相當資本主義和高度競爭──就充滿運動用語。你可能在一場面試中被投了「一記變化球」。你必須在生意上「擊出全壘打」。近來對於「在看台外思考」(意為跳出框架思考)──意指突破傳統──的要求被如此濫用，到頭來，在看台內思考反而才是不同流俗。

　　藝術、音樂和電影界也有所貢獻。「愛」真的「意味著永遠不必說抱歉」？「紳士」真的「愛金髮美女」？你的甜心是「你生命中的陽光」嗎？小說與電影中的老套主題和角色類型──浪跡天涯的牛仔，貧窮卻英俊、擄獲富家女芳心的男主角，苦悶的黑手黨老大──在我們真實但無法預測的世界中，提供了安慰和熟悉感。

　　所以，陳腔爛調的用處多多：在我們想不出話好講時提供協助，帶來娛樂和消遣，也維繫大家成為一個群體。而且它們也以許多方式，傳達我們心中的渴望。每個人不都或多或少希望能「從此過著幸福快樂的生活」？

解析

1. 文章提到 Clichés are safe and unprovocative，因此可知若某事是 unprovocative 則有 safe 的涵義；去掉否定字首 un- 後，provocative 一字應含有「不安全」之意，選項中只有(D)選項 **offended** 含有負面的意思。

2. 本題考的是細節的部分，文章第二段開始便提到習語會反映社會的價值觀，接著便以美國習語中充斥著運動術語作為例子，說明(B)**美國商業界中充滿競爭的本質**。

3. 文章雖然一開始提到使用習語讓人缺乏個性，同時習語傳達出使用者不真誠且膚淺的一面，但作者並不認為會造成(B)(C)這種現象，而且最後一段再次重申習語的功用，因此推論出作者雖然認為習語**不真誠但卻是不可或缺的**，故選(A)。

4. 本題考的是文章的主旨，文中並未提及(A)習語的起源，也沒有勸人(C)不要使用習語，而(D)選項只有點到文章第二段的重點，從第三題的詳解中可知，應選(B)。

5. 此句放在(D)的位置，一方面承接第一句 So clichés have many uses，另一方面最後一句的 live happily ever after 也為此句「**傳達人們心中的渴望**」作了一註解。(A)的位置在舉例說明習語，(B)在說明習語反應的社會價值觀，(C)在說明習語的來源，均不適合。

compatibility n. 適合	condolence n. 弔慰	inherit vt. 繼承
unprovocative adj. 沒有爭議的	characterization n. 角色人物刻畫	mafia n. 黑手黨
aggressive adj. 積極的	elaborate vi./vt. 詳細解釋	

27 橄欖油：「新一代」加州葡萄酒
Olive Oil: The "New" California Wine

翻譯

「你聞出什麼？」她問。

我傾身向前，聞聞她手裡的瓶子。

「花香味。」我說。她的臉皺了起來。顯然，我還有很多要學。

你覺得這兩人在討論什麼——酒？再猜一次吧——是橄欖油。確實，好的橄欖油能像好酒一樣在舌頭上留下複雜細緻的感受。可能嚐起來有草地清香或辛辣感；可能讓你想起蘋果、堅果或巧克力。越來越多具有頂尖品味的美國人嚷著要最好的橄欖油，而他們也會得到。**過去十年來，美食橄欖油事業在好萊塢之州持續蓬勃發展。**

在橄欖油生產上，由向來以葡萄酒業聞名的加州領先群雄，並非純屬巧合。加州擁有地中海型氣候，適合生產葡萄和橄欖。如今，橄欖在出產葡萄酒地區如那帕、索諾瑪和曼多西諾郡等地欣欣向榮。

加州橄欖油業者就像他們遠在歐洲的同業一樣，逐漸學到這門生意的訣竅：他們知道頂級橄欖油出自於人工採收的橄欖，並且必須立即壓製成油。除此之外，頂級橄欖油應透過「冷壓」法製成，因為熱度會對味道造成負面影響。

隨著更多美國人意識到健康飲食的重要，他們發現地中海式烹調法——以新鮮蔬菜、魚和肉為特色——**正可以滿足需求。**這種菜餚需要最高級的橄欖油，而美國人越來越精通選擇正確橄欖油的複雜門道。使用高級橄欖油的實用大原則之一是：灑一點在已經準備好的食物上，而較廉價的橄欖油則用來烹調食物。想來盤烤茄子？生菜沙拉？熟度剛好的牛排？先確定你找到最合適的橄欖油，享受探索「液態黃金」這個刺激新世界的樂趣吧。祝你胃口大開！

解析

1. 此為文章主旨題，一開始提到美國人越來越喜歡食用橄欖油，接下來提供橄欖油相關的知識，如生長環境、製造過程與烹調方式，故選(C)為橄欖油瘋狂。選項(A)是第三段的主旨，(D)是第四段的細節，文章並未提到(B)。

2. 本題考的是文章細節，雖然文章第一段提到美國人在飲食上越來越講究，但最後一段也提到(C)美國人**越來越重視健康**的飲食。

3. 此句的連接詞 As 有「隨著…」的意思，下一句也提到美國人越來越會選擇上等橄欖油，語意上是承接著因果關係而鋪陳下來的，因此可推測地中海飲食正是美國人(B)所想要的菜餚。雖然地中海食物是 exotic 和 tasty 的，但本文強調的是健康觀念，故不宜選(C)。

4. 本題考的是文章細節，(D)選項是錯的，因第三段提及頂級的橄欖油在採收後應立即榨汁，且要以冷壓法製作。選項(A)在第三段有提到製作上等的橄欖油必須用人工採收的橄欖；(B)在第二段有提到適合種植葡萄的地方也適合種植橄欖樹；(C)在最後一段有提到若用橄欖油來烹煮食物時，則選擇較便宜的橄欖油。

5. 第一段引出主題：橄欖油，最後提到美國人吵著要橄欖油，而他們也能取得這樣食材，因此這空格填入(A)，正好說明在加州就有生產橄欖油，同時也可接續第二段說明加州的氣候適合橄欖的種植。(B)選項無法接第二段，若放入此句，之後還必須說明美國從這些產地進口橄欖油，才能接續前一句；(C)選項雖呼應本文前面對於橄欖油味道的敘述，但卻未進一步的說明，不適合放入此句；(D)選項應放於第三段，說明如何做出上等的橄欖油。

---

crease vi. 弄皺　　coincidence n. 巧合　　counterpart n. 同業　　cold-pressed adj. 冷壓的

fit the bill 適合需求　　adept adj. 內行的　　intricacy n. 錯綜複雜　　drizzle vt. 噴灑

翻譯

　　如何讓通常由女性購買的商品對男性也具吸引力？如何讓一個小小音樂播放器成為年輕世代「必備」的時尚物品？廣告必須在一種深刻的文化層次上吸引目標消費群。影像、顏色和音樂必須特別針對他們的品味仔細安排。**兩個成功廣告──萬寶路香菸和 iPod──分別展現兩個不同時代的廣告商如何成功做到這點。**

　　在一九二〇年代和一九三〇年代，萬寶路香菸主要以女性消費者為取向。「如五月般溫和」正是萬寶路的招牌口號。然而在一九五〇年代晚期，萬寶路進行一場形象大轉變。在平面媒體和電視上，粗獷的「萬寶路男人」以男性消費者為目標被介紹出場。新廣告描繪一名牛仔騎在馬背上。他一面從事陽剛味十足的戶外活動，一面抽著香菸；且播放著撼動的背景音樂。廣告成功達到效果，到了一九五七年，男性已經開始**成群結隊購買這些產品**。美國牛仔形象完美代表了美式男性自由。

　　二〇〇三年，蘋果電腦展開一項以年輕人為對象的全球性廣告活動，促銷該公司的新型 iPod 迷你音樂播放器：在明亮背景襯托之下，剪影狀的人物手中握著他們的 iPod 隨音樂舞動。觀眾聽到嘻哈樂、電子樂和另類搖滾，屬於當代年輕人的音樂。蘋果電腦選擇將廣告設置在年輕人聚集之地。所以在倫敦，你可以在維京唱片旗艦店、地下鐵站和公車候車亭看到廣告。在蒙特婁，iPod 的剪影圖貼滿麥基爾大學地鐵終點站。五〇年代的廣告商會對這種策略大感吃驚：五十年前，主要廣告媒體只有印刷品和電視。

　　因此，雖然跟過去幾十年的廣告相比，今日廣告已經大不同，也更複雜而多層次，但仍必須讓我們有共鳴。如同巴布‧加菲德在《廣告時代》所指出：「(廣告) 必須能夠觸動我們、瞭解我們，(並) 反應我們的生活。」

解析

1. 本題考的是細節的部分，第二段後半提及萬寶路香菸新的廣告中有出現騎馬的西部牛仔 (a cowboy atop a horse)，從事戶外男性的活動 (manly outdoor things)，再加上撼動性的音樂 (stirring music)，故選(C)。

2. 此段提到萬寶路香菸新的廣告是針對男性消費者，又提到 The ads worked.，可知這廣告有達到所設定的目標－有**許多**男性消費者購買該牌子的香煙，故選(A)。

3. 文章第三段說到蘋果電腦針對年輕的消費者促銷 iPod Mini 音樂播放器，因此選擇**年輕人聚集的地方**設置廣告，接著便提到題幹中出現的這些地方，故選(C)。

4. 本題考的是文章的主旨，也就是第一段所提到的 The ads must appeal...to the targeted buyers.，故選(B)**市場取向**。

5. 文章第二、三段分別說明萬寶路香菸和 iPod 如何在廣告上成功地運用針對消費族群的策略來促銷商品，故選(D)。整篇文章都沒有提到(A)進行市場研究和(C)有關消費者基本權利等問題，故(A)(C)選項不適合；(B)選項提到現在的廣告越來越不精緻複雜這樣的說法和全文內容並不相符。

campaign n. 活動	must-have n. 必備之物	slogan n. 標語
drove n. 群	silhouetted adj. 輪廓的	congregate vi. 群聚
medium n. 媒介	multilayered adj. 多層的	gallop vi. 奔跑

翻譯

　　最近一項對英國學童進行的調查顯示，學生中有百分之十曾寄出具有威脅意味的電子郵件或手機簡訊給另一名學童。雖然校園欺凌事件已經折磨許多孩子數年之久，這種被稱為「網路霸凌」的新型態殘酷舉動，使惡劣行徑到達一個新而令人擔憂的程度。

　　網路霸凌行為最大的壞處在於，它不會僅止於學校。事實上，有些網路霸凌者大量透過電子郵件、網路聊天室、手機簡訊或部落格寄出惡意郵件，二十四小時，全年無休。對遭受這種霸凌行為的學童來說，根本沒有解脫之時，就算離開學校也一樣。

　　網路霸凌行為可能包括言語嘲弄、惡毒批評某人外表，甚至死亡威脅。但無論程度如何，受害者都對網路霸凌行為感到難受至極。悲哀的是，有些孩子被這些欺凌行為逼到走上自殺一途，而其他孩子則退縮到不敢交朋友和避開家人，甚至要求轉學或搬家。**這些反應恰恰顯示出這項問題的嚴重程度。**

　　要遏止網路霸凌行為，必須要孩子們、家長、校方、甚至警方展現堅定的態度。遏止言語嘲弄可能只需家長或校方對欺凌者的家庭打一通電話，但對於威脅要殺害或嚴重傷害某人的欺凌弱小者，警方必須介入追蹤這些人。此外校方也應該展開具體行動，透過學生教育和新反欺凌規定，防止網路霸凌行為繼續發生。

　　學生和家長們都應該切記一點：透過採取實際行動和連繫相關單位，網路霸凌行為是能夠被遏止的。嚴重威脅行為需要警方處理，將作惡者繩之以法，而較輕微的情況則需要校方介入，以確實矯正問題。

解析

1. 本題是考那一項**不是**網路霸凌和其他欺凌行為的不同處。由第二段可得知其最大的不同是，網路霸凌不只出現在校園內，也不僅只是肢體上的欺凌。而非威脅的訊息使網路霸凌和其他欺凌方式有所不同，故選(C)。

2. 本題考的是如何正確處理網路霸凌的行為。從倒數兩段中可得知(A)**家長應介入這些行為的發生**，為正確選項。文中並無提到(B)需曝露欺凌者的身份。文中提到有生命威脅的欺凌訊息出現時要通知警方，並不是(C)所有惡意的訊息，故不正確。文中並無提到(D)要學生不要太在意對外表的評論。

3. 本題考的是作者鋪陳這篇文章的方法，從第一段解釋什麼是網路霸凌問題及影響，再敘述應如何面對解決這種問題，可得知作者用的方法是(B)。

4. 單字 "fortitude" 從上下文來看，應該是指學校、家長甚至警方必須採取的手段來對抗網路霸凌。最好的答案應為(A)**堅定的態度**。不是(D)衝動、(B)熱情或(C)犧牲。

5. 本句的前文應該要有對於網路霸凌的反應，所以最適合的位置應為(B)，因為前文提到被欺負的學生種種會有的**負面反應** (driven to suicide, withdraw from friends...)。

bully vt./n 欺凌、霸凌	schoolyard n. 校園	tormented adj. 受折磨的
mean-spirited adj. 惡意的	cyberbully vt. 網路霸凌	taunt n. 嘲笑
relocate vi./vt. 遷居	fortitude n. 勇氣	rectify vt. 修正

30

全球暖化會導致世界政治衝突嗎？
Will Global Warning Cause Worldwide Political Conflicts?

翻譯

　　毫無疑問，地球正處於全球暖化期。科學家預測，洪水、海水位上升、乾旱和其他與氣候有關的災難會在未來幾十年大幅增加。

　　對溫帶氣候區國家來說，全球暖化效應也許不如南美和非洲等地接近赤道地區國家嚴重。而這些被預期到的效應很可能導致政治衝突，特別是在「富有」和「貧窮」國家之間。

　　衝突可能起自於排放二氧化碳，該物質將能量和污染困在大氣層內，使整個星球變熱。許多「富有」國──特別是北半球國家──比「貧窮」國排放出更大量二氧化碳。**然而較貧窮國家卻更為全球暖化所苦，即使這種現象並非它們造成**。這使得「貧窮」國對造成污染的「富有」國產生敵視。

　　沙漠化──土地變成沙漠──是全球暖化效應之一，也是另一個政治衝突肇因。以蘇丹的達佛地區為例，該地區正經歷全球暖化所造成的一場政治和生態大災難。主要因土地逐漸變成沙漠而導致的衝突，已經使超過二十萬人死亡。

　　與沙漠化現象相對，冰河融化會導致海平面上升，可能使低窪國家如孟加拉地區數百萬人民被迫遷往較高地帶，在這些難民遷徙到其他國家時，就可能爆發政治衝突。

　　以上兩個例子強調，因全球暖化導致的世界氣候變化，如何可能導致全球各地出現政治衝突和戰爭，因為數百萬人必須找尋新的家園，逃離升高的水平面和沙漠化的土地。

解析

1. 本題考的是細節的部份，從第三段可得知為(C)富裕的國家比貧窮的國家製造出更多 **(the lion's share)** 的 CO_2，也是造成衝突的原因。

2. 本題考的是 "temperate" 的同義字。根據第二段的上下文，countries with temperate climates 比起接近赤道炎熱的國家，受到全球暖化的影響較小，因此 temperate 應該是(C)「**較為溫和**」之意。

3. 第四段和第五段說明全球暖化所會帶來的政治衝突，分別是沙漠化和融化的冰河所帶來的難民問題，所以最適合的答案為(D)。

4. 根據第四段，**蘇丹的達佛地區**因沙漠化，造成生態上和政治上的災難，故能推論出**政治上的動亂**，答案為(A)。從這段無法推論出(B)蘇丹一定會和鄰國有衝突，(C)的敘述則應該要出現在有洪水的國家，此段也並未說明全部達佛的土地都沙漠化了，故(D)不正確。

5. 本句最適宜放在為何貧窮的國家受到全球暖化影響的段落，最適宜位置為(C)，前面說明富有的國家製造較多的 CO_2，但卻是貧窮的國家受到較多的影響，因此會怨恨富有的國家。**However** 開頭的句子會與上一句有轉折的語氣，因此不適宜放在(B)。

temperate adj. 溫帶的	equator n. 赤道	desertification n. 沙漠化
glacier n. 冰河	low-lying adj. 低窪的	subsequent adj. 隨後的
arid adj. 乾旱的	famine n. 饑荒	devastating adj. 嚴重破壞的

31 忘了毒針吧：黃蜂加入偵測炸彈行列
Forget the Sting: Wasps Recruited for Explosive Detection

翻譯

　　用狗來偵測飛機行李內的毒品或炸彈已經行之有年。但科學家徵召了一種新動物——黃蜂——來找尋這些藏匿物。這個名為「蜂探」新發展出的炸彈偵測系統是為了預防恐怖活動的情報單位而開發，利用小而不會螫人的黃蜂來尋找藏在機場和過境關卡處的爆裂物。

　　「蜂探」是將五隻半吋長的黃蜂置入一根塑膠管內，管子一端為螢幕，另一端是攝影機。螢幕讓空氣能進入管子中，而攝影機則跟一台筆記型電腦連接，監看黃蜂的行為。當黃蜂聞到牠們訓練要找出的化學物質味道時，牠們會飛向管子螢幕那端，表示牠們在附近聞到了爆裂物的味道。

　　生物工程師訓練這些黃蜂對味道有反應的方式，是每次黃蜂暴露在爆裂物質下時，都在管子的同一個地方提供糖水。經由這個過程，牠們學到，爆炸物的味道會帶領牠們得到一頓甜美大餐。這個因巴甫洛夫的狗而聲名大噪的「古典制約作用」訓練，對所有動物都有效，包括人類在內。事實上，蜜蜂也已接受這種訓練來偵測地雷及其他爆裂物。

　　跟狗比起來，黃蜂的優點在於牠們不昂貴、容易餵食跟照顧，此外還能在幾分鐘內就被訓練好。相較之下，狗則要經過數月時間訓練才能完成同一項任務。黃蜂的嗅覺也較佳。

　　憑藉如此生物工程技術的進步，有一天與眾不同的昆蟲跟動物也可能會擔任原本只適合人類跟狗的工作。而也許在十年內，我們就會看到機場警察擺弄著一管管黃蜂尋找毒品跟爆裂物，而不是牽著以皮帶拴住的狗。

解析

1. 本文在說明黃蜂可以取代狗成為查緝爆裂物的利器，利用此點作為背景知識，再從此句的上下文，可知當黃蜂嗅到特定的化學物質時，會飛到管子中有螢幕的一端，可知此時<u>在這附近</u>有爆裂物，故選(D)鄰近區域。

2. 此為文章細節題，第二段提及利用蜂探，要將黃蜂放在塑膠的管子中，管子一頭有銀幕，另一頭有連結到筆記型電腦的攝影機，故不需要(B)拴鍊。

3. 本題考的是推論的能力，第三段提到在訓練黃蜂時，科學家使用糖水當獎勵，因此在訓練的過程中，動物若能達成指定的動作，則被給予獎勵此行為，故選(B)。

4. 本題考的是各段落的主旨，第一段主要在引出主題蜂探；第二段在說明如何利用蜂探來查緝爆裂物或毒品；第三段說明這項訓練背後所仰賴的古典制約作用；第四段在說明蜂探勝於狗的優勢；最後一段則預言未來蜂探會被廣泛運用，故選(C)。

5. 空格前提到過去是用狗查緝毒品或爆裂物，而空格後則提到現在可以用黃蜂來執行這項任務。由於空格後已經提到「新型的炸彈偵測系統」，所以空格要說明這種新的系統為何，因此選(D)。而一再提及狗兒的(A)(B)選項都不適合，雖然(C)選項有提及黃蜂，但此句屬於細節的部分，無法用於承轉語意。

---

recruit　vt.　徵召

consistently　adv.　持續地

terrorism-prevention　n.　恐怖活動防治

classical-conditioning　n.　古典制約作用

vicinity　n.　鄰境周圍

leash　n.　拴鍊；皮帶

22 號難題：從小說到現實生活
Catch-22: From Fiction to Real Life

翻譯

當我們被迫要在兩害相權中取其輕時，美國小說家約瑟夫·海勒為這個兩難狀況提供了一個簡短而精彩的描述：22 號難題。在他的小說《第 22 條軍規》中，有是一條戰時空軍飛行員必須面對的虛構軍規：如果一名飛行員持續執行危險的近戰任務，卻不要求卸除這種具高度威脅生命的勤務，他一定瘋了。但如果他要求上級許可不去執行這些任務，就表示他還有理智，因此必須繼續執行下去。

「難題 (catch)」一字，意指一個隱藏的問題，或在情況內不樂見但必須克服的部分。例如，你獲得了一個高薪的新工作，但有個「難題」：這個工作需要值夜班。這表示有個壞處 (上夜班) 也同時跟著好處 (高薪的工作)。

然而，22 號難題的情況不同，因為並沒有好處存在。以下是另一個 22 號難題的例子：不運動對健康不好，但如果你在一個空氣污染嚴重的都市中運動，對健康也不好。所以，在 22 號難題的情況中，無論你做什麼決定，都是輸家。

海勒的小說是一部重要諷刺作品，描寫存在於戰爭背後的組織機構，並嘲弄官僚們為了控制人民思想跟行動所用的荒謬概念跟瘋狂語言。散見於小說中的對話跟主題表現出海勒對戰爭的痛恨。虛構的 22 號難題呈現了海勒對戰爭的想法，而他必定非常樂意見到，在該書出版後不到十年，這個詞就已成為日常生活用語之一了。

譯註：本文為求符合原意而作此翻譯，台灣已出版之書籍與電影譯名則為《第 22 條軍規》。

解析

1. 第一段主要是說明 catch-22 這個字彙為原先一部小說的名字，小說中說明了(C)這條杜撰出來的軍規互相矛盾之處。本段尚未詳細舉例可使用 catch-22 的情況。

2. 根據第一段說明，catch-22 原先為(D)一條杜撰的空軍軍規衍生而來。

3. 根據第二段的說明，catch 有「隱藏的困難」之意，故(A)為正確選項。文中並無提到小說家 Heller 對戰爭所造成的民族主義的看法，故(B)為非。(C)選項不是 catch-22 的情況，所以不正確。《第 22 條軍規》這本小說並不是對選舉制度的諷刺，而是對戰爭及體制的批評，故(D)為非。

4. 由 "in an effort to control people's thoughts and actions." 可推論出 "bureaucracies" 應是指(C)運作政府組織的人。

5. 本句是說明在 Heller 的小說中，充滿了對戰爭的批評及厭惡，與第四段整段文意最為符合，故選(D)。第一段在說明 catch-22 的源由和本質。第二段在說明 catch 的字意。第三段說明會使用 catch-22 的情況。

dilemma n. 進退兩難的情況	undesirable adj. 不受歡迎的，討厭的	satire n. 諷刺作品
bureaucracy n. 官僚	exemplify vt. 舉例	vicious adj. 惡意的
natonalism n. 民族主義	manifest vt. 明白表示	

而你還覺得「糖」有害身體呢！
And You Thought Sugar Was Bad for You!

　　只要讀讀與健康相關的新聞標題，就會看到許多報導指出，可樂跟碳酸飲料中過多的糖份、咖啡因以及人工甘味劑會如何戕害身體。但你可知道，當喬治亞州，亞特蘭大市的藥劑師約翰・潘伯頓發明可口可樂這種嚐起來甜甜的飲料時，其中一項成分是如今被列為嚴重違法毒品的古柯鹼嗎？

　　可口可樂上市早期，潘伯頓其實想比照在歐洲非常成功的古柯酒(一種酒跟古柯鹼的混和物)，嘗試發展一種「健康飲料」。他並沒有製造能解渴的飲品，在這項新產品中，他使用了古柯鹼和可樂豆，用以獲得刺激性的效果。**當時，古柯鹼被視為一種新的奇蹟藥物，有助於緩解疼痛並使人新生精力。**它出現在無數非處方用藥中，例如喉糖碇——用以治療喉嚨痛——以及其他止痛藥。

　　然而，到了一九〇四年，政府對一些公司在產品中使用古柯鹼感到相當憂心，因此可口可樂及其他公司被迫將產品中與該藥物有關的成分移除殆盡。不過，這並未阻止可口可樂成功變成廣受歡迎的飲料，因為它仍含有大量咖啡因，飲用可口可樂的人還是能一下子「精神大振」。雖然美國政府試圖迫使可口可樂公司將咖啡因排除於其飲料成分外，該公司最後還是勝出，讓其他產品也能含有咖啡因。

　　時至今日，可口可樂，或常被稱為「可樂」，已經成為世界上最廣為人知的品牌了。除了一些極細微的調整之外，它仍使用一百多年前同一套基本配方——只不過少了古柯鹼！

1. 在文章中並無討論**在可樂中加入古柯鹼會產生的副作用**，故答案為(A)。從第二段可以找到(B)(D)。在第三段中說明了可樂成份的變化，故可推論出(C)。

2. 從第二段 "he used cocaine and kola nuts in this new product for their stimulating effect" 和第三段 "for it continued to have lots of caffeine, from which Coca-Cola drinkers would still get an energy "boost" 兩句可推論出古柯鹼、可樂豆和咖啡因應該都有(C)提神的作用。

3. 從第三四段可得知，現在的 Coca-Cola 和原本的配方相去不遠，只是少掉了政府所不允許的古柯鹼，故選(B)。

4. 從下句 "allowing for other products to include caffeine as well" 可推論出，可口可樂在和政府對於可不可以在飲料中加入 caffeine 的爭論中，應該是獲得勝利的，才能讓其他產品也能含有咖啡因 (caffeine)，故 prevail 應為(D)「獲勝」之意。

5. 本句提到古柯鹼最適合放在(B)。前一句說明可口可樂有使用古柯鹼，接著說明它的功效及被使用在那些方面。

caffeine n. 咖啡因	artificial sweetener n. 人工甘味劑	cocaine n. 古柯鹼
thirst-quenching adj. 解渴的	myriad adj. 無數	over-the-counter adj. 非處方的
throat lozenge n. 喉糖碇	prevail vt. 戰勝	vitality n. 活力
consent vi. 同意	compensate vi./vt. 補償	intervene vt. 干預

別把那些漫畫書收起來
Don't Put Those Comic Books Away

翻譯

　　過去，漫畫在大多數學校裡都聲名狼籍。老師禁止它們出現在教室裡，且許多學校不允許學生在校園內看漫畫。不過，一個名為「漫畫書計畫」的新方案，不只把漫畫帶入校園內，還鼓勵學生看、寫跟畫它們──就在學校裡頭！

　　「漫畫書計畫」始於二〇〇一年，是一所小學內的課後社團活動。發起人麥可‧布里茲是一名來自哥倫比亞大學的教育工作者，他相信這門藝術能被運用在鼓勵學習上。布里茲尤其主張，漫畫書有助於激發校內讀寫能力，特別是在學生們創作屬於自己的漫畫書時。

　　「漫畫書計畫」最初吸引一些喜歡視覺藝術的學生加入，不過，參加該社團的學生也很快體認到好的寫作的重要性。舉例來說，學生們能夠在自己的漫畫書中畫場景圖案，但他們也必須為自己的角色想對白。**學生們接受指導，學習如何寫下自己的故事概念，以及為情節寫出大綱。**隨著時間過去，學生們必須在一段長時間中寫下、修正並編輯自己的故事，學生的寫作和閱讀技巧大有進步。而且因為他們總是在尋找新創意和靈感，社團中許多學生開始增加閱讀量──不只限於漫畫書，也包括傳統文學，如小說和短篇故事等。

　　基於這次首度實施的成功，「漫畫書計畫」如今被位於紐約及美國各地其他城市的另外四十五所學校採用。因此在未來，托這項創新計畫的福，漫畫書可能不再是校園中的犯規份子，而是受歡迎的有價值學習工具。

解析

1. 此為文章主旨題，第一段為主題「漫畫書計畫」；第二段說明計劃的實施與目的，第三段說明此計畫可增進學生閱讀與寫作能力；最後一段說明這計劃漸漸受到大家的重視，故最適合的標題為(D)。文章雖有提到這個計畫的創辦人，但並非主要在介紹布里茲，故(A)不適合；(B)(C)的敘述則太過於籠統。

2. 此為文章細節題，第三段最後提到學生閱讀傳統小說的原因：they were always on the lookout for new ideas and inspiration，故選(D)。

3. 此為文章細節題，答案(C)為文章第二段提到 comic books could help to boost literacy in schools，以及本文最後一句則點出在未來漫畫書可能會被認為是幫助學習的利器。文章第二、三段都有提及到布里茲提出此計畫的目的是透過漫畫的創作來提升閱讀與書寫的能力，而非著眼於視覺藝術這一部分，故(A)不正確；最後一段提到此計畫目前在美國許多其他城市被採用，故(B)不對；第二段提到，此計劃一開始是以課後活動的方式進行，而非(D)所說的。

4. 最後一句後半部為 but 所引導的子句，在語意上有一轉折，故 outlawed 一字應與後半句中的 welcomed 意思相反。此外，文章一開始提到以前漫畫書被認為是不良書刊、甚至被禁止，故選(A)。

5. 此句在(C)的位置，用以說明此計畫在學生學習寫作上的幫助：從編寫對話、擬定大綱，到最後書寫、修改與編輯，正是一個引導寫作的方式。此句為細節，時態為過去式，不適合放於(A)；(B)應該要放入布里茲提出此計畫的想法或目的；(D)出現的段落在講述現在與未來可能出現的狀況，故不適合。

| spur | vt. 刺激 | boost | vt. 促進 | literacy | n. 讀寫能力 |
| integrate | vt. 整合 | immortal | adj. 不朽的 | irrelevant | adj. 不相關的 |

35 今日模特兒業：一切在於新
Modeling Industry Today: All About the New

翻譯

　　崔姬。詩恩・辛普頓。在一九六〇年代，翻開每一本時尚雜誌，都會一次又一次看到這些女性優雅地躍然紙上。那時，流行界只需少數不僅能在紙頁上發光發熱，又能立即締造銷售佳績的超級巨星。這些人——幾乎全為女性——所到之處皆受到皇室般的款待。然而情況已不再如此。沈浸在資訊和媒體中的今日年輕人，要求不同形象持續翻新湧入。他們怎麼想一而再再而三看到同一個人呢？太沒意思了。

　　網路在模特兒業此番轉變中扮演著非常重要的角色。跟前一世代比起來，今日年輕人看到的形象多了許多。他們變得更容易感到無趣，而且要求視覺上不斷的變化。白皮膚、金髮和碧眼已不再是評判某人非常有吸引力的前提了。人們更能接受不同膚色和五官的人。事實上，不具有完美均衡五官者，反而比臉龐較對稱者更受青睞。不過，今天的世界頂尖模特兒，很可能在短短幾季之後就變得「過時」了。

　　越來越多名人步上超級名模的後塵。現今知名運動員跟超級巨星們兜售著各類商品，從手錶、早餐穀片到電話系統都有。但如果那位超級巨星不再具有國際號召力，他或她的市場價值立刻消失，高額的佣金亦然。

　　這一切之中有好消息：你不再須要是完美化身，才能做個成功的模特兒。但也有壞消息：就算你好運成了頂尖模特兒，也別期待能保持多久。永遠會有新的人出現將你取而代之。

解析

1. 根據全文，作者認為現在的模特兒及明星名人，是很容易受到汰換的，因此可推論出(C)。作者在本文中只提到現在的模特兒不一定是要金髮或身材完美，但並沒說成功的模特兒一定不能是金髮或身材完美，因此(A)不正確。文中並無提到(B)。崔姬等模特兒的成功和現在在模特兒界的流行是不相符的，故(D)不正確。

2. "prerequisite" 根據上下文推論，應是(B)指「先決條件」之意。

3. 根據第一段 (**young people of** today demand a constant new influx of different images.) 及第二段 (**The Internet** plays a huge role in this transformation of the modeling industry.) 可推論出答案為(A)。

4. 根據第二段的描述，人們現在較喜歡(B)有特色的臉孔，而不只是金髮碧眼或完美身材的模特兒。

5. 本句中的 "they" 應該是指 young people，最適合放在前面是描述青少年的段落，故選(B)。

---

information-and-media saturated adj. 沈浸在資訊與媒體的		influx n. 湧入
prerequisite n. 必要的條件	knockout n. 令人印象深刻的事物	hawk vt. 兜售
adulation n. 奉承	paparazzi n. 狗仔隊	

翻譯

「新年快樂！」準備沮喪一番吧。

一名英國心理學家宣稱，一月二十四日是一年中最令人憂鬱的日子。他表示，在新年過後三週，耶誕節歡樂氣氛的餘韻已經消失，只留下一堆帳單待付。新年的決心——關於要怎麼減肥、運動跟戒煙就會讓你成為一個很棒的人——這些已經成了過去式。而令英國人生活更加慘淡的是，惡劣的天氣毫不留情地持續著。

威爾斯的卡地夫大學教授克里夫·阿爾納博士表示，一般說來，英國的冬天並不好過。所謂「SAD」，即「季節性情感失調」猖獗不已。SAD 是一種跟缺乏日光有關的沮喪狀態，很少出現在陽光充足氣候區的居民身上。但在英國，冬天惡名昭彰地陰霾灰暗，約有三分之一人口苦於正如其名的 SAD 症狀。一小部分未接受治療的人甚至連生活都無法正常進行。

因此，阿爾納教授有一整季 SAD 好發的時間可選為他的一年最沮喪日。一月二十四日雀屏中選——或許該說不幸中選。這是由一個將七種因素考慮在內的方程式得出，這些因素包括天氣、耶誕節過了多久、無法堅持決心、負債程度月薪收入、低動機，以及執行的需要等等。阿爾納教授是為了一家旅遊公司製作出這個算式，該公司想知道，什麼時候人們最想逃離英國來趟假期。

當然，任何方程式都簡化了真實生活情境，但其他心理健康專家也原則上同意阿爾納這項令人沮喪的發現。也許這位教授下一個計畫可以著實開心點，告訴我們一年中最快樂的日子是哪天。八九不離十，時間不會落在冬天。

> 譯註：英文中 sad 正是悲傷沮喪之意。

解析

1. 開頭的這句話 (Happy New Year! Get ready to be depressed.) 在祝福完新年快樂後，卻馬上接著說準備好沮喪吧！作者用的是一個前後對比 (contrast) 的方式，故選(A)。

2. 此為文章細節題，第一段提及一月二十四日是最憂鬱一天的原因。而(C)應改成 people are unable to keep their New Year resolutions。

3. 此句之後提到，此疾病在陽光充足的地區是很少見的，但在冬天氣候陰暗的英國有三分之一的人為此疾病所苦，因此可推測 SAD 在英國是很常見的，故選(D)。

4. 這也是文章細節題，答案出現在第四段的最後一句：Arnall produced the equation for a travel company that....，故選(D)。而(A)(B)(C)在文中並未提到。

5. 由於空格出現在文章的最後一句，此句需要有總結全文或預測未來的作用，應選(B)。從上文可知由於英國冬天陰冷，使人產生憂鬱之感，因此可推測最快樂的日子不會出現在冬天；前文中並未提到阿爾納在預測何時是最憂鬱的一天是件艱困的任務，故不適合選(A)；雖然有時公式會過於簡化一些問題，但醫師大體同意阿爾納的看法，至於其他醫生和病人對此新發現會有什麼看法，似乎很難在此馬上做出結論，故(C)和(D)都不恰當。

afterglow n. 餘韻	stack n. 堆	resolution n. 決心	fabulous adj. 極好的
relentlessly adv. 無情地	rampant adj. 猖獗的	candidate n. 候選人	equation n. 算式

電子郵件可能讓我們變成膽小鬼
Emials Can Make Cowards of Us

翻譯

瑪莉，

我們曾經很開心，但我們別再見面了，好嗎？

我有了新對象。　彼得

你能想像瀏覽自己的電子郵件時，竟發現原本以為情投意合的男友發了這麼一封信給你嗎？當另一個人毫無心理準備時，電子郵件可不是個說再見的好方式。**然而，人們已經越來越少面對面溝通複雜的情感。**他們讓電子郵件替自己做這件事。

當某人讀你寄去的電子郵件時，他或她閱讀該訊息時你並不在場。該人無法從訊息本身抓出準確的口頭或情感上的微妙暗示，即使你用了再多微笑面孔或「LOL's」亦然。因此當你使用電子郵件時，要多體貼別人的需要。想想以下情境：你最好的朋友嚴重冒犯了你，而你非常憤怒。你可以寄一封氣急敗壞的電子郵件給她或他，說她或他是多差勁的人，或者在 My Space 交友社群上對該人發表一篇惡毒的評論，讓全世界都看到。但這真是解決問題的最佳方式嗎？你可能在短時間內覺得痛快，但這種惡意行為暴露出你自身的缺點，更甚於另一個人的。

如果你想跟男朋友或女朋友分手，請盡量別用彼得那種方式。如果他遇見了新歡，應該和瑪莉直接溝通清楚。面對面講最好，但在電話上與當事人說也尚可接受。當然，用這些方式過程會難熬許多，但採取這樣的行動展現了勇氣，以及更重要的是，對他人的體貼。別讓電子郵件使你成了一個膽小鬼。

> 譯註：此為英文語境下的電子郵件用語，可代表 "lots of love's"，即「充滿愛的」。

解析

1. 此為文章主旨題，第一段先利用一個實例引出越來越多人用電子郵件的方式來分手，第二段則解釋為何用這種方式來談分手不恰當，最後則說明較好的分手方式有哪些，故選(B)。文中並未提到(A)(C)(D)。

2. 從上下文中，可知不論是寫黑函或在網路上張貼惡意中傷他人的言論都是「不好」的行為，因此可猜出 malicious 一字含有負面意味的意思，故選(C) **spiteful**。

3. 本題考的是辨認指涉詞，讀者或許會誤以為 it 代替的是最接近的動作 (speaking face to face 或是 talking to the person on the telephone)；但若仔細閱讀包含有 it 的這個句子可知 these ways 才是指分手的方式，而 it 實際上指的是分手這樣的舉動，選(D)。

4. 本題考的是推論題，從第二段最後的敘述可知**寫黑函這樣的行為只是自曝其短**，故選(B)。在最後一段開始，明確指出寫電子郵件分手的方式是不好的，故(A)不對；從第二段的第二及三句可知，無論多少表情符號，都無法讓對方感受到寫信人的情緒反應，故(C)也不對；而最後一段提到面對面的分手雖然困難但卻是一種有勇氣與體貼的表現，故(D)不對。

5. 此句放在(A)的位置，在閱讀時就可發現空格後句中的 they 前方並未出現代替的名詞，放入此句，they 所代替的就是 individuals，同時文意上也剛好有轉折：使用電子郵件分手不是好的方式，但越來越多人這麼做。(B)(C)的位置是討論利用 email 的缺點，而(D)前文作者則提出了較適合的方法，均不恰當。

---

coward n. 懦弱	accurate adj. 準確的	verbal adj. 言語的	scenario n. 情境
write-up n. 評論	malicious adj. 惡意的	charitable adj. 仁慈的	spiteful adj. 惡意的
voluntary adj. 自願的	introverted adj. 內向的	inflict vt. 使遭受，把…強加於 (某人)	

翻譯

　　在電視出現的早期，許多電視節目為了滿足逐漸起步的市場而製作。其中有猜謎節目跟特殊才能表演秀，讓普通人也能藉著展現他們的知識或才能，有機會上電視贏得獎金或獎品。隨著電視觀眾逐年增加，這些類型的節目也越來越受歡迎。有些節目由地方製作，讓普通民眾能出來秀，但也有其他節目標榜知名度甚高的名人。由於大眾對名人跟他們公私生活的迷戀，過去幾年裡誕生了所謂「真人實境秀」的節目。

　　真人實境秀內容五花八門。有些要人做些極度危險的特技或噁心技藝來贏得獎金。有些則請了過氣名人跟其他人住在一個封閉空間中，在一個應該是「真實」的環境裡，讓觀眾能觀看及享受他們的日常互動。但據說在，這些秀中某些對話和行為是經過安排或變動的，原因是出於「收視率考量」。

　　最糟糕的例子之一也許是「美國偶像」，該電視秀有項眾所周知的不成文規則，盡找些沒有半點才能的人上節目，只為了讓他們在全國，甚至全球觀眾面前，被所謂的裁判奚落嘲弄。該節目使一個公然在台上被嘲弄的競賽者憑添娛樂價值。的確，「美國偶像」產生了一些明星。然而說穿了，像「美國偶像」這類電視秀，重點只在侮辱人，並讓人們看著當事者失敗，蒙受羞辱跟落淚。不幸的是，許多人愛看這類電視節目，而且收視率屢創新高。有些心理學家表示，人們喜歡觀看其他人失敗，以掩飾自己在生活中的不如意。

　　所以，「真人實境電視秀」是否真的呈現了現實？

解析

1. 此句之後提到實境秀的內容各式各樣、包羅萬象，有挑戰特技，噁心的任務等，故選(A)。

2. 本題考的是細節的部分，因文中並未提到人們喜歡實境秀是因為(C)喜歡這種節目所呈現的現實面。第三段提到觀眾喜歡看的是(A)別人的失敗；第一段最後有提到對名人的迷戀和想窺探名人的公眾生活和(B)私生活；第三段開始也提到實境秀常找一些(D)普通人完成困難任務，這些都是實境秀受歡迎的原因。

3. 本題考的也是細節的部分，(D)為正確。第三段明確指出「美國偶像」這個節目的目的是要羞辱 (to humiliate) 參賽者；文中提到這個節目有國內，甚至是全球的觀眾，故(A)不對；同時這類型的節目收視率創新高，因此(B)不對；文中雖有提到心理學家，但是引用這些專家的看法說明這類節目受歡迎的原因，但心理學家並未參與實境秀的演出，故(C)不對。

4. 本題考的是推論的能力，雖第一段看似客觀地說明實境秀發展的由來，但第二段從用字 disgusting 和 supposed to be a "real" environment 可知，作者不喜歡這類節目的內容，也懷疑這些內容是捏造出來的，加上在第三段作者認為這類節目的目的是 mock, humiliate, watch the failures of others (都是負面的)，故選(A)。

5. 第三段前半在說明這類節目的目的，空格之前提到 mock，之後提到 humiliate，而(B)選項也提到 to be publicly ridiculed。整篇文章都沒有提到(A)綜藝節目或情境喜劇；(C)(D)選項應出現於第二段最後，接前面所提到的實境秀不見得是真的，有時為了節目效果，也會造假。

| encompass vt. 包括 | stunt n. 特技 | feat n. 技藝 |
| rating n. 收視率 | ounce n. 一點 | despise vt. 鄙視 |

生態流行熱
Eco-Chic

翻譯

　　不久前在台灣，上千人花上好幾個小時排隊，願意付離譜的高價，以獲得一個上面印有環保標語的帆布袋子。對這些人之中的大多數而言，環境並非真正重點所在。如果是，他們可以不用如此**大費周章**，他們可以以非常便宜的價格就可買到類似袋子，或免費從政府單位取得。他們那麼做的主要原因在於，當時那種袋子是必買的時尚物品。

　　大部分現代人都意識到需要保護環境。大部分人也都做了份內之事：回收、減少使用，並盡力重複利用。然而，悲哀的是：許多人只有在自己方便、別人在看，或覺得那樣很流行時才這麼做。

　　環保油電混合動力車 (hybrid) 就是個好例子。它們已經上市多年，卻被社會大眾普遍忽視。人們繼續購買並且駕駛耗油量大且高污染的休旅車。直到許多好萊塢名人開始開環保車後，這些車輛的銷售率才開始增加，**原因是現在擁有一台這種車才「流行」**。另一個例子則是：為了不浪費更多寶貴資源，倡導利用回收布料製作衣服。消費者認為他們在假日購物時，同時也在保護 (拯救) 地球的行列中。然而，一個令人震驚的現象是「綠色貨幣」的銷售：個人可購買來讓自己繼續污染及耗損自然資源；而這些銷售所得收益，照理將給私人機構或非政府組織繼續進行環境保護研究。

　　過去幾年來，環保意識已大幅提升。然而，廢料、污染跟自然資源耗損量卻每年都在增加。拯救環境的唯一方法，就是時時刻刻保有環境意識，而非只在方便或流行時才這麼做。

解析

1. 本題的(A)錯誤在於，名人有助銷售環保的環保油電混合車而不是 SUVs。根據第三段對於 "green dollars" 的描述可以推論出(B)。從第一段排隊買包包的例子可以推論出(D)。從最後一段作者的陳述可以推論出(C)。

2. 根據上下文，很多人排很久的隊去買很昂貴的環保包。作者認為如果真是為了環保，應該是相反的做法，人們應該會花較少的錢，及用較不麻煩的方法，故選(B)。

3. 此句主要是提到，綠色貨幣 (green dollars) 的銷售會用在環保的研究，故選(D)。

4. 整篇文章作者提出現在社會中一般人士因為方便或流行而購買環保商品的心態，由最後一段可推論出作者對這種現象的批評，故選(C)。

5. 本格應放在好萊塢明星開始風行環保混合動力車之後所造成的影響，故選(D)。(A)和本段句意相反。本句後面的句子為 "Another example..."，所以不會再出現新的例子，故(B)為非。(C)無法連結兩個說明「不是為了環保而環保」的例子。

---

chic　n　時髦高雅	queue　vi.　排隊	outrageous　adj.　毫無道理的
hassle　n.　麻煩	hybrid　n.　(環保) 油電混合車	gas-guzzling　adj.　非常耗油的

是傻瓜還是天才？
Idiot or Savant?

翻譯

　　在業界有個觀念，如果某人擁有許多高級證照，那個人不可否認地必定非常聰明。然而，一個擁有博士或企業管理碩士學位的人，也可能是以班上最低成績畢業，勉強才獲得學位。英文「素人天才」這個字原為法文。形容一個人擁有天生而超群的智慧；是個天才。達文西就是個著名的素人天才。他多才多藝，擁有橫跨藝術到工程等許多領域的技術和知識，而且多半是自學而成。

　　擁有特別天賦的人通常並不自覺。他們可能具有解答謎題或解開密碼的才能，而這些常令人們驚訝不已。當他們進入高等學習機構時，可能會對課程感到無聊，因為學校所教的東西他們已經懂了。大部分人通常會輟學，原因不在於成績不及格或經濟問題，而在於他們認為那是浪費自己的時間。有些人覺得這些高等學習機構太封閉，不允許自由思考。有些則因放棄自己的機會被認為是傻瓜；然而，他們大多不太在意那一紙文憑。他們會更想繼續做自己有興趣的事。有些人成功了，有些沒有。但一旦他們成功，往往成就極為非凡。

　　Google 的創設團隊，以及蘋果電腦的創始人史提夫賈伯斯，都是拒絕體制的人。他們走出學校做自己有興趣的事，然後變得非常成功。最成功的故事應該屬比爾蓋茲。他自哈佛大學輟學，開始依自己的想法做事，在父母的車庫裡開了一間公司。他的公司如今被稱做微軟，而他是世界上最有錢的人之一。他到底是傻瓜，還是天才呢？

解析

1. 這篇文章主要是在說明，有些(B)天資聰敏的人，在學校課業表現不佳或對課程不感興趣，但用自學的方法達到很高的成就。

2. 本句主要是說得到學位的人很可能在班上畢業時成績墊底，根據此語氣 "barely made it through" 應該是勉強通過的意思，故選(A)。

3. 在第一段中，作者先提到一個非英文的外來單字 "savant"，然後提到達文西(A)來說明 "savant" 的字義是指像達文西這樣天資優異的人，可以透過自學的方法，精通很多學科。

4. 本題考的是推論的部份，最後一段提到史帝夫賈伯斯不喜歡固有的學校系統，而是自己去創業，根據第二段，這樣的人常是覺得學校教的東西沒有挑戰性或太制式化，故可推論出(C)。從本文無法直接推論出(B)和(D)這樣的論點。

5. 本格應描述對學習感到沒興趣，而從學校離開的學生的心態，故選(C)。(A)在說明資優生的家長的養育態度。根據上下文，此格不會提到學校老師的心態，故(B)不正確。這一段都無提到這樣的學生在工作場合的情形，故(D)不正確。

| savant n. 天才 | polymath n. 多才多藝的人 | institution n. 機構 |
| anti-establishment n. 反體制 | tackle vt. 應付、處理 | |

自工業革命以及為一般民眾而開始大批製造商品後,商品設計就大多走平實及實用路線。隨著競爭日益激烈,商品設計和市場行銷也越來越受重視。以往,男性是家庭中賺取生活費和做決定的人,因此大部分商品設計和市場行銷都以他們為主要對象。第二次世界大戰後,更多女性進入職場,成為薪水階級。商品生產者發現了這個新市場,開始製造對女性有吸引力的商品。**然而,這些商品通常沿用同樣的設計,只是顏色為粉紅色或粉色系,有個可愛名字而已。**隨著時間過去,許多公司發現到,若要在這個市場保有競爭力,就必須特別為女性而設計商品。**她們的需要跟需求必須被考量到。**而這意味著精緻化、使用上的順手,以及設計感。受到影響的商品從汽車、電腦到其他電子產品都有。商品的市場行銷方式也有所改變,以期對更多女性有吸引力。

以電子產品為例,商品設計考量到應符合更小的手、較短的手指使用,可放進手提包內攜帶,以及其他因素如較長的指甲等。今日,行動電話顏色多采多姿,而非過去到處都是的黑色和銀色。它們也有不同款式和特色,以符合各種品味。舉例來說,有些內建數位相機的行動電話,將自動對焦設在約手臂伸直的距離處,因為據觀察發現,許多年輕女性喜歡和朋友自拍。就連一向以青少年和年輕男性為主的電玩工業,也越來越重視女性玩家,因為近來研究指出,女性在現今玩家中佔了百分之四十三。電視及電腦遊戲開發者開始設計以女性為主角的冒險和角色扮演遊戲,希望能吸引女性玩家。女性市場商機龐大。女性比男性更有流

行意識,她們較常更換手機、數位相機或其他物品,以保持與時下流行同步。誰知道呢?也許未來,在你走進一家電子產品店時,會有「女性」和「男性」的商品區也不一定。

1. 本題考為女性設計商品時<u>不需</u>考慮到那一項。由第一段 "This meant compactness, ease of use and style." 可得知需考慮精巧、操作便利及風格,由第二段開頭也可推論出設計女性商品會考慮到她們的體型,本文並未提到需注意(D) **all-in-one function**。

2. 根據上下文,their needs 這裏指的是(C)**女性**的需求,已開始被廠商們所注重。

3. 在此句中提到女性對潮流較敏銳,比起男性更容易去更換購買新的電子產品,因此可推論出女性的市場應該是(B)**獲利很高的** **(profitable)**。

4. 本題是考對全文的了解,第二段中可推論出(A)(D)。第一段,針對男性的商品並不注重設計,可推論出(C)。第一段也說明在二次大戰後,女性投入職場,有經濟能力,廠商開始注意到女性市場,故並不是在此時(B)**才開始注意商品的行銷**。

5. 此句應放在段落中有說明開始有針對女性設計的商品,故選(A)。(B)位置應放關於開始注重女性設計的商品,(C)位置應放考慮到女性體型的設計,(D)位置應放關於女性電動商品的設計。

bland adj. 平庸的	utilitarian adj. 實用的	breadwinner n. 負擔家計的人	gear vt. 調整
compactness n. 小巧	accommodate vt. 適應、遷就	portability n. 可攜帶、輕便	
ubiquitous adj. 到處存在的	built-in adj. 內建的	cater to 滿足需求	protagonist n. 主角

翻譯

在女性加入職場工作行列以及配方奶粉被發明之前,餵母乳一向相當普遍。在七〇年代,女性解放成了重要議題,工作機會也增加時,許多女性開始轉而以奶瓶餵寶寶。有些女性甚至決定不餵母乳,認為那會影響她們的身材。

世界健康組織估計,每年有一百萬名寶寶因腹瀉而死亡或生病,原因來自於未清潔乾淨的奶瓶或以不潔淨的水沖泡配方奶粉。專家們強調:餵母乳是讓寶寶能存活下來的關鍵,特別是在寶寶剛出生後。新生兒的免疫系統尚未成熟,無法保護他們不受無數細菌、病菌或其他侵略者的危害。雖然母乳的確切性質很難理解,但其中有許多獨特成分是特別設計來保護寶寶的。母乳中含有活細胞、賀爾蒙及酵素,它們的分子結構是配方嬰兒奶粉無法重製出來的。再者,如刊登在《新加坡醫學期刊》上的一篇報告所指出,母乳會隨著時間而改變,以符合嬰兒吸吮母乳的不同時期,初乳和後乳就是一例。嬰兒配方奶粉很不幸地只能為寶寶提供「固定」模式的營養。它並不符合生理原則。因此,餵母乳或人乳本身仍是給嬰兒的最佳贈禮。

除此之外,餵母乳的過程中包含許多擁抱、依偎以及眼神接觸,對於親子關係的建立有極大幫助。餵母乳的女性罹患乳癌的機率比不餵母乳的女性低了一半。若全程餵食母乳,一天還能消耗 250 大卡的熱量,因此是幫助母親減去懷孕所增體重的方法。

因為母乳確實是嬰兒理想的食物來源,聯合國建議能夠餵母乳的母親,在嬰兒出生後前六個月都餵食母乳。如果你無法全程餵母乳,應該至少考慮餵上半程。

解析

1. 本文主要是(D)探討餵母乳的好處,第二段說明它比配方奶粉良好的地方,第三段也說明餵母乳對母親的好處。

2. 第一段說明了以前母親不願意餵母乳的原因,其中包括了女性開始進入職場,女性的解放運動,配方奶粉的誕生及擔心影響身材的因素,但沒提到(D)家庭暴力的問題。

3. 從 "1 million babies die or fall ill every year from diarrhea picked up from unhygienic bottle feeding or from formula milk powder mixed with unsafe water." 可推論出 "diarrhea" 這個字應該是(C)「喝了不潔的水會產生的疾病」。

4. 從第三段 "Women who breastfeed have half the risk of developing breast cancer than those women who don't." 可推論出(B)。(A) 不正確,應該是有一百萬的嬰兒因腹瀉而死亡或生病。(C)的 couples 應改為 mothers and infants。(D)文中並無提到。

5. 本句應放在段落中有說明母乳和沖泡奶粉的比較,故最適合放在(C),解釋說明前一句提到母乳的成份,並承接下文,比較和奶粉的不同。

breastfeed vt. 餵母奶	workforce n. 工作	formula milk n. 配方奶粉
liberation n. 解放 diarrhea n. 腹瀉	unhygienic adj. 不衛生的	immune adj. 免疫的
foremilk n. 初乳 hindmilk n. 後乳	physiological adj. 生理上的	hormone n. 賀爾蒙
enzyme n. 酵素 molecular adj. 分子的		

43 整型手術跨海之旅
Round-the-World Plastic Surgery

在現今的全球市場，無論什麼事情，只要價錢最划算，人們就算踏遍世界也在所不惜。最令人趨之若鶩的划算交易中包括了整型手術。大多數人都渴望變得更美麗，而許多人會橫越地球達到這個目的：但前提是價錢必須最划算。

已開發國家如美國、英國及日本的人會到泰國、馬來西亞、匈牙利及捷克等國家旅行。他們先做太陽浴，在沙灘上打發時間。**然後就去動手術了。**這種「保健之旅」套裝行程生意正蓬勃發展，有數千名接受手術者及全世界各地提供手術服務的業者參與其中。

舉例而言，「美麗人士」是一家以英國為據點的仲介業者，安排英國客戶到捷克進行手術。一年之中，這家公司就送了超過兩百名英國人到布拉格去。整個套裝行程包括一週的食宿、一名當地導遊，以及一次抽脂手術。費用呢？三千美元，約為一千七百英鎊。若在倫敦，一個人的費用就要兩倍。

但還是有缺點。雖然醫生也許會說英語，很有可能護士和其他提供服務的人並不會。如果回去後出現併發症，該人要如何獲得立即治療呢？手術是有風險的；到海外去讓一名不認識的醫生治療，更是危險。

台灣也慢慢進入保健之旅的市場中。這個國家以提供價格合理的雷射眼部手術而聞名：在當地能以相當於美金一千元的價格進行眼部手術，幾乎比世界上任何國家便宜。在台灣病患也獲得擔保，能擁有最高級的醫療環境。

想要改頭換面的慾望，往往壓過了所有對於進行海外整型手術風險的擔憂。無疑地，在未來幾年，醫療旅行的生意只會越來越興隆。

解析

1. 根據第三段的描述，「美麗人士」並無提供(B)手術後的諮詢服務。
2. 本題考的是推論的部份。根據本文人們到別的國家做整型手術，主要是價格的因素，故(A)為非。最後一句也指出這樣的風潮只會更流行，故(B)為非。從對於台灣雷射眼部手術的描述，也無法推論出(D)。在第二段提到提供保健之旅的國家均位於東南亞或東歐，因此可推論出(C)**當地手術費用較低**。
3. 第四段說明了在海外做整型手術的風險，及缺點 (drawbacks) 其中第二句指出的是(B)**語言溝通和手術後諮詢的問題**。
4. 從下一句 "No doubt the medical tourism industry will only grow in the years to come" 可得知在海外做手術的風潮只會更盛行，因此可推論出，人們對追求美的渴望會(D)**優先於任何可能隱含的危險**。
5. 本格主要應是描述在國外做整型手術的人，欣賞完風光之後，接著會做的事，因此選(D)。本文並無提到器官捐贈，故(A)為非。(B)和前後文意不連貫。(C)的前文應說明病人該如何度過恢復時期，故不正確。

---

round-the-world adj. 環繞世界的　　sought-after adj. 深受歡迎的　　bask vi. 曬太陽

package n. 行程　liposuction n. 抽脂手術　　complication n. 併發症　LASIK 雷射矯正手術

expertise n. 專業　falter vt. 遲疑、減緩　　take heed of 留意　　come to terms with 設法忍受

在古埃及，電燈是亮的？
Were the Lights on in Ancient Egypt?

翻譯

對於古代文明如何能創造出屹立至今的歷史遺跡，許多人做出推測。埃及金字塔就是一個例子。他們有人力，有工程知識，但他們如何照亮工作現場呢？幾十年來，這點難倒了許多科學家。有人認為他們由內向外建造，所以光線並不是個問題。有人主張，他們造出一些特別的井狀通道探入金字塔裡，將光線引導入內，再折射到需要光亮的地方。

然而，一個古代電池被發現後，證明了古代人已經具有電力知識，該電池如今被稱做「巴格達電池」。它的設計很原始，是一個泥土罐子，有鐵和銅製的棒子並被緊緊固定在罐子上，罐內裝著一些微酸性溶液。它只能產生極少量的電力，而且會需要將數百個串連在一起才能產生作用。此外，之前也沒有跡象顯示，有任何能用這種電池製造光線的裝置存在，直到後來，在石雕上發現了類似古代電燈泡的圖，它如今被稱為「丹德拉之光」。所以，可能埃及人曾有工作用的光源存在。跟它一模一樣的設計在許多年後出現，而且成功發揮功能。然而，沒有其他證據顯示它們曾經存在過。

有些專家仍然堅持，埃及人在建造金字塔時曾有電力照明，因為在牆壁或隧道和走道的天花板上，幾乎沒有發現任何煤煙痕跡能顯示使用過火炬或油燈。

也可能，埃及人曾得到來自外星人的援助。而且，無論他們是誰，都在完工後把工具也一起帶走了。

解析

1. 本題主要考的是文章的主旨。全文主要是(C)探討古代埃及人的照明技術及一些發現。文章並非只在說明金字塔的照明設備，故(A)不正確。(B)的敘述太為籠統，本文不只著重在神秘的古埃及文明，本文也並沒探討(D)古代科技如何影響現在的技術。

2. 根據上下文，很多人都對古文明的文物感到奇妙並想去(A)猜測背後的技術或原因。

3. 在這一句的前一句可得知，古埃及人可能有一個像電燈泡的(B) **light source**，它的石雕也被發現，但卻沒有留下實質證據。

4. 由第二段第一句可得知，故(A)古埃及人對電已有初步的了解，不正確。由倒數第二段可得知，沒有煙灰 (soot) 的存在說明了古埃及人沒有用油燈而可能使用電力，故(C)不正確。根據第二段，巴格達電池的存在，只說明了埃及人對電的知識，但沒有製作出足夠的照明，故(D)不正確。由第二段關於燈泡的壁畫，可推論出(B)。

5. 此空格應說明科學家對古埃及人如何處理照明問題的各種解釋。(D)選項和照明無關，(B)選項並非科學家會有的觀點，(C)句子中的 also 表示前面也該出現解釋照明技術的句子，故不正確，答案應為(A)。

| speculate | vt. | 推測 | monument | n. | 遺跡 | baffle | vt. | 困擾 | shaft | n. | 通道 |
| crude | adj. | 原始的 | extraterrestrial | n. | 外太空生物 | loathe | vt. | 憎恨 | emitting | adj. | 釋放的 |

45 跨越文化差異
Crossing Cultural Borders

翻譯

「我的中國學生問我一個月賺多少錢時，我嚇了一跳。雖然我們德國人很直接，但談論錢還是太隱私了。如今我明白，對他們來說那只是在聊天，一種表現出興趣甚至友善的方式。」瑪麗亞‧舒密特，德國籍老師。

「德國人實在積極過頭。他們跟你握手的時候，會用力到捏痛你。」克麗絲汀‧林，新加坡籍行銷主管。

「我的日本朋友有點怪。她話不多，但在談話過程中，會發出許多嗯聲跟從鼻子發出的雜音。」萊賀德‧克雷格，德國籍會計師。

每個國家本身都有一套看待肢體行為、語言和人際關係的方式。以上例子中，有些溝通的小問題是因一方對另一方不了解而產生。例如，日本人說話的方式較為審慎，有許多轉折。那些嗯和啊聲表示他們正注意聽，而當中的沈默其實意味著他們正在構思一個周詳的回應。但對於一名健談的義大利人，或愛聊天、習慣立即反應的美國人來說，你可以想像這樣的談話方式會造成一些困擾。

在今日的世界裡，許多公司橫跨數個國家，跨文化的生意往來每天都在進行，因此文化上的溝通誤會有可能造成嚴重影響。例如，德國人認為強而有力的握手方式是一種自信的展現。如果在工作面試時，你的握手不夠結實有力，等於可以直接走出房間回家算了。

然而，尊重他人文化，不只是條列出一些可以做和不可以做的事情而已。你必須對他人文化背後的價值觀和哲學有所理解。我們常聽到亞洲跟西方價值觀的對比，亞洲人多麼尊重團體和階級倫理，還有美國人多麼愛競爭和個人主義。沒有哪邊本來就比較好或比較壞，而陳腔爛調和刻板印象也可能會誤導。此外也總有個

人習慣存在。概論式說法是有用處，但只在於提供我們一個基本概念，做為起點，開始互相合作。有智慧地運用這類說法，並永遠保持一顆開放的心，才是優良溝通技巧的關鍵所在。

解析

1. 本題考的是文章主旨，全文著重在(C)**不同文化有不同的溝通方式**。文章並未強調造成誤解的原因，也沒有特別說明那些禁忌要避免，故(A)(B)不正確。文章中雖提到每個文化的特色，但並無強調應向其他文化學習，所以(D)不正確。
2. 由開頭三段引述可得知德國人覺得中國人愛問私事，但並非指中國人說話較直接或德國人對話完全不觸及個人話題，故(A)(C)不正確。日本人在對話中常會發出鼻音，不代表日語中有很多這種音，故(D)不對。第二段引述中可得知(B)**德國人握手時非常強而有力**，甚至會痛，進而產生誤解。
3. 本題考的是文章細節，由最後一段得知，中西方對階級的意見不同和西方人較重視個人主義，故(A)(B)正確。由第一段最後一句中的 "used-to-instant-response Americans" 可得知(C)為正確。(D)選項不正確，因為日本人用沉默來表示正思考該如何回應，並非不同意。
4. 本題考的是反義字，由下文 "turn-taking"、"formulating" 得知應為「經過仔細思考」之意，故反義字為(A) **impulsive(衝動的)**。
5. 本題句子之後的段落應是提醒讀者(C)**除了該做及不該做的事情之外**，對於各國文化的了解還需注意什麼。(A)是說明各國不同的溝通方式，(B)應是說明了解不同溝通方式在貿易往來的重要性，(D)應為建議讀者如何溝通的結尾句。

intrusive adj. 侵擾的	physicality n. 身體	blip n. 盲點	turn-taking n. 轉折
formulate vt. 制定，準備	voluble adj. 愛說話的	used-to-instant-response adj. 習慣立即反應的	
hierarchy n. 階級倫理	inherently adv. 本來地	quirk n. 習慣舉動	merit n. 優點

翻譯

　　詩人和賀卡公司利用書寫永恆的愛，賺進大把銀子，但一名康乃爾大學教授指出，永浴愛河只是個神話。辛蒂・赫桑教授認為，實際上，浪漫的愛情只能持續十八到三十個月。

　　赫桑教授對愛情進行一項研究，訪問了來自三十七種文化背景的五千位人士，並要成對伴侶接受醫學測試。她發現，在求愛期，有三種化學物質——多巴胺、催產素和苯基乙胺——會在腦中合成，產生我們稱為「愛」的一種強烈感受。赫桑教授也發現，男性比女性受這些化學物質影響的速度更快也更強烈。

　　然而，赫桑教授發現，對兩性來說，這些化學物質的作用都很強，也曇花一現。「愛」只持續到伴侶能交往、成為配偶，或許再產生一名後代為止。隨後，這些化學物質就會失去效力，而「愛」的激烈感受也消失了。愛情似乎是一種生物學機制，幫助人類種族存活。

　　赫桑教授表示，一旦激情消逝，有些人就去尋找新伴侶。舉例來說，女星葛妮絲・派特洛曾相信男星布萊德・彼特是她的夢中情人，但在他們交往到第三十個月時，她和他分手了。她承認布萊德・彼特並沒有變，但她對他的感覺已經不同了。其他伴侶們持續在一起的原因，有大部分出於習慣。一名結婚五十四年的女性表示，她對丈夫感受到的激情，在婚後幾年就消失了，但有其他牽掛使他們的關係值得繼續維繫。

　　在《仲夏夜之夢》中，莎士比亞曾指出：「真愛的路途從來就不平坦。」如果這名劇作家知道，真愛的路途也非常短暫，不知會作何感想？

解析

1. 本題考全文的主旨。整篇文章主要是在敘述(D)科學上的一些研究，發現人類在戀愛時，腦中會分泌化學物質，而產生熱戀的感覺，然而卻不能持久。(A)(B)本文均未提到，(C)的敘述太過廣泛，本文主要是探討愛情的部份。

2. 從第二段最後一句可得知，在戀愛時，男人比女人受到腦中化學物質影響更大，故(B)不正確。

3. 在第三段中，由下文 "Love lasted only long <u>enough</u> for couples to court, mate and perhaps produce an offspring." 可得知腦中分泌的化學物質的效力是(D)短暫有期限的。

4. 在最後一段引用莎士比亞說的話 "The course of true love never did run smooth." 說明了(C)真愛的過程常充滿障礙困難。

5. 此段主要應是說明戀愛時，為何腦中會分泌化學物質，故選(A)來做為本段的結論。(B)和前一句並無轉折連結的作用。(C)應該放在介紹這些化學物質作用的段落。(D)應該放在第二段，說明化學物質對兩性影響的地方。

course	n.	過程	subject	vt.	使接受	courtship	n.	求愛期	dopamine	n.	多巴胺
oxytocin	n.	催產素	phenyl ethylamine	n.	苯基乙胺	transitory	adj.	短暫的	potency	n.	效力
elusive	adj.	難懂的	formidable	adj.	驚人的

翻譯

那是很糟糕的一天。在大雨滂沱中，我撐著一把滴水的傘，飽受頭痛之苦，開始走上斑馬線。突然間，一輛賓士車疾駛而過，濺起一大片雨水，潑得我們全身濕透。我不假思索地衝口而出一些不太好聽的咒罵。

我兒子小手還緊緊牽著我，他認真地抬頭看我，然後說：「媽咪，你不應該講那種話。你應該說：『噢，天哪』之類的。」

信不信由你，我當上母親時心懷大志。畢竟，我被賦予將另一名人類教養成人的機會。我兒子會有媲美 (前南非總統) 尼爾森・曼德拉的建立國家的智慧與勇氣。而我也將會在這過程中，變成一個更好的人。

然而，要當個好母親真是難上加難。我讀遍所有育兒書籍。要攝取營養。好，小孩子應該吃健康的食物，但我自己還是比較喜歡垃圾食物和甜食。睡覺時間？要有紀律而且堅持一貫，因為睡眠很重要。不過我之所以那天如此糟糕，是因為前一晚我熬夜看電視。我當然可以叫兒子照我說的話做，而不是照我的樣子作。但人們說以身作則最重要。所以我拖著兒子踏遍公園 (大自然)，雖然我真正想的是去逛街，我會拍拍貓和狗 (愛護小動物)，雖然我得不斷壓抑自己對毛茸茸生物的恐懼。感謝老天，我兒子沒說他想養寵物。

當個睿智的父母就像在演戲，而就算真正的演員也沒辦法每一次都演好！所以現在，我把所有希望都寄託在他的基因上，祈禱儘管我這個樣子，我的孩子還是會成為一個良善的人。畢竟，曼德拉不是生長在一個不公平、混亂的環境中，身邊還有許多行為不佳的大人？

解析

1. 根據全文，作者應該是(C)一名在扶養小孩的過程中，遇到困難且感到困惑的母親，並不是小孩行為不好或她在工作家庭兩者之間無法取得平衡。

2. 根據第二段小孩說的 "You shouldn't use words like those, Mommy" 可推論出水濺到作者身上時作者應該是說了一些咒罵的話語，故選(B)。

3. 根據第四段的描述，作者為了好好撫養小孩，常必須犧牲自己的喜好 (junior should eat healthily but I rather like junk food and sweets myself.)，故選(A)。此段只知道作者不喜歡小動物，不能推論出(B)；作者也沒用任何文字描述犧牲自己的喜好是很值得的，故(C)不正確；此段並沒有提到作者原先對營養或自然的想法，故(D)不正確。

4. 作者在最後一段提到曼德拉生長在混亂的環境，成長後仍有所成就。這不是為了比較他和自己小孩的相似度，而是覺得自己不是一個很完美標準的母親，希望小孩還是有機會成才，(C)減輕自己的罪惡感。

5. 此句在說明作者也會在這個過程中成長，前面的句子和段落應該會提到要撫養小孩的過程，故最適合的位置為(B)。(A)的位置應說明會如何扶養小孩，(C)位置應說明身教的重要性且時態不合，(D)應解釋身教的困難之處。

strand vt. 受困於	drench vt. 使溼透	expletives n. 咒罵
parenting literature 育兒書籍	pin vt. 使寄託	decent adj. 正直的
desperate adj. 孤注一擲的	strike a balance 取得平衡	abide by 忍受

48

樂活 (LOHAS) =「快樂生活」：為了地球好的世界性潮流？
LOHAS = "Happy Life": A Worldwide Trend for the Good
of the Planet?

翻譯

　　樂活 (LOHAS) 是「健康而永續的生活方式」的縮寫。**樂活消費者和公司致力於拯救環境、促進世界和平，以及實現社會公平。**因此，在樂活圈裡，人們偏好有機食物和替代性能源；投資在具有社會意識的公司上；並引進西方醫學領域之外的另類醫療行為。以下簡短概述這個正徹底擴張的樂活圈幾項重點。

　　永續的經濟方式。致力於達到樂活目的的公司和組織，會確保他們所進行的活動具有生態性、達到成本效益平衡，並能盡可能讓最多人受惠。在樂活圈中，降低碳排放量或支持小額借貸給第三世界國家居民的公司，都是領導先驅。

　　活得健康。長年來，有機、自然食物這部份累積了樂活市場的主力。在美國，有機食物的銷售額一年超過四百億美元。雖然如今有機食物佔了美國食品銷售總額的百分之一至二，專家預估，未來還會升高到百分之五至十。

　　另類保健醫療。這部分包含了一些醫療方式，它們不屬於「科學」或以醫院為據點的保健體系之內。此類醫療方式包括針灸、草藥、足部反射以及按摩等。研究顯示，這些另類療法確實能節省開銷；它們能讓人們保持在更健康的狀態，且持續更久。

　　個人發展。生活在高度壓力下的現代人，正尋找和平及寧靜。美國人對提供沈思和冥想活動的組織趨之若鶩。瑜珈愛好者如今已達數百萬，世界各地都有人參加瑜珈課程。

　　樂活品牌的商品如今正被引進到台灣。長久以來有著高經濟成長和工業污染，台灣人也發展出對環境和健康生活方式的關切，這點並不令人訝異。政府正從事一項大規模資源回收行動，並強制公司和一般大眾遵行有效利用能源的政策。

　　LOHAS 的中文譯名為「樂活」，意指快樂生活。似乎台灣人也正在尋找對地球更好的解決對策，以期讓我們──和我們的地球──更加快樂。

解析

1. 本題考的是選出那一項**不是**樂活的定義和做法，由第五段可知追求樂活的人會參與 contemplation 和 meditation (沉思冥想)，故(A)為真。由第一段得知樂活注重對環境及資源的保護，故(B)為真。由第二段可知樂活支持借貸給貧窮國家的公司，(D)為正確敘述。本文中並未提及**追求樂活是要當個 SOHO**，所以(C)不屬於樂活的定義。

2. 本題考的是文章的細節部份，由第二段之中 cost-effective, ecological 等字可得知，注重樂活的公司會尋求環保有效率的方式來促進 sustainable economy，故選(A)。

3. 根據上下文，美國有機食品的銷售一年超過 400 億，可見 lion's share 應是**強調佔有的數量很多**，故選(B)。

4. 由最後一段可得知，(B)**很多和樂活有關的產品已經引入台灣**，台灣人民和政府也越來越願意參與這項風潮。(A)(C)(D)本文皆未提及。

5. 本題的句子主要是在說明**支持樂活的人們和公司的理念**，最適合擺在解釋樂活的段落，因此擺在(A)，後面的句子 (Hence,...) 用來進一步說明支持樂活的人會做的事。

acronym n. 縮寫	sustainablity n. 永續	carbon emission 碳排放量
standard-bearer n. 領導先驅	garner vt. 收集累積	acupuncture n. 針灸
reflexology n. 足部反射療法 (腳底按摩)	contemplation n. 沉思	prototype n. 原型

翻譯

　　他是一名熱心參與地方政治的律師，一名冠軍運動員，曾在世界盃、歐洲盃和殘障奧運會的田徑及高山滑雪項目中贏得十四面金牌、九面銀牌和六面銅牌。他也是個熱衷於法國號的吹奏家，一年舉行二十五場演奏會，已經發行三張專輯，並剛完成一趟日本巡迴演奏會。然而這些都只是他的興趣。他的主要職業是領導一個有四百名員工的政府部門。

　　你可能會心想，這必定又是個自我滿足慾太強的成就追逐者。**然而事實上，馬提斯‧伯格非常平易近人，戴著一副眼鏡，微笑時總是露出酒窩。**但他的成就確實令人驚異，因為他是名「沙利竇邁寶寶」。

　　沙利竇邁是德國葛盧南道藥廠研發的一種藥物，主要販售給孕婦抑制害喜和幫助睡眠。該藥物在安全測試尚未完成之前就上市，結果導致五〇年代晚期至六〇年代早期約一萬名寶寶生下來就嚴重畸形。當時馬提斯的母親只吃了一顆，但傷害卻已造成。她的寶寶生下來就有兩隻鰭狀手臂，短得只能碰到自己的腋窩。

　　馬提斯回憶童年所遇到的困難。「我有三個難關要克服：我有雙短手臂，滿頭紅髮，而且口音跟別人不一樣。日子不太好過，例如我不會被邀請去參加聚會活動或生日派對等等。但我並非什麼受害者。」孩童時期的不順遂，有親密的家庭支持來抒解。「我們幫他選擇一項自己喜歡的樂器。我們覺得法國號最適合，因為他只需用三根手指就可以操作好閥門。」他母親如此回答，她本身就是一名音樂家。在被問到，是否這些成就都是對自己身體殘障的一種補償心理使然，這名四十五歲，已經為人父的男子微微一笑說：「不會啊，我覺得如果我是個『正常』的孩子，也同樣會做這些事。讓自己有紀律，只是在對抗我天生的懶散。」

　　如果人格也有比賽，馬提斯‧伯格一定能獲得另一面金牌。

解析

1. 本題是問那一項**不是**馬提斯的興趣之一，從第一段可得知他是個律師，喜歡運動和滑雪，吹奏法國號，開音樂會，但並無(A)**指揮音樂會**。

2. 本題是問 malformation 的反義字。在第三段中可得知，吃了沙利竇邁的孕婦都生出有 severe malformations 的小孩。馬提斯出生時手部畸形，因此此字應該為「畸形或不正常」，反義字應為(B)「**正常**」。

3. 本題考的是細節部份，從倒數第二段可得知，馬提斯做這麼多嘗試，並非(B)**補償自己的肢體缺陷或紀念母親**，而是對自己的要求。

4. 由本文最後一句可得知作者認為如果有人格方面的比賽，馬提斯也應該拿冠軍，因此可推論出(C)**作者對他評價很高**。

5. 本句有 Yet 開頭，必定和前一句有語意轉折的作用，所以最適合的位置在(B)，用來說明原本讀者可能認為他是個自滿的人，然而他卻是**很平易近人**。

Paralympics n. 殘障奧運	overachiever n. 成就追逐者	pharmaceutical adj. 醫藥的
adequate adj. 適當的　malformation n. 畸形	soothe vt. 使鎮定	valve n. 管樂器活塞
grin vt. 微微一笑	deformity n. 畸形	hospitality n. 好客　immunity n. 免疫力
dosage n. 劑量	bespectacled adj. 戴眼鏡的	dimpled adj. 出現酒窩的

50 鐵窗後的幼犬
Puppies Behind Bars

翻譯

　　長久以來，狗都被用來幫助行動不便者，尤其是盲胞。不幸的是，要訓練一隻狗到能做好這樣的工作，需要花上約兩年時間和兩萬五千美金的費用。但在一九九七年，葛羅莉雅·吉波·史托嘉創設了「鐵窗後的幼犬」這個非營利組織，讓有許多時間可用的監獄受刑人，以義工形式為基礎，擔任主要訓練工作。

　　起初，許多人對這個計畫感到相當擔心，尤其是在矯正機關中狗狗們的安危。為了減輕大眾疑慮，「鐵窗後的幼犬」計畫不讓曾犯下重罪的受刑人和任何動物一起工作。而且，有意願參加計畫的受刑人，都必須先接受完整的面談審核程序，有暴力傾向的受刑人會被剔除。

　　一旦加入該計畫，受刑人必須參加兩週一次的訓練課程。其餘時間，他們就跟分配給自己的幼犬生活在一起，教導牠們基本技巧如上廁所、依命令坐下和站著，以及在擁擠的地方走動而不致於感到混亂的能力。十六個月後，受刑人就要將自己的幼犬交給專業犬隻訓練者，進行最後五個月的訓練。

　　茱蒂·古德曼是第一批接受從「鐵窗後的幼犬」訓練計畫中畢業的狗兒的人士之一。因為實在非常感動，她前去拜訪狗兒被養大的監獄，對訓練者們表達感謝之意。「他們非常引以為傲，也確實應該如此，」她表示，「因為他們做得太好了。」

　　也許這項計畫中，最大的受惠者是受刑人。**在訓練動物的過程中，他們學習到有耐心與責任感**。最重要的是，他們得到了只有幼犬能給予的，一種無條件的愛。受刑人羅斯福·路易斯這麼談到他的幼犬，「約書亞幫我找回了心靈

的平靜。」

　　看起來，「鐵窗後的幼犬」給了每位參與者一項新的「生命鞭策」。

解析

1. 本題考的是文章的主旨，全文主要是介紹讓受刑人訓練導盲犬的計劃，(B)**能帶來很多助益**。不是講(C)照顧流浪狗的機構，不是(A)會幫忙監督犯人的狗，也不是(D)幫助盲人及犯人的義工。

2. 本文考的是細節部份，由第二、第三段可得知受刑人必須通過面試，參加兩個禮拜一次的課程，教導狗技巧，但不用(C)**陪伴他們直到給新主人前**，而是把狗交給訓練師做最後五個月的訓練。

3. 從第二段可得知，要參加這項計畫的受刑人<u>必須通過嚴格的審查，以便過濾</u>或是(D)**淘汰**有暴力傾向的人。

4. 根據上下文，此段應表示茱蒂古德曼對受刑人訓練狗的成果印象深刻，所以 They 應該是指(C)**受刑人 (Inmates)**。

5. 本題這個空格應解釋<u>說明這個計畫對受刑人的好處</u>，所以適合的答案為(A)。(C)是指每個囚犯都能這樣貢獻社會，(D)則說明囚犯這樣可以反省過錯，均和此項計畫較無關。根據上下文，此空格並不會出現新的主題 (the physically-challenged)，故(B)不正確。

inmate n. 受刑人	weed vt. 除去淘汰	recipient n. 接收者
beneficiary n. 受益者	janitor n. 監獄看守人	invalid n. 傷殘者
detained adj. 扣留的	trainee n. 實習生	

英文讀寫萬試通

車昀庭／審定　三民英語編輯小組／彙編

全書16回＝閱讀技巧篇+實戰演練篇

・Unit 1~3：
說明閱讀技巧，彙整大考閱測題型、考古題並
提供1篇仿大考閱測。

・Unit 4~16：
文章主題豐富、由淺入深。每回提供1篇閱測
和2題問答題(仿大考寫作)。

・解析本：
提供文章翻譯、答題思路與範例。可搭配選修
課程。

WRITE RIGHT, No NG
英文這樣寫，不NG

張淑媖、應惠蕙／編著　車昀庭／審定

Write Right！讓所有文章都不NG！

・由「句子擴充」、「內容構思」的概念談起，
引導你從最基礎的寫作開始。

・提點常見的寫作錯誤，如標點符號、時態等，
替你打下紮實的基本功。

・介紹常見文體，包括記敘文、描寫文、論說
文、應用文等，讓你充分學習。

・補充自傳、讀書計畫等寫作技巧，幫助你為生
涯規劃加分。

・循序漸進引導，按部就班練習，自學、教學都
不NG！

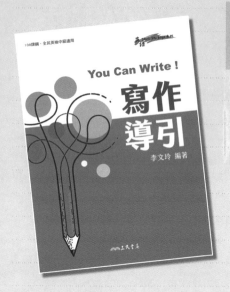

You Can Write!
寫作導引

李文玲　編著

大家一起來「寫」拼！

- 從寫作概念的介紹到各種文體的寫作策略，循序漸進。
- 近百題的實戰演練。
- 每章另闢小單元，分享寫作小技巧與常面臨的問題。

關於 Reading Power

這是一套為愉閱英語而生，

一套能體驗英閱樂趣，

精選閱讀　精采內容

★ 理論篇針對閱讀能力的提升，分析探討六大閱讀技巧。

★ 精選50篇多元主題文章，廣泛閱讀各類題材。

★ 測驗篇的試題結合理論，讓你深入理解，實際活用。

★ 符合大考中心公布之字表範圍，讓你輕鬆迎戰大小考。

★ 解析本詳列中譯、難字提示、試題說明，達成自我評量之功效。

一套能開拓視野見聞，

一套能厚植英語實力，

一套讓人愛不釋手的系列叢書。

三民網路書店
www.sanmin.com.tw

「精選閱讀」與
「翻譯與解析」不分售
80734G